Raven's Prey

Raven's Prey

by SLIM RANDLES

McRoy & Blackburn, Publishers, Ester, Alaska

© 1998 by Slim Randles
Published by McRoy & Blackburn, Publishers
P.O. Box 276
Ester, Alaska 99725
Printed in the United States of America

Book and cover design by
Paula Elmes
ImageCraft Publications & Design
Fairbanks, Alaska

ISBN 0-9632596-8-7 (paperback)
ISBN 0-9632596-9-5 (casebound)

CHAPTER 1

I t was the wrong kind of day for death.

Lazy long summer day in late July, soon to be sliding toward the icy rains of August. Teeming with noise and fun. Before Buck walked the short distance from the village to my cabin, I'd just been sitting there listening to Stravinsky, watching black-capped chickadees flit-doodling around in the birch trees high above slate juncos dancing on the ground. Four trillion bugs singing like a chorus of chain saws. Blackwater pockets in the muskeg boiling with life; the creeks near the cabin waving the thorny hellish whips of the devil's club.

Death seems to hurt more, seems to count for more, on a day promised to life.

I watched Buck pour a cup of coffee from the pot on my stove.

"Are you sure about this?"

Buck nodded. "I'm sorry."

"They didn't say anything on the radio . . . about Bill. Didn't give any names."

"Karen called," Buck said. "Asked me to tell you."

The news without names had been scary enough. Even in a land of incredible beauty and occasional violence, when you hear that someone slips the familiar mental boundaries and kills his tent mates, it gets your attention. It gets everyone's attention. Little else had been on the radio news all morning: four men found dead in the Talkeetna Mountains. You hear news like that and say, boy, that's a shame.

But Bill Turner . . .

"Karen's a mess," Buck said.

I nodded.

Life bubbling everywhere and Bill was gone. Bill, who had had the future mapped out. Bill, who had known exactly what he was going to do for the next thirty years until he retired.

"Want me to fly you in?"

"Oh . . . no thanks, Buck. I can use the drive."

"Yeah," he said, patting me on the shoulder. "Need anything . . . call."

"Thanks."

Hell of a morning. Hell of a beautiful morning. Hell of a tragic morning. I walked out to the dog lot and fed and watered the eight huskies. They wanted to leap and run and maybe go fishing, but that would have to wait. We were all waiting through these summer days. The team waits for those first leaden snows of October so they can run again. I wait until the velvet has been scraped off the antlers of the moose and caribou. I wait until the largest and nastiest of Alaska's animals are at their peak and the game regulations say it's all right. Then I set up the white canvas wall tents on the other side of the Alaska Range, beyond the big white mountains, and I take my chosen hunters in for a few weeks they'll remember all their lives.

In the meantime there's fishing and fixing this log home that has been in my family for generations now, and listening to some Mozart or Brubeck on the stereo and cutting firewood. There's always firewood to cut.

But now, even the waiting will have to wait.

Bill's dead and Karen wants me to come to Anchorage, and that's why I spent a hard hour first with my splitting maul, readying firewood I wouldn't need for three months.

I wanted that time. I wanted to look at the seasoned logs of my comfortable home. I wanted the time to look at each of the dogs and their happy faces. I wanted time to try to deal with the feeling that rose in me like a ghost that says this will change things. This will change everything. Like putting a heavy red filter on the camera lens of the mind, things will forever look the slightest bit different.

I looked at the cabin and hoped I would have more years here, years where the sun will shine, unfiltered by pain, but now I couldn't be sure, because a shadow had crossed my life and blown the cold breath of death across my neck.

I cleaned up and changed clothes, then slowly drove the two hours along the forested highway to Anchorage.

〜

Bill and Karen Turner bought a sensible house in the Muldoon area of Anchorage three years ago. It had three bedrooms, just right for them and the children. Shelly must be about five now, and George . . . I think George is going on three.

George is named for me. In a way.

I have one of those Alaska names tourists have a hard time handling. On the birth certificate it's Jepsen George. The Jepsen comes from my mother's maiden name and dates back to some nasty folks from the North Atlantic who were heavily into pillaging others' villages from their home ports in Norway. My mother's side gave me the blue eyes and a fondness for polka dancing. The George comes from my father's side of the family, which is Athabascan, the Indian people who live in the interior of Alaska. In school, the kids shortened Jepsen to Jeep for me, and I've been Jeep George ever since.

In downtown Anchorage, about five miles from Bill and Karen's house, is the old movie theater with brick walls that made it through the big quake and a whole lot of little ones. If you go around to the alley and look, you'll see a door with Jepsen George, Guide and Outfitter, on it. Unlock the door, walk up a flight of stairs, and you'll find a cubbyhole I jokingly refer to as the office. It is used more often as a bedroom, really, but does have a phone and a desk and a shower and a few nice mounted heads and a wall with some framed pictures of hunters I've gotten particularly fond of over the years I've been guiding on my own.

Call it a poor man's hotel, anyway. About six years ago, I did a rather large favor for the man who owns the theater (and other downtown property besides). I refused to take any money for the favor and he painted my name on the door, put the furniture in, mailed me a key and said I was responsible for sweeping it out. He has never accepted rent for it.

Any number of people have seen the sign on the door, or read my name in the phone book and called me Mr. Jepsen, but I'm used to it. It's just one of those names. The George family gives me dark hair to go with the Jepsen blue eyes, and the combination makes me a hunting guide, a dog musher, and in winter a dancer of polkas down at the South Seas road-house at home in the little village of Kahiltna.

The dog musher part tends to make a man a bachelor, too, as a lot of women don't understand why a man with a college education will feed eight dogs just so he can stay away from a warm fire in cold weather. Most of us who do that aren't really good candidates for faithful attendance at delivery rooms or PTA meetings.

If I tried that for very long, I'm afraid I'd start remembering what the early morning sky looks like from my moose lookout hill over across the Alaska Range. During those winter-night PTA meetings, when the parkas are hung up and everyone is nodding off, too hot in three sets of long johns, I'm afraid I'd remember that night in the hundred-mile race when the dogs and I crossed the ridge and dropped onto the ice of Kroto Creek. As the dogs trotted ahead in a sinuous line on the meandering ice, the moon showed the black spruce timeless along the banks. Above all, it was quiet. On the slick ice, there wasn't even the usual crunch of snow be-neath the runners. The only sound was the occasional creaking of the sled as we cornered on the oxbow turns, and the ticking of a hundred and twenty-eight dog toenails on the ice.

After two hours of that, the temperature dropped, and just when I thought it couldn't get any prettier, the northern lights came out over Mount Foraker and made a liar out of me. The shaky green dream curtain gave depth to the fields of snow in the swamp systems along the creek. The dogs broke into a run, then, in pure joy. I let them. I understood. We were made for this, the dogs and I. We had our instincts, we had our training. We had our jobs, that cold night, and for a few hours it all came together, the team and I working in a smooth ballet, winding like a shad-owy, happy snake through a gentle frozen forest in the God-light of a winter moon. Later that night, when we reached Joe May's cabin, I almost hated to go in.

Sometimes Alaska is woman enough for a man. I'm not sure it's that way with me, because there are those times at night when I want to talk about things and no one is there.

There are those times.

But mine wasn't the way of life Bill Turner chose. And he did choose it. For some people, life just happens. For Bill, it was family all the way. He came to our little village of old sourdoughs and young homesteaders and

Indian families when he was very young, as a foster child. None of us knew much of his life before that, and I don't imagine anyone asked much. Those things aren't too important in Alaska. Up here, it's just today and tomorrow that count, and yesterdays are just melted snow and things that happened first.

Maybe it was something in the time before we met him that made him such a fanatic about family. When we were going through college and working the hunting camps and fish canneries together, Bill was as jovial as anyone. But inside him was this streak of stability that made the rest of us look at him a little strangely. The official state sport in Alaska is being spontaneous and dreaming big for eighty-five years before telling the attendants at the Pioneers' Home what you plan to do next year if you could just get out of this wheelchair.

Maybe for him it was just that the aching to belong was so deep it took the permanence of a rock to settle it. Bill's degree in engineering was as carefully planned as every other move he'd made in his life. He met Karen in college, and those of us around them knew they would be married. Marriage was a calculated move, but Karen wasn't. She was Bill's love, and could've talked him into being reckless, I imagine.

But she wanted him just the way he was. If ever a man was custom made to be a husband and father, it was Bill Turner. I was the only one who could tease him about it, though.

Bill and Karen even came to resemble each other some. It didn't take long. He got a little chubby and his hair thinned prematurely. Karen chubbed up a bit, too, but into a comfortable motherly kind of shape you'd expect of someone twenty years older who makes quilts. I realized, on that trip to town, they both wore glasses that gave the same general impression of steadiness, of maturity.

Bill loved that modest house in Muldoon. Each time I visited, I got a fresh tour of the place, with each new improvement pointed out in detail.

"Jeep, I don't believe you've seen the shelves I've built in Shelly's room . . . "

"Sure I did, Bill. Saw them last trip."

"That was May," he said with a smile. "You know how kids are. She decided after a couple of weeks she didn't like them, so I tore them out and put some thinner ones in. I think you'll like what I've done with them."

So I finished the tour, admiring the shelves as though I was the building inspector. I felt guilty each time this happened, but never said anything to Bill. To me, shelves are good if the books don't fall. Pearls before swine, I'm afraid.

The last time I'd been in the house was on the Fourth of July. Bill had just the right number of steaks and he naturally remembered how everyone liked them done. Besides Bill and Karen and the kids, there was me and a young woman from down the street . . . single and about our age . . . who owned her own home.

She had a pretty smile and listened to a guy's stories, but it didn't take. The steaks were great, though, and I really do enjoy meeting women. They say you never know.

That's what Bill always said. You never know.

"You never know, Jeep, when that lady who's right for you will be around the next corner."

"Thank you, Mother Turner."

"No, really. Like when Karen and I met. . . ."

"You met in your first year of college," I said, ticking the familiar points off on my fingers as we sat later by the little gas fire in his fireplace. "It was love at first sight. You were born to be married to each other. You'll live together until you're both a hundred years old, and lie side by side forever."

He grinned and shook his head. "You make it sound so . . . so planned."

I laughed so hard I choked on my soda pop. I like the orange ones.

That day, just a few weeks ago, Bill talked for more than an hour about the various insurance policies he had, and some bonds he was buying with each paycheck to salt away for the kids' college.

Bill Turner was a planned man. Had been. But now Bill Turner was dead. The kind of man he was, and the kind of friend he was, made it all the more shocking. He was the kind of guy you could picture retired and traveling in tours with Karen after the children were seen safely through the university and into taxpaying.

My gut had started to hurt. I hadn't been driving fast to that remodeled house in Muldoon. I knew I would never be fully able to remember it with laughter and smiles after this day. That is how the death of someone diminishes our own horizons, taking away little pleasures by tingeing them with pain.

I listened to the radio news again on the way in.

Four men working for the Shan-Dor Mining Company were found dead when a supply plane arrived in a remote camp in the Talkeetna Mountains. The state troopers are treating the deaths as homicides, and the names of the dead have not been released pending notification of next of kin. A source close to the investigation says a fifth member of the crew is missing and is being sought for questioning.

I'll bet he is.

Well, world, the name of one of those men was Bill Turner. William Henry Turner, actually. Bill Turner was there in my cabin on the fringes of Kahiltna the night I found my Grandpa George's body in his favorite chair by the stove. Bill was there all night, saying almost nothing, but keeping the coffee hot and listening to the ravings of a wild man. Well, actually a wild kid more than a man. My grandmothers had died when I was younger, and my Gramps Jepsen had died just the year before. My parents had both been killed in a plane crash when I was small. Chada, my Grandpa George, was all I'd had left. Then he was gone, and I was orphaned altogether at just that age when you turn from a child to a man. The village, which is the ultimate parent of any of us up here, accepted me as an adult after that, so I became one. It often works like that.

Karen met me halfway across the mowed lawn and threw herself in my arms and sobbed. We went in the house and I got her to the couch.

"Where are the kids?"

"Mother's. I wanted to get myself together before I told them. Oh Jeep, what . . . why did this happen? I don't even know what happened. They won't tell me!"

"What did they say?"

She pulled herself up straight and wiped her face. It was red and puffy and her hair was like damp seaweed. I'd seen her looking a lot better.

"Well," she said, trying to sound logical, "this morning a trooper came here with a minister. I don't even remember the minister's name, Jeep. He wasn't our minister. Do you think they just have a minister who does this?"

"I believe there are several who take turns."

"He was very nice and offered to call a friend or go for my mother. I forget his name. I don't even remember which church he was from."

"That's okay. What did the trooper tell you?"

She paused, trying to organize the hellish memory into something I could understand and that she would never forget.

"He asked me if I was Mrs. Turner. I said I was. And he said Mrs. William Henry Turner? I said yes. And he said he was sorry, but my husband is dead. Just like that."

"Sometimes it's best like that."

"But it was just like that, you know?"

"I know."

"So I asked him what happened and he said someone killed Bill and three other men in camp and they didn't know who did it or why they were killed."

"Where were they?"

"They were in a camp."

"Yes, I know. In the Talkeetna Mountains. But do you know where it is?"

"I don't know. Bill said he'd only be gone a couple of days. He would've been back here tomorrow. Maybe even tonight. Oh Jeep, he would've been back maybe tonight."

I just held her until the shaking subsided.

"I asked the trooper if they'd been . . . you know, dead very long? Like overnight. There's bears out there . . . and wolves."

"You shouldn't worry about that."

"The troopers are there now," she said. "They won't let anything . . . "

"Of course not."

"I haven't told the children yet."

I put my arms back around her and she tried to push her head through my chest as she sobbed.

"This wasn't supposed to happen."

"I know."

"I haven't told the children yet, Jeep."

"There's time."

"They know something's wrong, though."

"Yes."

"The trooper didn't say anything more. Why would anyone want to kill Bill?"

"Three other men were killed, too. Who knows how these things happen?"

Alaska can be a strange chemical brew. She tends to bring out whatever traits you have, but to ridiculous extremes. If, for example, you liked to tell jokes around the barber shop down in Kansas, you could become a laughing jackass in Alaska. If you were inclined to be a bit snappy at your neighbors down in Ohio, a winter or two in Alaska could leave you with a police record.

Or, in some rare cases in this state's history, if a person was strange enough, people could die in the far places, and the state troopers wouldn't know why.

It happened that way in the Cache Creek mining camps back in the 1930s. All they found were the bodies of the miners and their wives. The man they suspected had vanished forever. Some say he perished in the mountains, while others still say they know he made it back to Seattle.

Similar killings have taken place at the old ghost town of Kennicott and at Barrow. In each case, there seemed to be no obvious reason for the killings except that Alaska had finally snapped the fragile twig inside a human being that separates eccentricity from homicide.

In one of the breaks between tears, I broiled some mooseburgers for us. She ate a little, which is better than I thought she would. To me, even the succulence of moose tasted like cardboard.

When death hits, it seems to wipe the color and flavor out of every-thing. The outside world may look the same as it did yesterday, but death tars it with the blackness of shock and pain. About all you can do is tough it out and get through it.

My father's people have ways of letting these things work themselves out over three days. If that doesn't remove enough of the hurt to get back in life again, the potlatch helps later. Unlike the bizarre bankrupting blow-outs the Tlingit threw a century ago, the Athabascan potlatches are just little quiet parties, with food and presents for those who sat with the body and stayed and cooked for the family.

It seems to work well for us, and that's all that matters. Find something that works and use it.

It's times like these when I pity those who come from a single culture and a single set of customs. It must be sad to be stuck like that. I count myself lucky. The blue-eyed part of me can draw on Anglo America and the great brotherhood of the Sons of Norway. The dark-haired part can draw on thousands of years of animism, heavy medicine, omens, and my personal totem, the raven. And, if the pain or the situation seems too much for either of these methods, I have no hard-nosed ethnic qualms about mixing and matching until I find something that works.

Karen wasn't that lucky. She had a culture that came from California. As far as I could tell, it consisted of a frantic pinball game between large sterile office buildings, large sterile school buildings, large sterile shopping malls, and a house made of stucco and painted a color that wouldn't offend the neighbors. She had only her mother left of that culture. She used to have Bill, too, and that had been enough. Now Bill was gone. Karen will, I'm sure, pull out of this and take care of business, because she's that kind of woman. But that night she was jelly and nerves, all shaking on the couch, sometimes talking, sometimes crying.

It was starting to get twilight outside, so I knew it must be late.

"What do you want to do about the kids tonight?"

She took a couple of deep breaths and tried a shaky smile.

"I don't want to frighten them when I'm like this. I guess I'd better call Mom and see if they can stay over."

"Good idea."

She did. But her mother, in confusion, had told Shelly and George that Daddy had been in an accident and couldn't come home any more. They wanted to know why, and Grandma didn't know what to say next.

"I'd better go over there," Karen said, giving me a long hug and kissing me on the cheek. She gathered up her coat and hat and took my hand again.

"Thanks for coming. I needed you here. I'll be okay now. Well, I don't know if I'll ever be okay again, actually . . . "

"Yes, you will."

"I guess I have to, for the kids. What am I going to tell them, Jeep? They'll want to know what happened and why. And so do I. I couldn't think of anyone else to call."

"You did the right thing."

"Would you find out for me? Would you talk to someone and learn what really happened? The trooper wouldn't tell me anything."

"I'll see what I can do."

"Thank you, Jeep. Will you be in Kahiltna?"

"I'll stay here in town at the office tonight so I can use the phone tomorrow."

"And you'll call me?"

"Just as soon as I know something."

I knew, even then, that there would come a time I'd wish I hadn't made that promise.

CHAPTER 2

I awoke with the light, which comes early this time of year. The morning, which is really the middle of an ordinary night, is the only nice time to be in Anchorage, because ever since it was simply Mile 114 on the Alaska Railroad, it's been trying to act like a big city. Lately it's been succeeding.

I rolled up the sleeping bag and stuffed it into the closet, took a quick shower and dressed, then walked the few blocks to Ship Creek.

It's not much to look at any more. The creek empties into Cook Inlet right at the base of downtown Anchorage. The raging tides here regularly transform Ship Creek from a placid sheet of water with waterfowl on it to a series of killer mud flats.

This morning it was mud flats, and that was all right because I was in a mud-flat mood. For once, I didn't even mind the encroaching industries around the creek.

But the day coming on was beautiful: clouds to the east over the Chugach Mountains and just the pale pink of eternal snow on the base of McKinley, a hundred and fifty miles away, beyond my village of Kahiltna.

The sky becomes light gently this time of year. There are usually a few lights left on in the sleeping city, and a few blocks away on Fourth Avenue there is still activity around the bars. The girls are still standing their eternal watch on the sidewalks, hoping for construction workers. But even on Fourth Avenue it's quiet now, as if in deference to the coming day. Tony and the band have gone home from the Montana Club. Only the winos are left, along with those few people, usually men, who find life so terrifyingly lonely here they have to cluster together to weather it through.

I like to take an early morning walk to Ship Creek when I'm stuck in town, because there is often life in it. Some ducks or geese. I've seen musk-rats in there, but they were a little farther upstream toward the boundary of Elmendorf Air Force Base. Near there is a pond where the hot water from the base's boilers empties out. A handful of hardy ducks tough it out there all winter and are celebrated throughout the city.

Down the inlet, I could see the offshore rigs and their tiny flames amid the vastness of the ocean. Somehow, the magic of visiting Ship Creek early in the morning didn't work this day, so I walked back up the hill and drove out a ways to Peggy's Airport Cafe for breakfast.

By eight I was back in the office over the movie theater, making some calls. My pal at the Daily News hadn't been told any more than the rest of us about the killings, but he knew it was up in the Talkeetna Mountains, which I'd heard on the radio anyway.

A call to Shan-Dor Mining Company narrowed the hunt a bit . . . after five minutes of listening to some nineteen-year-old girl tell me no one was available to talk to me. No, Mrs. Shannon wasn't taking any calls. No, Mr. Dorio wasn't taking any calls, either. What exactly did I want? Yes, that was certainly a terrible thing. We're just . . . well, we don't know what to think about it here. Maybe if you call in a few days? Where did it happen? Look . . . maybe I shouldn't tell you this, but it was at a place called Mur-der Lake? Can you believe that? Murder Lake? It's even on the map here. Next to a place called Stephan Lake.

She pronounced it "Steven" instead of the correct Alaskan pronuncia-tion of Step-ANN. It was named for Chief Wasilla Stephan, whose family was murdered just a few miles away and many years ago at Murder Lake. Grandma George always said we were related to him on her side of the family.

I thanked the girl and hung up and thought about it for some long minutes. Murder Lake. There weren't three people who lived within twenty air miles of it. It is a place of incomparable beauty, with spreading forests, lakes dotting high tundra ridges, and mountains that shoot up from the tundra, making secure homes for Dall sheep. It is good hunting country. I guided that area years ago as an assistant guide for Bob Gordon. Some open country, but a lot of taiga forest as well . . . black spruce and birch in the lower areas, dissolving into the hells of alders up higher where the soil thins and the tundra takes over.

I called trooper headquarters and asked to talk with Captain Strickland. I didn't really expect him to be there, and he wasn't. Jim Strickland is one of the finest woodsmen I know and I pretty much guessed where he'd be.

"Captain Strickland won't be back in town for several days, sir," said the voice of a young police officer. "He's pretty busy right now, but perhaps I could take your name and phone number?"

"Is he working the homicides at Murder Lake?"

"I'm sorry. We never give out that kind of information."

"Well, would you please tell him Jeep George called and it's important?"

"Jeep George the dog musher? Yes sir, I sure will. Uh, Mr. George, I don't think it would hurt anything to tell you Captain Strickland is working that mining camp case, yes. We don't expect him back for a few days."

"Can you tell me anything about it?"

There was a hesitation.

"No sir. I prefer you get anything like that from Captain Strickland. He's in charge of the case."

"Thank you, officer. I appreciate it."

"Mr. George? I've heard a lot about you from the captain and some of the other officers. The captain has talked about you ever since you traveled together on the Iditarod race. Would you mind answering a question for me?"

"I believe I owe you one."

"Well, the captain told us a story about when you two got to Nome and were out celebrating later. I was just wondering . . ."

"Does this story have to do with the cavernous size of the urinal and how slippery the floor is in the Board of Trade saloon?"

"Well, yes sir, it does."

"I'm afraid it's all true."

I could hear him laughing as I hung up.

It took me some time to locate Karen's mother's number, and I was a bit ashamed that I hadn't learned much, but it was nice to hear Karen's voice sounding at least like a shell of what it had been two days ago.

"How are the kids taking it?"

"Oh God, Jeep, that's the worst of it now. They don't understand it."

"Neither do I, Karen."

"This not knowing is driving me crazy. I want to do something. We can't even have a funeral for a while, you know? Because it's a crime and all."

I said I was going to be gone a day or two and hoped I would learn something by then. She God-blessed me and I told her to kiss the kids for me. You have to say something.

Then I called Buck Davis and asked for a ride to Murder Lake.

He picked me up at Merrill Field in the Super Cub and in minutes we were flying into the southern foothills of the Talkeetna Mountains, headed for Murder Lake.

"I can put down on that little strip in this Super Cub," Buck yelled back.

"Good," I yelled forward.

Buck Davis has the lean face of one who has seen everything twice and is no longer startled by the bizarre things that occur in bush Alaska. He grins a lot beneath his thatch of slightly graying brown hair. This morning the hair jutted out from beneath a gimme cap singing the praises of Olympia beer, his favorite brand.

Down there now, sliding along beneath us, was the country of legends and delight, and horror and death. It's the land of moose and sheep and gold and people who never come back and maybe, just maybe, a killer. When you fly in a small plane in Alaska, distances are so deceiving, because it can take you days to cover ground on foot that can be covered, literally, in a minute or two in a plane.

"You want some music?" Buck yelled, waving a harmonica and smiling.

I grinned back. Not exactly the headsets and stereo music of the big jets, but he tries.

"I guess not today."

"Okey doke."

If you've lived in the Bush for any length of time, you begin to collect a list. It's called The People I've Known and Loved Who Have Been Killed in Plane Crashes. As the years go by, the list grows.

Sometimes you can take it out and look at it and wonder about it. These were guys who didn't have time to get old or sick. They had split seconds, if any, of pain, and then they were forever young, forever up there in some canyon. Oh, the bodies come back, except where it would endanger others to recover them, but those pilots are still up in those canyons. They are still wondering why they turned the corner and found that fog bank and no room between the canyon walls to turn the plane. Still wondering why they took that chance and tried to make it back to the airstrip in the rain instead of sitting there overnight and trying again in the morning.

Buck Davis is one of the few I'll ride with any more, and he does all my flying for me. It would probably be a convenience for me to learn how to fly a plane, but I have no intention of doing that. I have jousted with machinery since I was old enough to throw a wrench at something. Last year, my truck broke down and left me stranded on the highway four times. Buy an airplane? No thanks.

Buck once told me he always carried precious cargo, by which he meant himself, and that he looked forward to becoming a grandfather someday. I like a pilot with that attitude.

The nose of the Super Cub pointed up and we headed for sheep country. We began seeing rocks and snow beneath us now as the ground climbed steeply to try to meet us. We both looked down, almost automatically, and found a herd of Dall ewes and lambs trailing along a ridge off to the right. At this time of the year, the rams are still off by themselves. The sheep appear to be snow white, and it comes as a shock to see them after the first snowfall, when they prove to be slightly yellow, like a polar bear.

Then the Super Cub's nose pointed down again and we descended into the valley of the headwaters of the Talkeetna River. We followed it upstream and at last found the small lake that had earned its hideous name almost a century ago. The tiny landing strip lay to the west of the wall tents of the camp. Two jet helicopters were parked just off the strip in some berry brush.

Buck dropped the little Super Cub down for a close look and dragged the strip, flying over it low to make certain there were no obstacles to landing there. He checked the "Alaska windsock"—the tattletale strip of surveyor's tape on a stick at the north end of the runway—for wind direction.

A half-dozen men were standing outside the wall tents about a hundred yards from the strip, and they all looked up at us as we buzzed the strip. Then we were up again, our flaps pulled, and Buck set the Super Cub down on the short bouncy strip like a friendly toy with its oversized tundra tires.

Before we could climb out of the plane, two uniformed officers approached to tell us this was a closed airstrip and did we have an emergency.

"No," I said. "But I need to talk to Captain Strickland."

"Are you from the press?"

"No. Tell him Jeep George is here, will you?"

The way the two officers looked at each other, I figured they were either a couple of dog mushing fans or had heard the urinal story. One stayed with us while the other walked down to the knot of men gathered by the tents.

Almost at once, the officer waved us in, and Jim Strickland himself met us halfway with a handshake and a hug.

"Jim, this is Buck Davis of Kahiltna."

"You have a good reputation as a pilot, Buck," Jim said. "And as a hospitable one, too. Is it true you serve beer to your passengers?"

"A dirty lie," Buck said, drawing himself up as though offended, "and if I did, it would only be for those in first class."

Jim laughed and clapped Buck on the shoulder.

"Can we talk, Jim?" I asked.

"I'll wait at the plane," Buck said.

"Come on," Jim said, walking down the airstrip.

Jim Strickland is the kind of guy who never should have been a cop. He doesn't have the right attitude. He doesn't believe everyone who jaywalks or shoplifts a loaf of bread should be gunned down for the betterment of society. As a unit, however, the Alaska State Troopers makes a point of seeking professionals for its force, professionals like Jim, and discourages hiring the other kind.

Jim has a bluff, rugged face with shocking red hair and a body like a fireplug. It's a good setting for the kind of man he is. Jim Strickland loves his wife, his kids, his sled dogs, his job and his beer, not necessarily in that order. And he's very good at what he does.

"One of the men killed here," I said, "was a guy named Bill Turner."

Jim looked at me. "How did you learn that?"

"His wife told me. We go way back, Jim. Bill was one of my closest friends. Like you. Like ol' Buck there. Since we were just kids. You know how it is in a village that size. He was a foster kid. My parents were dead. We parded up. I stood up for him at his wedding. He was my handler at the races."

Jim nodded. "I remember him now. What do you want from me, Jeep?"

"I promised his wife I'd see what I could learn about this for her."

"And it won't go any further." It was a statement, not a question.

"Of course not."

He walked and thought for a while.

"Let's find a sit-down log, Jeep."

We found one and Jim found a comfortable spot on it and filled and lighted his old curved pipe.

"This is a dirty business, Jeep. I've never had one like it, although I know there have been some in the past."

"What happened?"

"Best guess?"

"Best guess."

He looked up at the sky turning cloud gray toward the east.

"Well, there were five men here, working for an outfit called Shan-Dor. You familiar with them?"

I nodded.

"Two of the men were mining engineers, I understand. One was a young kid just out of college who signed on for some of the grunt work. Your pal Turner came up just recently to look the project over and report back to the office on their progress up here."

I nodded.

"The diggings are up there on the hill," Jim said. "There was one more member of the group. He was hired to cook and to rustle up firewood, whatever was needed. General swamper, you know. He took care of camp. He's also the one who isn't here."

"Name?"

He thought for a minute, still watching the sky. "Well, I think the press will get this pretty quick from the mining company anyway. It's a guy named Hendrix. Lee Hendrix. He's long gone by now, of course."

"On foot?"

"On foot."

"So what happened?"

"The supply plane came in here early yesterday morning. Nothing was moving. By the way, that plane was supposed to take your friend Turner back with it.

"The pilot walked over to the tents and found the bodies. Someone killed all four of them with a knife while they slept. Assuming it was Hendrix, and we have no reason to think it wasn't, he didn't steal anything from them, just walked away. There haven't been any aircraft in here since the murders but that supply plane and our two choppers."

"Nothing missing?"

"Nothing to write home about. All the scientific stuff seems to be here, the company says. Nothing of any value taken. He appears to have rummaged through the stores to get some food together, he has a sleeping bag with him, and we know he has a rifle. There are only four rifles here, and one of our planes was shot at this morning."

"Have any of your men followed his trail yet?"

"Through these blueberries? I didn't think you could."

"Could I have a try at it?"

"Why?"

"Why not? Might learn something."

"You let me know every detail."

"If there's anything to learn, yes, of course."

"Help yourself."

We walked into the compound of white tents and I noticed five sled dogs tethered on a picket chain behind one of the tents. There was an empty sack of dog food against the tent.

"Jim, did any of your men feed these dogs?"

He asked. No one had.

"Well, someone fed these dogs heavily just a day or so ago. Look at the uneaten food. See the empty sack there? See the string? That's the opening string. Someone opened a brand-new fifty-pound bag of dog food and poured it out to the dogs. All of it. Someone who thought these dogs wouldn't get fed for a few days. Whose dogs were these?"

"They belonged to one of the dead men, Jeep. The young kid just out of college. They say he was planning to winter in here and work them into a team."

"Anyone we know?"

Jim shook his head. "Up from Oregon, I understand."

I nodded and went to look for a trail.

What I had to look for here was physical trail. There are different kinds of trail, but I needed tracks. I needed broken branches. I needed to find some solid evidence to go on.

The camp was on the west shore of Murder Lake, and from there a well-used trail led up to the northwest about a quarter mile to where the diggings were. This, Jim said, was a prospect hole. Prospect holes are almost an industry in Alaska. Some old sourdough finds ore that assays out pretty rich, then sells the claim to an outfit like Shan-Dor Mining Company. Shan-Dor probably owned or leased rights to several hundred of these holes.

The more promising of these claims warrants a prospect team like the tragic one here. They fly in some sophisticated equipment and try to learn just how good and how big a find it is. This process takes anywhere from a couple of weeks to a few months. If one of these men was planning to winter here, this was more than likely one of those prospects that would become a mine.

So I avoided the trail up to the mine and the area around the lake and the path out to the outhouse and the airstrip.

Murder Lake is an area of stunted spruce in some areas, alders here and there, and muskeg down in the lower areas. Slightly higher on the slopes are thicker stands of spruce, pocked with the alders. Great moose country.

At that moment, it was man country, and I wanted to learn what kind of man would stab four men to death as they slept.

I found his trail about two hundred yards away from camp. At least, it was one possibility. Here was a man's trail. This man Hendrix, if that's who it was, was wearing large boots with fairly new tread. Ankle-fit hip boots. A man who knew what to wear in the Bush.

Following a trail in muskeg and the short timber isn't like tracking some-one on dry ground or (bless it) wet ground. Muskeg is a combination of rank blackwater pools choked with insect life and hummocks of short grasses. Muskeg heals itself much like these self-healing puncture-proof tires. You take a step and for a second the hummock gives beneath your foot, the grasses compress and the outer areas bulge upward to compen-sate for your weight. Then, when you step off, the hummock takes as long as ten or fifteen minutes to return to normal.

If a man can find a cold human track in muskeg, he's either a whole lot better than I am, or the luckiest devil in the mountains, or both.

What I found, at first, was a tiny bit of cloth hanging around a foot up on some blueberry brush in the middle of the muskeg flats to the east of camp. It was dark green, wool of some kind, perhaps what my German hunters called loden cloth. I put it in my pocket and took an overall look.

If this was our man, and the green wool came from his trousers, he was heading to the east. I lined up the approximate area where he'd be leaving the muskeg for higher ground and walked over there.

I walked in large crescents, each one farther out from the muskeg, until I found him. Found his tracks, that is.

At first there were several boot tracks, then a few broken branches. Then I got lucky. Up here, where the ground rises steeply, our man tripped over an alder root and fell.

Here were the knee impressions where he went down and there, just to the left of them, was something even more important. It was a round pug mark, punched into the ground, and it spoke volumes.

I took the lightweight aluminum tape measure given me by one of my hunters—it had his company's logo embossed on the outside—and measured the pug. It was over three-quarters of an inch across. I spread the debris away from it and could find no other marks next to it. I compared the distance between his knee mark and boot mark to my own.

Then I followed his trail through the easier-going soil until I had a pretty good idea how big this man was and which direction he was heading.

Jim Strickland was waiting when I got back to the camp. "Well?"

"Well, Captain," I said, "he has blue eyes, grew up in a poor section of Liverpool, speaks with an Ethiopian accent and likes food heavily laced with curry."

He grinned. "You go to hell."

"I'm afraid I'm no Sherlock Holmes," I said, "just a hunting guide. But I'm willing to bet you the rifle he took is either a .338 Winchester Magnum or a .375 Holland & Holland Magnum."

"The company told us he carries a .375 H & H."

"And it has a scope."

"How the hell you know that?"

"He tripped up there and the muzzle went into the ground. From that I could tell the size. A thirty-caliber muzzle will make a mark just under three-quarters of an inch. There was no mark from a front sight, so I'm guessing it's a scoped rifle.

"This is a big guy, I'm guessing. Over six feet. Wearing green wool trousers"—I handed him the scrap I found—"and is either a very experienced hunter or a professional guide."

"How did you figure that out?"

"The mark the rifle made in the ground was of the muzzle, which means the muzzle was hanging down. That's how guides carry them. Two reasons: keeps water out of the bore, and you can bring it up for a shot faster that way.

"Also," I said, "he had covered the muzzle with something . . . Oh, it could be a cellophane cigarette pack wrapper, or even a piece of Scotch tape. An uncovered muzzle would punch quite a different hole in the ground. It would leave a ring, like this." I drew a picture in the dirt.

All the officers were now listening. I looked around and smiled and shrugged.

"And . . . if you don't already know it, he's right-handed and a big fella."

"Six four, around two hundred twenty pounds," Jim said.

I nodded. "A couple of other things, Captain. He left here at night, and it has rained since."

"That fits."

"His tracks," I said, "head fairly straight for that divide up there. My guess would be he'll head across the Su toward the Nelchina."

Jim motioned me aside, and we walked out past the woodpile.

"We know where he is . . . or about where he was this morning, anyway."

"The plane that was shot at?"

"Yeah. Search plane, flying over the headwaters of the Susitna, got shot at. Right through a float. Monster exit hole in that pontoon."

"A .375 would do that."

"Sure would. We're warning pilots to stay away from that area for a while."

"You going in after him?"

"I'm not going to read this in the paper?"

"Nope."

"I can't see getting anyone else killed by this nut, can you? It won't bring any of those poor guys back. It won't bring back your friend Turner, either."

"I can't believe you're just going to sit here and let him go like this, Jim."

"You have to see it my way, Jeep. The way he's headed . . . you know the Nelchina? It's what . . . a hundred and fifty, maybe two hundred miles across before this guy gets to a roadhouse or a highway. And he'll be lucky to make ten miles a day out there."

"I agree. If he sticks to the swamps, he'll be lucky to make half that."

"That's my point. Also, he may just wander around out there. Good men have done it before. Those lakes in the Nelchina all look about alike now, don't they?"

"If," I said, "this guy Hendrix were some cheechako just off the boat who somehow managed to talk his way onto a mining crew and then conveniently went nuts, I'd agree with you. Let Mother Nature take care of the case. A man who doesn't know his way around probably wouldn't survive."

"That's my thinking exactly, Jeep."

I looked at Jim. The usual grin was a firm straight line now beneath the level eyes with the laugh wrinkles. "Between us?" he asked.

"Between us."

"This man's insane. We haven't come up with any kind of a reason why he'd want to kill the other men in this camp, but he did. It was a dirty business. He did things that were . . . unnecessary? I guess that's the word. Unnecessary. And after the men had been dead awhile, the coroner says."

"Mutilation?"

"Yes. And he arranged things . . . like the men's clothes . . . in strange ways. Laid them out on the ground in strange patterns, like this." Jim drew a strange design that seemed a balanced figure of some sort with points on four corners.

"Some kind of cult thing?" I asked. "Witchcraft?"

"Our expert on that stuff doesn't think so. Basically, he says the guy's a nut."

"Jim, would you mind if I asked around a bit about this guy in town? It's for Karen, Bill's wife. She wants to know what to tell those little kids of hers, and I don't blame her."

"They have children?"

"Two of them," I smiled. "The little boy's name is George."

"After a nutty dog musher I might know?"

"The same."

"Parents should have more sense than that."

"That's what I told them."

"Look, Jeep, I can understand why you'd want to do this, but what good would come from asking around? We've been asking around. Good Lord, I have men asking around all over the place right now, believe me. But it's really to try to find some motive. We know Hendrix did this. Hundred-to-one odds. Thousand to one. No idea why."

"Then what harm would come of my asking a few questions?"

"Look, you are a good dog musher—well, okay, an adequate dog musher—and you're a great hunting guide and a super pal, but this is police work. Cop stuff. You leave it to us."

"Thanks, Jim," I said, shaking hands. "But I want to do something. If I learn anything interesting, I'll let you know."

"You'd better."

"See, it's just that I want to learn a bit about this guy myself. Curiosity, I guess. I'd like to know what would make a man kill his camp mates in such a way, then have the kindness to feed those dogs so well before he left. Jim?"

"Yes?"

"I wouldn't bet on his not making it across the Nelchina. This is a woodsman."

"Alaska kills woodsmen all the time," he said.

"And every day," I said, "people survive incredible trouble up here."

"That's true enough. Well, will you please give my condolences to Mrs. Turner?"

"I will, Jim, and thanks for filling me in."

"Wish I knew more about this myself. Please tell her that her husband's body will be released probably tomorrow, if not the next day. We'll call her."

"Thanks. I owe you one."

I turned to walk to the plane.

"Jeep . . . "

I turned back.

"I hear Hendrix has a girlfriend named Dottie who works some of the Fourth Avenue bars."

"Thanks."

"Watch your backtrail."

"You do the same."

Buck was sitting on the balloon tire of the Super Cub, talking with a state trooper who evidently had stayed with him for the whole hour we were there. We swung the tail of the plane around and I climbed in the back. Buck got in, pulled up the bottom half of the door, then pulled down the top until it clicked, and started the engine.

"Any sense in me asking any of the four million questions I have about this thing?"

"I made some promises, Buck. Not now."

"Later on, maybe?"

"Later on for sure."

He gunned it down the runway for about three hundred feet and then popped the Super Cub into the sky. Trees began disappearing beneath us.

"I'll take you anywhere except the headwaters of the grand and glorious Susitna River," Buck yelled back over his shoulder. "That nice fella in the uniform said it was bad medicine to fly there. Anti-aircraft guns. Surface-to-air missiles. That sort of thing."

"Very bad medicine. Back to Anchorage, Buck. Thanks."

He fumbled around in the little ice chest he kept up front and handed me back an orange drink. It tasted great. He knows I like the orange ones best. I have nothing against harder stuff but I have too much respect for those ancient Athabascan genes of mine to play Russian roulette with alcohol.

Buck whipped out the harmonica and waved it above his head as a question.

"Let 'er rip, Buck," I yelled.

Buck doesn't know how to play anything sad . . . says he has no time for sad songs. I was glad of it that day because the drone of the engine, the flash of the sunshine below on the black of the lakes, and the jaunty music were just about enough to wash from my mind some of the pictures that were haunting it.

Just about.

CHAPTER 3

By the time I'd showered and dressed and had supper, it was twilight again in Anchorage, but this time with the thick dark layer of rain clouds it's famous for.

As I started down one end of Fourth Avenue's section of seedy to semi-seedy bars, the rain began . . . cold, misty, gentle and sad. It was okay. I was in the mood.

The families of four men were torn apart on this slowly crying evening, the kind of evening when even the ravens huddle in back-alley doorways or go places only ravens know about.

Fourth Avenue itself is sad. The best thing that ever happened to Fourth Avenue occurred one day in March of 1964, when the west half of the bar district fell about thirty feet. The east side of the street stood miraculously unscathed after the worst recorded earthquake in history. The west side then humbly became parking lots that slope down toward Ship Creek, and a famous fast-food joint anchored one corner of the infamous old dive district. It's one of the places to go between five a.m. and eight a.m., the time when the law says the bars must be closed.

Every city has a Fourth Avenue. It is the place where broken dreams meet broken bottles. Where disappointments distill into a fulminate of desperation so thick you can taste it like the beer.

Maybe Anchorage is even more that way than other cities Outside, because this is a place where people come who are young, either in body or mind. They come with the dream of taking something brand new, or old beyond imagining, and somehow finding a way to make it work for them.

To find that little niche, or to make that big splash.

Alaska's population is the youngest in the nation, and the ideas are young and new. There is the feeling that nothing is impossible as long as you keep getting ideas and don't get killed by the cold or a bear or an airplane or the slashing sea.

For some, the only niche they find is here on Fourth Avenue. It's the last stop before Seattle or the grave. They can find something in the music and the beer and the laughing and the fights.

The bars are busy during their legal twenty-one hours a day, and these few short blocks have their own little society, too. At the head of the society are the bar owners, followed by the bartenders. The bar girls and dancers and customers and the band members are the great proletariat, and out in the back alley between Fourth and Fifth avenues are the police patrols. They don't have too much to do in summer; the bartenders break up most fights without any help. But in winter, the patrol cars prowl the alleys for sleepers. Sleepers will try car doors in the parking lots until they find one that is unlocked, then they crawl inside, fall asleep, and die.

Or they'll crawl into a dumpster and fall asleep, and maybe, just for a little while, dream that dream once again . . . of finding gold in the mountains . . . of starting an oil field corporation . . . of winning the Iditarod . . . of being the best seal hunter in the village.

Then they die.

The hookers patrol outside the bars, too—walking the sidewalks in summer and driving around the block in winter. Both the hookers and the cops circle the herd, waiting to pick off strays, each for their own reasons.

When a certain newspaper columnist left Alaska, he left behind a sign (without permission) at Anchorage International Airport. It read:

> *Welcome to beautiful Anchorage*
> *Nestled on Cook Inlet's shores,*
> *Where the hookers outnumber the oilmen*
> *And the poor folks outnumber the whores.*

Fourth Avenue is a lot like that. So traveling from bar to bar looking for a woman named Dottie on a rainy night seemed to fit. Fourth Avenue suits a rainy night, even if the view from the front doors of the bars can be breathtaking.

I found her at the third bar.

"The bartender tells me your name is Dottie," I said.

"Did you think that line up yourself, or was it written down in a magazine?"

"I'd like to talk to you for a few minutes, if you wouldn't mind."

"Look, pal," she said, slurring her words, but speaking as carefully as she could, "I don't know what Joseph told you, but if he let you think you'd get anything more out of me. . . . Where you from?"

"Kahiltna."

"Kahiltna. Kahiltna. Where the mountains are big and the men are bigger, right? Where the men are men and the dogs are nervous, right? I'm from Sleetmute."

I thought there was a touch of the village in her voice, and her hair was black. Dottie didn't stand more than five feet tall, but a lot of that had begun sagging lately.

She wasn't full Native, of course. The facial features gave that away. My guess is she's one of these special Alaskan combination plates . . . like me. She wore a good dress that had been on her too long, she had a ring on every finger, and smoked cigarettes from a cigarette case that cost twenty bucks at the airport gift shop. It was made in Taiwan, but had a totem pole on it and looked good.

"Sleetmute's a nice village," I said. "I've been in there a time or two."

"Yeah? Well, did you know that Sleetmute . . . good ol' Sleetmute . . . sucks? You ever see anything going on there? You ever see a Fur Rendezvous in Sleetmute? Oh, they got dogsled races. Big time. This kid against that kid. Winner gets a sack of dog food from the trading post, right? They race shki-doos for motor oil there."

When she pronounced Ski-Doo like that, I smiled. No one but a village person would pronounce it that way.

"In the summer," she said, waving an unlighted cigarette in the air until I got the idea and picked up her lighter and lit it for her.

"Thanks, bon soirée mon ami. That's French, you know. Means my dear love or something. Not that you're my dear love, don't get me wrong. We don't even know each other yet. I just like to speak French sometimes. A guy taught me some a couple years ago. He was from Canada."

"Sleetmute in summer?"

"Sleetmute? Oh, Sleetmute, of course . . . bon soire Sleetmute, of course. In the summer everybody fishes and cuts them open and dries them and gets eaten up by bugs. Fun, huh?"

"I guess some people like it, Dottie."

She looked at me funny with her eyes kind of squinty. "Who are you, anyway?"

"Jepsen George. Call me Jeep."

"Jepsen George call me Jeep, huh? Okay, Call-Me-Jeep. Why are you looking for me?"

"I need to talk to you."

"About what?"

"Lee Hendrix."

She made a pushing sound with her breath and looked at me again. "You his friend?"

"No."

"Good. I hate that creep. You a cop?" I shook my head. "Two cops asked me a lot of questions about him. They think he killed those men in the mountains."

I nodded.

"You're not a reporter, are you? I shouldn't talk to a reporter, you know. Everybody says so."

"I'm not a reporter, Dottie."

"Then who the hell are you?"

"I'm the best friend of one of the men who got killed in that mining camp, and I'm trying to figure out why this all happened."

She looked at me strangely for a minute, then spoke something in her language. It wasn't mine and I had no idea what she was saying. I smiled and gave her a greeting in Dena'ina from the Dash-qe-tana branch of the Athabascan family.

She grinned and shrugged. "I can't understand you and you can't understand me, Jeepsen George the Jep."

Then she began singing a song of the village in a high voice, a haunting voice, and the noises of the bar quieted a minute as two others joined her in song.

Then she stopped and they continued, yelling above Merle Haggard's best on the jukebox. You could almost smell the smoke from the spruce fires and hear the skin drums. Even on Fourth Avenue.

"Pretty, isn't it?" she said, smiling.

I nodded.

"Do you have enough money to buy me a steak?"

"Yes," I said. "Dessert, too."

"Maybe a bottle later on, Jeepsen?"

"We'll see, Dottie. But I'm good for a steak, anyway."

"Okay," she said, hopping down from the stool. "Let's go."

We went to a cafe where I knew she'd be comfortable. It was one of those service areas for Fourth Avenue; its only real rush came during the three hours in early morning when the bars had to close. The steaks they served there were just right, as the old joke goes: "If they were any better I couldn't afford them, and if they were any worse, I couldn't eat them."

Dottie knew most of the people in the place. It was the kind of cafe where steak was put on the menu because the owner thought it should be there, somewhere. No one asks how you like it cooked, and the waitress automatically brings ketchup.

Dottie didn't say five words through dinner, eating as methodically as she had probably filleted fish with an ulu a long time ago. No wasted movements. Do it first. Do it right. Get it done.

When she finished, she lit a cigarette.

"That was a good steak, Jeep. You're the dog musher, right?"

"Right."

"You don't win very often, do you?"

"Not really."

"Why not?"

"It's not that important to me. I enjoy the dogs and the driving, but if I had to get serious about competing, I'd have to feed seventy-five dogs instead of eight, cull the puppies mercilessly, and work too hard. The way I do it is more fun."

"I like fun," she said, taking a puff. "It's enjoyable."

Then she laughed. "I made a pretty good joke there, didn't I?"

I grinned. "Dottie, what's Lee Hendrix like?"

She thought about that for a minute and I knew the alcohol was beginning to lift a bit.

"Well, he's big and strong and quick. So quick you can't believe it. But I don't suppose that's what you want."

"How quick is he?"

"One day he was being a jerk and I started throwing things at him. You know. As fast as I could? He caught most of them and set them down on the table. He's that quick."

"Impressive."

"You're a strange one."

"Not really," I said. "Dottie, why would Lee want to kill those men?"

"I thought about it. I thought about it a lot since those cops came to see me. I don't know. If he could make money off them, he'd kill them."

"Did he make money off you?"

"Damn right. I fed that slob and took care of him. You know those fancy rubber boots that cost you a hundred dollars? Who do you think paid for his? But that wasn't enough for him."

"What was enough for him?"

"None of your business."

"I bought the steak."

"Okay . . . you bought the steak. Yeah, you bought the steak. What the hell, huh? Well, I had a good job. I worked for it real hard, you know? I went to school. I took the civil service test and I did real good on it. The agency hired me and I was doing okay there for a long time.

"Well . . . let's just say that my pay at the agency wasn't enough for him, all right? That satisfy you?"

"He wanted you to . . . moonlight?"

"My boss found out about it. She had a fit. All I have left is the moon-lighting now."

"I'm sorry, Dottie."

"Yeah, he was sorry, too. He found a younger woman about a month ago and moved in with her. That creep."

"Do you think he might be a little crazy in the head?"

"Jeez, to kill those guys? I think he must be, don't you?"

"You know him, Dottie. I don't. Did he ever do crazy things?"

Dottie fished another cigarette out of the totem pole case and waited until I lit it. I ordered more coffee. The waitress gave us one of those "Are you going to hang around here all night until I'm off shift and then not leave a tip?" looks, and cleared the table of all but the coffee.

"Crazy things. Well, let's see. He likes to hit people, but a lot of guys do that."

"Did he hit you?"

"Sure. What the hell. It happens. I didn't think it was right. I spent a long time in school and worked hard to get my job and come here, you know? Then some damn hunting guide thinks you should be hanging sheefish on a rack someplace and bangs you around. Helluva life, ain't it, Jeep George?" She smiled at me a little.

"He was a hunting guide?"

"Well, I don't think he ever had his own camp, you know? He just worked for another guide."

I nodded. "An assistant guide."

"I guess so. He worked for a guy named Red, I know. Talked about him some."

"Did he say what Red's last name was?"

"I don't think so. I don't remember if he did. Sorry. He used to say Red would disappear up in those mountains some day, though, and no one would ever find the body."

"He didn't like Red?"

"Honey," she said, "Lee doesn't like anyone." She laughed. "Well . . . dogs, maybe."

"He had a dog?"

"No. Just liked them. Used to say they were the only pure creatures on earth. That they wouldn't hurt a man or stab him in the back."

I remembered the fifty pounds of dog food that had been poured out for the dogs by a man who had just murdered and mutilated four men.

"People had stabbed him in the back?"

"He thought everybody did. He thought I did. Honest, I never looked at anybody else, and he got every cent I made."

"How long were you two together?"

She looked at the ceiling and squinted. "Off and on, I guess about four years."

"Off and on?"

"You know how it is. He'd stay around in the winter for a few months, then go off somewhere. If he wasn't working a construction job, he was on that fishing boat. I got to hating that fishing boat."

"Which fishing boat was it?"

"Its name? I don't know. I'm sure he told me, though, honey, but I'm sorry, I just can't remember."

"That's okay."

"I'm afraid I'm not much help, Jeep. I want to help, too. You're nice to a girl. You got a wife or anything?"

"No wife or anything," I said, smiling.

She smiled. "You're too smart for that, right?"

"Right."

"And I bet you treat ladies real kind, too."

"Thanks, Dottie. That's a nice thing to hear." I stirred some sugar into my coffee. "What was Lee like when he was home?"

"Lee. Lee. Always about Lee. Do we always have to talk about Lee?"

"I'm sorry. It's very important."

She sighed. "Well, sometimes he was nice, you know? That's why I let him come back. Sometimes he was nice. He liked to go out, too, and sometimes he'd take me with him. But there were some times when it was like I wasn't even there. He'd maybe just call me names. Bad ones. And I hadn't done anything. And he'd say he was going to get a boat and he was going to be free. Said he'd get rid of an albatross. He said I was one, and a friend looked it up for me at work. I was still working for the agency then. She said it was a bird. Like I'm a bird?

"See, that's crazy, isn't it? He thinks I'm a bird. That's something crazy, seems to me."

"Did he say anything else that was crazy?"

"Just about getting a boat. He said he was going to get a boat and then he'd be master, you know? And he used to say poetry things about boats. Rhyming things about boats, crazy stuff like that. I told him I thought it sounded like fun, and I could go along and cook for him, but he said women were bad luck on ships and I had to stay on land where I belonged.

"Well, I got a little mad at him, you know? So I told him a fishing boat wasn't a ship, and if I was good enough to cook for him here, I could cook there. And you know what he did? He hit me, mean like. And then he laughed. It was about two weeks later he told me to make more money. Said he needed it for the boat."

"And you started moonlighting?"

She shrugged and looked down into her coffee cup. In the harsh fluorescent lights of the cafe, I could see the start of wrinkles near her eyes.

"You're nice," she said, finally. "I'm embarrassed talking to you about it."

"I think I have the picture," I said. "He needed more money to buy a boat and that was why."

She nodded. "Well, said he needed boat things, anyway. Radios, things like that."

"And your boss found out?"

"Somebody in the office found out and told my boss. You can't even think how mad she was, Jeep. It was like I disgraced a family or something, you know? Maybe I did. She said we were supposed to set examples for the needy people we were helping, and I was nothing but a . . . Fourth Avenue girl, you know?

"I promised to quit, and I meant it. I worked there twelve years, Jeep. Twelve years and I never did nothing like this before. I guess I'm a jerk, too. I went to school to learn to do this. I went to school under a program, you know? And my boss, she hired me twelve years ago, and now it was just gone, just like that. And when Lee found out, I told him and I was crying, you know, and he just laughed and said I was stupid, and now how was I going to make enough money? Then he got really mean. He didn't hit me, but he called me names and said I was only fit for the land and he walked away. He was gone four days."

"But he came back."

"He came back, for one night. He got up in the middle of the night, took all the money out of my purse, and moved in with another woman. I saw her. She's younger than me."

"When was this?"

"About a month ago, I guess. Maybe she made him cuckoo. I don't know."

"Did you know he'd gone to work for that mining company?"

"No. He musta done that after we broke up."

"What kind of music does he like?"

"What?"

"Music. What kind of music does he play on the radio?"

"Rock stuff, mostly, but sometimes the weird stuff, too."

"Weird stuff?"

"You know. Orchestras. Opera stuff. Violins. Sometimes he'd talk about the boat and he'd get that station on the radio and he'd turn it way up. Sometimes the landlady had to come and tell him to turn it down. He always did, though, because he didn't want us to get kicked out."

"Did he mention any favorite composers, Dottie? You know, like Mozart or Beethoven or Bach?"

"Beethoven, I think. Did he write the real loud stuff that sounds like war?"

"That's the one."

"He likes that loud war stuff. He said some of those songs were written hundreds of years ago. Is that true?"

"Yes."

"Hard to believe, isn't it? That a song can last that long, I mean."

I grinned. "That song you sang in the bar tonight, Dottie. How old do you think that is?"

She thought a minute, then grinned. "Pretty darned old, I guess."

"Did he stay awake late at night?"

"Sometimes. Why are you asking these questions?"

"I want to learn as much as I can about him."

"You wouldn't like him. That's all you need to know about him."

"But did he like late night? Or did he like to get up early in the morning?"

"Early. He likes to get up early. It drove me nuts. I'd work for him all night, then he'd get me up to fix breakfast for him. He'd say, 'Daylight's burning, baby, get busy.' Never knew what he meant by that. He'd finally get out of there, and I could shower and go to work. While I had my job."

I nodded, and gave her one of my cards with the Anchorage phone number on it.

"If you can think of anything else about Lee that would help me understand him a little, please call this number, will you? I probably won't be there, but a nice girl named Betsy will take the message."

"Are we all done now?"

"We're all done."

"Would you like to maybe get us a bottle and come up for a while? I mean, it would be friendship only, Jeep. We're friends now, aren't we?"

"We're friends now, Dottie. You bet." I slipped her a ten. "Why don't you take this and get that bottle, Dottie? I'm worn out. You understand, right?"

"Oh, I understand, all right," she said, and her mouth and eyes squinted down into something I didn't like to see. I knew now how she'd look at eighty, if she survived Fourth Avenue. "I understand I'm not good enough. . . ."

"Now, Dottie . . . "

"Dammit, don't talk down to me! I had my belly full of that in the village, and I don't need to get it here. I guess I'm supposed to smile now and go out to the kitchen with the other women, aren't I?"

Her lip quivered and she turned away for a minute and then wiped her eyes.

"I'm sorry," I said. "I didn't mean to get you upset, really . . ."

She turned back to me and shrugged. For a minute she just looked at me, then she started to smile. She reached out and gave my arm a squeeze. "No. I'm wrong. Oh boy, I don't know why I said that. Hard to know just what . . . well, I don't know what to say."

"Hey, it's okay. I'm like that all the time," I said.

She tucked the ten away, then straightened her dress.

"You asked me if I understood," she said, "and I think I understand a lot, Jeep George. I think maybe you are a gentleman and a pretty nice guy."

I laughed. "I'll bet you say that to all the dog mushers."

She took my arm as I paid the check and watched the relief spread over the waitress's face, then we stepped out together into the strange summer twilight and achingly fresh rainy air of Anchorage.

"I'll see you around, huh?"

"Sure thing, Dottie."

"Are you going to try to find him?"

"Of course not."

"Good. He'll kill you."

"You think he killed those men, Dottie?"

"Of course he did." Then she was gone down the long block to the noise and rain and muddled lives of Fourth Avenue.

CHAPTER 4

"Are you going to sleep all day, or will you buy a girl a cup of coffee?"

The light hit my eyes from the windows where she'd slashed back the curtains. It was blinding and I threw my arms across my eyes to shield them.

"You just break into a man's home when he's asleep, huh?" I said to Betsy, who was already making some coffee over in the corner. "You need to be more considerate, Miss Kelley. For example, what if I had been . . . shall we say entertaining in here?"

"Not a chance, Jepsen George. Dottie called me this morning. Asked me if I was your girl. Said you two were just friends and had a nice long talk and boy were you ever a gentleman and boy was I lucky. When I told her I couldn't even stand to be in the same room with such an ugly man, she told me I was nuts."

"Hey, I'm in a sleeping bag here, you know?"

"Ah . . . is the big tough Alaskan hunting guide bashful? Well ah declare, ah'll just avert my glance so you-all can get dressed. Theah, darlin', is that moah to yoah likin'?"

Her Sarah Bernhardt pose, wrist against forehead in feigned distress, started me laughing as I pulled on a pair of blue jeans. She always gets me laughing. It's one of the things I like most about Betsy Kelley. She is a very efficient maker of hunt reservations and answers the phone for me wonderfully. But it's more than that. She makes me laugh, and I love that.

Betsy is a regular woman. By that I mean she's attractive enough with her face and figure and all, but no one would ever ask her to pose for Answering Service Digest's centerfold. It's only after you get to know Betsy that you learn how beautiful she is.

She has this hair, brown as a Circassian walnut rifle stock, long hair that is brushed until it shines, and it acts as a frame for two deep green eyes that seem to be emeralds in a face that is almost always smiling.

She should have children. They would grow up laughing all the time. Sometimes I think I'd like to be the father of those kids, too. And there are times when I think she might even go for it. But I keep thinking that if I really care about her, I wouldn't saddle her with a man who lives in a tent five months of the year and with eight dogs the rest of the time.

But in the middle of winter, when I'm in the home cabin there just a short walk from Kahiltna, I get to thinking about that laughter. When it gets bad enough, I just pull on my parka and dancing mukluks and head through the trees to the South Seas roadhouse and order up some orange drink and some polka dancing.

Betsy is one of the world's special people.

With the cobwebs washed away by coffee and some splashing of cold water, I was able to enjoy looking out across most of the roof of the movie theater and on across Knik Arm to the trees on the other side and the swelling masterpiece beyond that is Mount McKinley, North America's highest peak.

"Okay," Betsy said, "who's Dottie?"

"Jealous?" I asked, grinning.

"Oh yes, dear heart. Why, when I heard her say your name . . . the way she said it. Jee-e-ep. Long, drawn out, sexy. Oh wow, I thought, there goes any hope I may have had for a happy future. I'll apply for convent duty tomorrow. Right after lunch. Now who's Dottie?"

I spent the next hour telling her what I could about the murders and what I had learned. I didn't tell her things I shouldn't, and I knew that what I did tell her wouldn't go any farther. She's that kind of woman.

"Well," she said, "Dottie said she has a message for you. She said she looked into your soul last night and she wants to say don't do it."

"I wonder what she means by that?" I said.

Betsy looked at me and got up and did the honors on coffee. "Don't you know?" she said.

I shrugged.

"Oh, a shrugging question, is it? Is Dottie perchance Native? That would explain it. Ignorant white girl born in Chicago can't understand deep meanings, so we just beat the drum and shrug and boy howdy are we ever deep and primordial. Something like that?"

I was laughing so hard I spilled my coffee.

"Now tell me," she said, "what did dear ol' Dottie—she sounded a bit drunk when she called, by the way —"

I nodded.

"—what did she see when she looked deep in your soul?"

"A mess at the moment, Bets. Just a mess in there. Nothing sorted out. No way to go. No path out of the mess. I think I'll just ask some more questions and see what happens. I can't think of anything else to do."

"Are the troopers going after this guy?"

"They have men stationed at what they call 'strategic locations' along the Glenn and Richardson highways."

"What? Couple hundred miles to cover there?"

"Something like that."

Betsy looked out the window at the mountain and then at me. She even looks good with no makeup and just a windbreaker and jeans on and just morning. Just good. A regular but special kind of good.

"I imagine what the troopers mean," I said, "is they'll have extra patrols on the roads, and will be checking empty cabins in the basin and keeping an eye on the roadhouses in the area."

She looked at me. "Well, that will make it handier for him, won't it? He'll have all these police officers he can give himself up to, won't he?"

"I don't think that's too likely to happen, Bets."

"Of course not, Jeep. I was being facetious. That's spelled f-a-c-e . . . "

"I'm sorry, Betsy, I'm not too sharp this morning."

"It wouldn't be that what Dottie saw in your soul was that Jepsen George, the said-to-be-best hunting guide in Alaska, might be thinking of doing a little hunting before the regular early moose season opens, would it?"

I looked at her, trying not to show anything on my face. It didn't work. "Jeep?"

"Not bad," I finally said, "for an ignorant white girl born in Chicago."

She was silent. She looked out at the Alaska morning. "I hope you aren't serious, Jeep."

"Me too. Maybe they'll pick him up when he crosses the highway. Maybe he'll starve out and turn himself in. Maybe some bear will do us all a favor and eat him. I vote for all of the above."

"But you don't think any of those things will happen, do you?"

"No. I don't."

"Is he good?"

"Very good."

"Then leave him alone."

"Even the good ones make mistakes."

"Who made you the police force, Jeep? We pay them. They know what they're doing. Let them do it."

"Do you remember Bill Turner?"

"Of course."

I just sat and stared out the window for a while, trying to draw some strength from that monstrous mountain out there. I longed to see a raven fly across my path this morning, some indication that what had been creeping more and more into my mind and heart wasn't just craziness. Thinking like this can't really take place in the city, though. Here you have all the cars and lights and people talking and sales over at the J.C. Penney store. A lot of people make bad decisions in cities.

Serious decisions have to be made on hilltops, where the world can be seen and judged but not heard. You must put it first where it belongs and not let it get too important for itself. My Grandfather George used to go out and sit on a hill behind the airstrip when he needed to think. In the last few years, I've come to understand why, more and more.

"I have to learn more about this guy."

"Why?"

"For Karen."

"Are you sure?"

I looked at her and smiled. She looked my way, with a raised eyebrow, and smiled. Betsy is like a part of you that can't be lied to. A part, like your conscience or soul or personal totem, that would never forgive deceit.

"Between us?"

"Of course," she said.

"Maybe part of it is for Karen. The only problem with that is, the more I learn about Hendrix, the more I don't want to tell Karen about him. If this were just a case of some guy getting bushy and killing his roomies, that's one thing. People get bushy. People kill their pards out there sometimes.

"But how do you tell her about the evil? There were things done. . . . and how do you tell her that the same monster who killed her husband as he slept for no apparent reason then took time to feed five dogs before he left? How can you give her those permanent nightmares, because that's what they'd be.

"So I sit here trying to fulfill my promise to her, by learning what I can about what happened, and it's becoming a little like Uncle Remus' tar baby. The more I try to push this away in my mind, the more mired I seem to be getting. But right now I believe I'll make sure Danny can handle the early hunters in case I might be a little late, and I will ask some more questions."

"When will you be going to camp?"

"A few weeks. Three. Maybe four. I have hunters in about four weeks, I think . . . "

"Four and a half."

I nodded. "And I'll need a couple of weeks to set up camp and get some wood cut."

"I don't like the way this conversation is going, Jeep."

I looked at her and smiled, and then I reached across and took her hand. It shocked me as much as it did her, I believe.

"Bets, all I'm doing right now is asking some questions. Let's just leave it at that, okay?"

She squeezed my hand and smiled.

"Sure. What can I do to help?"

"Think you can locate Danny for me? If you can, tell him I'd like to see him this evening, if I could."

"He won't be hard to find. He calls all the time, wondering if you've been asking for him yet."

"He's a good man, Betsy. You can always trust him to do his best. And, unlike some other assistant guides I've had, he doesn't mind listening."

"I'm sure I can find him."

"Good. I need to locate a hunting guide named Red today. Would you ask Danny to meet me for a burger at the Westward Coffee Shop about six?"

She stood and put a hand on my shoulder. "Sure."

"You're the best, Bets."

"Bet you can't say that three times in a row real fast," she said, and went out the door.

CHAPTER 5

According to the Alaska Department of Fish and Game and the Alaska Professional Hunters Association, there were five registered guides who went by the name Red.

Their records showed the only one who had hired Lee Hendrix was Red Tanner, a man of my acquaintance and one who held my respect as a fair-chase guide. Fortunately, he lived in Eagle River, about fifteen minutes north of downtown Anchorage. He told me to come out for lunch.

There were a few blood vessels in Red's face that had broken, but his stride was that of a man of forty and not of sixty, which I knew him to be. When Red Tanner began guiding, horses were the only way of getting to camp, which lengthened hunts and eliminated a lot of hunters who weren't willing to spend some serious time looking for game.

It was a time I believe I would have enjoyed very much.

"Jeep! Good to see you!" he said, walking out to the truck. "What's it been? Two years?"

"All of that, Red."

"Too damn long, anyway. Come on in."

The Tanner house was one of those substantial places, with imported brick fireplace, a lot of triple-thick windows and beige carpet everywhere. Some fine heads hung in nearly every room. It is the kind of house a sourdough who's spent years living in a log cabin dreams about having if only he had the money.

"You met Clo before, Jeep?"

"Mrs. Tanner. Nice to see you again."

"Just Clo, young man. I'm not old enough for the Mrs. stuff yet."

"All right, Clo," I grinned. "Thanks for asking me out."

"Let's go sit and talk before lunch. Want coffee? Me neither. What's this about Lee Hendrix?"

"They think he killed those men up in the Talkeetnas."

"Jeez Louise! Are they sure?"

"Sure looks like it, Red. They got there and found four men dead and Hendrix gone with a rifle, a sleeping bag and some food."

"He still carrying a cannon?"

"Company says he owns a .375 H & H."

"That's Lee. He likes them big like that. Likes to talk about how many foot-pounds of energy one of those things has. It bothered me about him. I'm a man who believes in shot placement. Too much chance of wounding an animal by shooting something that could cause you to flinch. I'd much rather have a hunter use something sensible that he can handle, and place that first shot properly."

"I agree."

"What do you shoot for a backup rifle, Jeep?"

I grinned. "Thirty ought-six."

"See?" Red said, slapping me on the back. "I use a seven-millimeter Remington Mag, but that's just because I found one that fits me and it gets the job done. A .30-06 will take care of anything in North America if you place your shot properly."

He looked at me. "Thirty ought-six? I'm beginning to believe some of the stories I've heard about you."

"Some guides carry cannons to make their hunters feel more secure, I know," I said.

Red nodded. "And some guides can shoot those big guns all day and shoot them well, too."

"Can Lee Hendrix shoot that big cannon?"

"Good question. And the answer is, I'm not really sure. There were two occasions on bear when he didn't place those backup shots too well and it scared hell out of my hunters. I was never certain whether Lee got rattled by the bear or by the recoil, you know?"

I knew.

"Anyway, after that, I pulled him off bear duty and sent him to moose camp. He worked moose and caribou for me the rest of the season, and I don't believe he had cause to use that rifle of his again."

"It's scoped, right?"

Red nodded. "Three to nine variable, I believe. It's been a couple of years now, and it's hard to remember everything, but Lee's a hard man to forget."

"Likable?"

"Yes and no."

"No!" said Mrs. Tanner, sharply, sticking her head around the corner.

"Aw, Clo," Red grinned. "You just didn't like him."

"That's right, I didn't. And you didn't either, did you?"

"At first I did, Jeep. He comes on real friendly, like a big ol' pup or something, you know? Then later, well . . . it's like you've let something into your house that you're afraid has outgrown your ability to handle it. It's an uncomfortable feeling.

"But to answer you, Jeep . . . Lee's the kind of guy who is real likable to some of your hunters. But they're mostly the ones who shouldn't be up here. You know the type—they know everything. They complain about how expensive everything is. They try to cheat you every step of the way, and somehow or other you get the feeling if they couldn't shoot a rifle, they wouldn't have any sex life at all. You know the ones I mean?"

"I've met a few. Thankfully I don't get any of those any more. I have a very small operation: just me, an assistant guide and our cook, Mary. We won't take anyone we don't know or who isn't recommended to us by a hunter we trust. I've dealt with a couple of those like you described, when I was an assistant guide, and that was enough for me."

Red whistled. "Well, I think you did the right thing. You see, I sometimes have twelve camps going at once. It's a little slower now, but it's still a big operation. Sometimes I think guiding the way you do it is the way to go."

"Guiding the way I do it," I grinned, "lets you live in a three-room log cabin near Kahiltna rather than a beautiful home like this one."

Red nodded. "Yes. Yes, I guess that's true."

"Any idea where he might go, Red? He headed east from Murder Lake in the Talkeetnas . . . at least for the first ten miles or so."

"Hmmm. That's not my part of the country. I don't know much that's out there. He'll end up going across the Nelchina, won't he?"

"If he keeps going that way, yes."

"Ocean, maybe," Red said. "He loved the ocean. It used to irritate me some, too, I must admit. Here we had these paying hunters in the middle of a paradise of mountains and this loudmouth would be going on about the ocean. Used to work on a fishing boat and liked it."

"That's what I hear."

Red stood up and motioned for me to follow him. We went into a carpeted bathroom large enough to camp in and he closed the door while we washed our hands.

"I had to let him go," he said in a quiet voice, "when I found him playing a bit fast and loose with the game laws. I've asked myself many times, Jeep, whether I should've maybe turned him in to Fish and Game right then and let them come after him. But I didn't. I thought of the hassle, of the paperwork at Fish and Game, and I had a camp full of hunters who wouldn't understand. Instead I just gave him his time and had him flown to town."

"I can understand that," I said.

"But Clo wouldn't," Red said.

"I understand that, too," I said.

"Thanks, Jeep," he said, looking relieved. "I've always run a straight camp."

"Everybody knows that, Red."

He smiled.

"Is he good in the woods, Red?"

"I'd have to say he's pretty good. Maybe very good."

"Good enough to make it to the ocean from the Talkeetna Mountains?"

"Who knows? Am I good enough? Are you good enough? Well, barring catastrophes I'd have to say yes. He can feed himself, certainly, with no problem. He's weatherwise and isn't going to get lost, certainly, and he's a good tracker."

"Good tracker?"

"Very good tracker."

"Thanks, Red. If you think of anything more, give me a call, will you?"

"Got a card?"

I gave him one. He stared at it for long moments, then looked at me until I started to get embarrassed.

"You need anything? I have a warehouse full of gear."

"Thanks, Red," I grinned. "Just learning a little bit, that's all."

"Sure," he said, smiling and opening the bathroom door. "Don't you know it isn't nice to lie to old people? Clo! Can you feed a couple of hungry guides?"

"I've been feeding hungry guides since you were too young to care, Red Tanner. Did you wash up?"

"Yes, Ma'am."

"Well, it's ready."

CHAPTER 6

D anny Manning was already in the coffee shop and well into his third cup by the time I arrived. We greeted each other warmly, much as brothers would, I imagine. Danny would make a great younger brother.

He's a grown man but has worked for me since he was a teenager, for nearly five years now. He has become a very good guide during those years, but what is more important, a genuinely good man. I like him very much and trust him completely.

Even now, in July, Danny wears a cartridge slide on his belt (empty, of course) to let people know he's a guide. He "signs his work," as the saying goes.

If intensity were money, Danny would be rich and we'd all work for him. His angular features, jutting chin and high cheekbones seem to go well with his attitude, which is something akin to an Olympic sprinter's in the blocks. Whatever the job, Danny is ready. He is so ready that sometimes I have to tell him to relax a bit and not try to do everything today. Being in the Bush relaxes him a little, but it takes about a month.

The evening crowd was just coming in. The coffee shop at the Anchorage Westward Hotel has absorbed so many ideas, has seen so many brainstorms fall flat, has probably laughed at so many harebrained schemes concocted here that it's a wonder the building doesn't either laugh or cry itself into rubble. This is the traditional place for the young people with beepers to meet. This is the very room where much of the very first Iditarod Race was put together, back in 1972 and early 1973 by Joe Redington,

Senior, and a handful of believers. This was where a lot of the figuring came about for the Trans-Alaska Pipeline, for the Alaska Native Land Claims Settlement Act, for nearly every big decision to hit Alaska. Every politician in the state knows this coffee shop, and most of them decided to run while in this room.

It is also the place of the semi-con men, those purveyors of dreams who talk just outside reality but not so far out as not to be believed. It is easy to do this in Alaska. It is easy to be believed in this room. This is the place where everything's possible. A musk ox ranch? A new type of bush plane? A new resort that caters only to the thousands of Japanese tourists who come here each year? Why not?

There's the money, of course. That's what most of these talks are about. "I'll meet you at the Westward at ten," and the talk is on. Can we promote something from the oil companies maybe? Or the state? It has a lot of money. I hear there are investors in Seattle just waiting to get into some of this up here. . . .

The coffee shop at the Anchorage Westward should be designated a Historic Dreaming Room some day, for a great deal of what Alaska became and did not become started right here.

Up on the top floor is a fancy restaurant and bar with one of the most spectacular views in the world, but it is down here in the coffee shop that Alaska's new ideas have taken form. They hope, these people with the little pagers on their belts and in their purses. They hope, and they work. Maybe this time it doesn't work out, but look what happened with the Iditarod, and it started right here in this room.

Each table has a story . . . a different one each day. About the only thing the stories have in common is they are all vibrant ideas. They are as wonderful and wild and scary as the country itself, which is part of its charm. It has always been that way here: gold mine or lead, millionaire or bum.

Even the vanilla in this room has chocolate syrup on it.

"Did Betsy fill you in on what's going on?"

"No. She said you were going to be busy for a while and said you wanted to see me."

"You bet. Let's get something to eat and then we can talk."

I filled Danny in the best I could without betraying confidences, but it wasn't easy, what with his interrupting every twenty seconds with a question.

"Anyway," I said, "I'd like you to be ready to go open camp and maybe even handle the first few hunters yourself. They're two nice guys from Anchorage who are meat hunting, and you don't really even have to guide them, but if you feel like giving them a hand, go ahead. They're really just paying for the use of camp and Mary's cooking."

"When will Mary come to camp?"

"A few days before the hunters get in. Remember to get all our firewood cut and split before the season opens. I don't want to be using a chain saw or splitting maul when we're supposed to be quiet in the mountains, okay?"

"Sure."

"Burn the garbage."

"You don't have to tell me that, Jeep. I'll take good care of your camp and your hunters, too. But when are you coming to camp?"

"Well, that's just it. I'm not real sure right now. Chances are I'll be out there with you and we'll set it up together. Maybe do a little scouting around together, count some sheep. But I may be called away for a while on business or something, and if I am, I just wanted to check with you to make sure you didn't have any questions."

"Would this be Lee Hendrix business?"

I shrugged. "Things come up."

"Right," he said. "Things come up."

"Better get the cook tent set up first, so Mary will have a place to stay. Sweep it out good before she gets there, too, will you? You know how she likes it clean."

"Jeep, I also know how to haul water and cut wood and find moose and unzip and subdivide same. It's what I do for a living, remember? You taught me, remember?"

"I'm sorry, I don't mean to pick on you. I have other things on my mind these days, I guess, and it's hard to think right."

"Like this guy Hendrix?"

"Mostly like Karen Turner and her children."

"You going to see her again soon?"

"Tonight."

"You tell her for me . . . well, you know, Jeep."

"You bet I will. She'll be glad to know you're thinking of her."

"Boss?"

I grinned. "Any time you call me boss, I know . . . what is it, Danny?"

"Betsy says you've been asking a lot of questions about Hendrix."

"Every question I can think of."

"Why?"

I sipped on my coffee and looked across the table at him. He's a man now, and part of my little family of friends.

"Because, Daniel, when you are after a bear you must first learn what the bear eats. You must learn how old the bear is, how fast it is. You must learn to recognize its track among other bears' tracks. You must get to know how good its sense of smell is, how keen its sight, its hearing. You have to be able to know what it will do when confronted by any number of different situations."

"Jesus, Jeep!"

"Not one word to Betsy, or anyone else right now. This will be between us."

"Of course not. You want me along? You know, two sets of eyes."

"I'm counting on you for early moose season, Danny. You will have to run camp while I'm gone. And look, I may not even go, you know. They may arrest this guy any day now. Who knows? A couple of days of rain and he could just walk out to the nearest highway and give himself up."

"But you don't think he will."

"I think it's unlikely."

"Don't worry about camp."

"I'm not. You just get Buck to fly you in when the time comes. He'll bring in Mary and the hunters, and you can send a shopping list back out with him if a lot of our food has been ruined or anything."

"That's a pretty solid cache," Danny said. "It'll be all right."

As with many tent camps, the only permanent structures there are the pole frames over which the tents are stretched and the board floors we flew in there, sometimes only two boards at a time, over maybe four years. The rest of the gear—tents, stoves, tables, chairs and food enough for a month or two—is kept for seven months of the year in a cache (and I've always thought it appropriate that that's pronounced "cash," since a good one is like money in the bank). Ours, like most, looks like a small log cabin on four tall stilts.

"Danny? Does your mom still know how to make those piroshkis?"

"You know she does."

"I'd like to buy about four dozen from her. Would you ask if she could do that for me in the next day or so?"

"Anything special you want in them?"

"I don't care," I said. "Anything she puts in them is fine with me."

I must admit I'm hooked on these holdovers from when Alaska was called Russian America. They are simply bread dough wrapped around meat, vegetables, fruit, whatever, and baked in the oven. If you're like me and don't care what's in them, eating each one is like biting into a birthday present: you don't know what you're going to get, so you get the nourishment of a piroshki along with the anticipation of Christmas.

"I'll throw in some moose jerky, Jeep," Danny said. "I have about five pounds of it at home."

"I have plenty of that, but thanks."

"I wish you wouldn't do this."

"I'm just asking around right now, that's all."

"You need four dozen piroshkis to ask questions around Anchorage?"

The kid's coming along all right.

He thought a minute. "It's the time that's worrying you, isn't it?"

"Well now," I grinned. "I believe I trained you right."

"He'll have more darkness to travel in soon, and crummy weather so planes can't spot him," Danny said.

"He may not make it that long, Danny, or he may get to where he's going before the rainy season hits in full."

"Either way," Danny said, "he's gone."

"Either way."

"Does Jim Strickland know how you're thinking?"

"If he doesn't, he's not as bright as I give him credit for."

"And?"

"Well, we'll see what Jim says, won't we? Maybe they've changed their minds and are going after this guy. There are good trackers on the force. I know two of them to be excellent men.

"Thing is, this isn't going to be one of those cases where a fugitive hijacks a car or takes hostages and tries to drive through a police roadblock someplace and is either captured or killed. He's either too smart or too crazy to do that. My vote is for smart, but it doesn't matter. So I'm hoping Jim kicks loose a couple of trackers on this guy and they nail him out in the bogs someplace. As I said, they have men who can get the job done."

"But not as good as Jeep George."

I grinned. "You can tell I pay you a salary, can't you?"

I stood and left a tip.

"If I don't see you before you go, Jeep, I'll leave the piroshkis in the office."

"Thanks."

"And you be careful."

I looked at him. "Looking stupid is only my disguise," I said, winking at him and shaking his hand.

Karen looked as though someone had pulled the plug on her life's juices. Her face was as gray as the housecoat she wore. An older woman was sitting on her couch, and I recognized her from many years before as Karen's mother.

Karen and I went in the kitchen and sat down. I told her as many of the things I'd learned as I felt like telling her. The things that wouldn't burn nightmares into her. She sat very quietly through the telling and then thanked me.

She got up and made a pot of coffee, and I kept waiting for some sort of reaction. It was awkward for me. It was probably awkward for her, too.

"Do you think he'll die?" Karen asked suddenly.

"What?"

"The man who did it. Hendrix. Do you think he'll die in the Bush?"

"Maybe. Who knows? Anything can happen out there."

"You're lying to me, Jeep. You're lying to me to make me feel better, just like you did before."

"When did I ever lie to you?"

"When you said you told me all you knew about what happened to Bill. I learned from the wife—I guess widow now—of one of the other men why we can't see Bill before he's buried."

She sat down and cried, and I walked behind her and put my hands on her shoulders. You know, massaged a little. Probably a futile gesture, but what else could I do? Husband butchered? Here, let me rub your shoulders and all the hurt will go away. So I stand here with nothing to say as my best friend's wife shakes with grief. Then I got a very selfish feeling that had no place in what was going on. For a quick moment, I thought that if a woman ever loved me that much, I'd feel as blessed as the ground at first snow. With my life, I'd worry about her. But it might be worth it, someday.

"Coffee's ready," I said, digging into her kitchen shelves for mugs.

"I can get that," she said, jumping up and wiping her face on her sleeve.

"Haven't you heard about the revolution?" I asked. "Haven't you heard that we mustn't stereotype ourselves into roles just because of gender? Look, woman, I've read all the books and I've been practicing, and rather than let you think your old friend Jeep isn't modern, I learned how to pour coffee."

She tried to smile, then stood and hugged me. I hugged her back.

"I can't stand to think of him out there," Karen whispered into my shirt.

"Who?"

"Hendrix. He's out there, walking around free after destroying the lives of all of us."

"I don't like it either," I admitted. "You take sugar?"

She nodded and sat down to her coffee.

"He's walking around out in the woods, getting away with murder, and the police aren't going to do anything," she said.

"Sure they are, Karen. Look, do you know how difficult it is to find someone in an area that large when he wants to be found? Sometimes it's impossible. Sometimes they find the guy's body and sometimes they don't."

"With Hendrix, he doesn't want to be found. He's already shot a hole in one airplane, so the police don't want to look for him too hard from the air, and frankly I can't say I blame them."

She just looked at me.

"Look, Karen. Even if this man weren't armed with an elephant gun, it would be almost impossible to spot him from the air. He is undoubtedly walking only after dark or when the weather is too rough to fly. With the short nights right now, that will slow him down a lot, and the slower he goes, the better chance the police have of getting him. There is more chance of him getting hurt, or getting killed, or getting hungry, or giving himself up."

"Do you think a man who has committed four murders will give himself up?" she said.

"Giving himself up would be crazy," I agreed, "but so is killing four men, so who knows?"

"You don't believe he'll give himself up, though, do you? And you don't think he'll get killed out there, either."

"I don't think so."

"What's going to happen?"

"My guess is he has someplace to go to, a place where he knows he'll be safe. I think he'll head for that. He needs to get there between now and snowfall, though, because he'll leave tracks in the snow you can spot from a satellite. When the rains of August come in a week or so, he'll be able to travel more during daylight hours, because he won't be afraid of aircraft seeing him. But he'll leave good tracks in the mud."

Karen looked at me and didn't say anything. She just kept looking at me.

I smiled. "I thought maybe I might take a hike out that way and see if I can tell which direction he's going."

"You're a poor liar, Jeep."

"That's twice tonight you've said that."

"What do the troopers say?"

"Well, I haven't exactly discussed this with them, you understand."

"Jeep, I want Lee Hendrix to be punished for what he did, but if he hurts you. . . . Maybe you're right. Maybe he's crazy enough he'll forget how to feed himself out there, or he'll give himself up."

"Maybe. Anyway, it's nothing to worry about, Karen. I'm just going for a hike for a few days or so to get in shape for hunting season. I can read sign fairly well, so maybe I can give the troopers a tip on which way he's heading."

"Isn't there some state statute against lying to a widow in her own home?"

"I sure hope not."

I got another hug before I left, and gave a couple with kisses thrown in to George and Shelly—carefully, because they were already asleep.

On the way back to my office that evening, I asked myself some searching questions. How much of my desire to do a little tracking was from my sense of civic duty, loyalty to an old friend, or a love of justice? How much of this was due to one tracker thinking—and I was embarrassed to even bring the thought out into the open—that here at last was prey worth his talents? It was an uncomfortable question, so I forgot it and drove back to the office and tried to get some sleep.

It wasn't easy any more.

The first couple of nights in town are usually all right. Then you sort of get some Anchorage under your skin. It's like going to one of the old Native funerals and hearing the drums. Then you are singing, so you begin to feel the earth beneath you and the magic of chulyen, the raven, wash over you; and then the drums become you and you are the drums. Your body beats, and everyone's body beats, and the house beats, and changes happen then. The frame house slides back two hundred years and becomes the *gazhee* of our fathers. There are the skin sides and roof. There are the communal belongings piled against the walls, just as they are in the old stories. There is the head of the clan, with his face painted black in grief and mourning, and he is dancing, and you can sometimes see these things when the drums beat. Maybe if my family had all come to Alaska from Norway I wouldn't hear these things or see these things, but I can't know that.

It can get that way in Anchorage because Anchorage gets to be like a drum. At first it's the little street noises that annoy you. Later it's the traffic, making the ground shake a little. But after a few days in the office-cum-bedroom I keep here, Anchorage makes the peace of Kahiltna and the mountains vanish. Anchorage lets the sleek black bird live here, but it reduces *chulyen* to eating garbage scraps, not salmon. He must pick through the worst of life for his living here, not through the best. The ravens of Anchorage do it because it is an easier way to live. Just as the people do.

But always there's this beat beneath Anchorage that hits you about the third night. It's a jumble of noise and too many things going on. Late at night, when a man is lying on his couch in a sleeping bag, watching the curtains flash off and on with some faraway neon, it is not a time for rest. The body feels the warmth of the sleeping bag and wants to sleep. The mind asks questions.

Most men my age have a wife, a child or two, and maybe a little house. Maybe like the one Bill and Karen . . . well, like Karen and the kids have . . . out in Muldoon.

But I don't.

I don't really have what most men (and I'll bet most women) consider a career. I like what I do, and it pays the bills as long as the bills don't get too big. But is this what I'm supposed to do?

One of the problems with Alaska is that you can actually be a screaming eccentric and no one will bother to let you know. Alaska takes such pride in its eccentrics, they are considered normal. Alaskans often have to venture into Canada or the Lower Forty-eight to check in with polite society and see if they still fit. Or if they ever did.

Sometimes it is a question of looking for, and finding, something inside you, or outside in the mountains, that brings about a balance—a tuning of nature with what is inside us. It happens to some people. It happens to me.

The nervousness hits me about the third night in Anchorage. It's dark now, passably dark for this time of year, so I lie there and try to picture what Lee Hendrix is doing. He's moving, of course.

If he stays to tundra ridges, he might make ten miles during one of these short nights. Then, too, his travel is hampered by having to keep searching for a place to lie up during the daylight hours. This may take him several miles off his path to whatever his sick mind is seeking.

When daylight comes, he'll have to be holed up. He can't have a fire during the day, even in the thickest of spruce stands. The smoke would give him away.

When the rains come at night, he'll have to keep walking. In daytime, in his brushy hole, he can rig a shelter of some kind, or he may be carrying a lightweight tent.

But these things take time to set up and take down. Hendrix is moving for his life and he must know that. He must know, even inside his own twisted mind, that he must keep going. That may be where he'll slip up. Maybe, with the ghosts of dead men riding him down those long tundra ridges, he'll make a mistake.

Maybe. Not good enough odds to take to the bank, of course.

But maybe the brain that drove him to unspeakable horror might also push him from the tundra ridges to the seemingly endless muskeg swamps of the Nelchina Basin, where he might make a mile a day. Or he might be sucked below by the keepers of the underworld.

When I'm thinking of wheres and whens and hows, my Norwegian ancestry takes over. When it came to dealing with facts and problems and logistics, it was hard to beat my grandfather, Roald Jepsen. He was one of the kindest men I ever knew and also the most practical.

Gramps, it was said, built the best sluice boxes in the gold fields. When you wanted a sluice box where the riffles always sat down in the slots without a wiggle, you went to Roald Jepsen and asked him for one. He just asked you how big you wanted it and that was it. Miners who had one of his sluice boxes showed them off to visitors like signed pieces of art.

Gramps built sluice boxes that captured gold, boats that didn't leak and, in the days before everybody went nuts over aluminum, pack frames that never rubbed sores and hung just right.

His tools were always sharp. Their handles never broke or wore away. The doors on his cabin always fit exactly, despite weather changes. His roof never leaked.

When you had a problem in the Bush, Gramps always took the practical approach.

"First," he used to say, "you sit down on a log. Then you think, and you think logically and you gotta think right. What is it you need? How many different ways are there of reasonably getting the job done with the tools and materials you have on hand?

"When, boy, you figure which one would be the best way to go, then you do it. Say you got a broken leg in the mountains? What would you do?"

And so I'd play the familiar game with him while he worked with a spokeshave or drawknife on a choice piece of wood. He'd work and listen, and I'd imagine myself in the woods with a broken leg. Then I'd start telling him some of the things I could do. He'd listen, nod and say "good" now and then, which always sounded a bit like "goot," and encourage me.

"You got a broken leg, how many things you gotta worry about?"

"Two," I'd say. "Take care of the leg, and get help."

"Good start," he'd say. "But I think four things."

He stopped and counted on his fingers. "One, get that leg splinted. Take care of your health, right. Two, you need some sort of shelter to get after you fix your leg. Don't do any good to have a good leg and freeze to death, right? Three, you need to find food and fix a way to cook it. Four, when you're all set up so you don't need to go nowhere, then you figure a way to signal or get yourself out of the woods."

He'd look at me. "You gotta think, boy. If you think, you're always going to be ahead of the man who doesn't."

So I've tried to do that. Each time a problem comes up, I try to run it through the checklist that Gramps taught me. What are the various things that could happen? What do I want to do about it? What do I want to do about it first? How many ways are there to accomplish this? Which of these would work best?

This method has kept me out of trouble many times and has gotten me out of trouble a few times when I couldn't avoid getting into it. I miss that good-natured old man with his missing teeth and his gray hair and his laughter.

Sometimes late at night, though, when I'm this tired, my mind seems to belong to the Athabascan half of my ancestry. And when I hunt, it goes back to about a half-and-half balance. The white guy half knows some good recipes for cooking a meal for a hunter in the field. The Indian-guy half finds game, sometimes, in a special way.

Chulyen, where are you now? Off to the places only ravens know about? Or are you picking through the debris of the alley behind Fourth Avenue, listening to country music and fights?

I remember you, Chulyen. It was the day when there was tracking snow and I was ten and Chada let me take the army rifle.

"You must not hurt the moose," my Chada, my Grandfather George, had said. "You must kill it or leave it alone."

I was carrying that heavy rifle and I looked up from beneath my marten-skin cap and nodded. We had gone maybe a quarter mile from his moose camp and a raven flew across our path, his wings beating that breathless sound as he crossed.

Chada nudged me. "Say good morning to him," he said.

"Why?"

"Because," he said, "it is to bring you good luck and keep Raven happy. Maybe he will show you a moose today."

"Good luck?"

Grandfather shrugged and grinned, the way I do these days. "It is kind of a nice old way of doing things, don't you think? And it doesn't hurt, does it?"

About that time, the raven turned from being on our right and flew back across our path to the left.

"Good morning, Raven," I said.

"Tell him you'll leave the gut pile for his children," Chada said.

"I'll leave the gut pile for your children," I called.

"And the eyes."

"That sounds awful."

"The eyes."

"And the eyes, too, Raven."

My grandfather smiled. "Maybe he'll like you."

As we walked along about half an hour later, we saw a raven flying down toward a creek from the alder thickets where we were.

"Chulyen," Grandfather said, nodding.

It may even have been the same one that had crossed our path earlier. It may have been another one. Alaska is full of ravens. But this one was flying that slow, deliberate way ravens have and heading down toward the creek.

Without saying anything more, Chada nudged me and pointed in the direction the bird went. He motioned for me to keep silent, too, and we started down toward the creek.

I heard the moose in the thicket along the creek and we worked our way silently, a step at a time, down from one spruce tree to another until we were about fifty yards from where the sound was coming. He motioned for me to stop and get ready and held his finger to his mouth again for silence. Quietly I worked the bolt of the army rifle until a cartridge was loaded into the chamber, then flipped on the safety. I put my left hand around a skinny spruce tree and stuck my thumb out to the right. I laid the fore end of the rifle across that, got the rifle comfortably settled and waited.

Then he stepped out. I had seen moose many times in my ten years, of course, but this was the biggest moose ever in the world because it was my moose.

I could hear in my mind Chada's admonition not to hurt him, so I put the sights on the exact spot where the spine crosses the shoulder blades, took off the safety, and squeezed the trigger.

The giant's four feet folded up against his body in midair and he hit the ground right there and it was his final place. It was my first moose, and he wasn't hurt, and it was the best day of my life.

After the moose died, Grandfather taught me to say a prayer of thanks to the moose for his meat. He pointed, and the raven was sitting in the top of a spruce tree about a hundred yards away.

His children got fat that day.

Since that day, I have had a special affection for Chulyen. When I hunt, his children eat. Sometimes when he crosses my path, it is a lucky day.

Sometimes it isn't.

One morning I was tired, broke, out of work and the truck broke down and I was hitchhiking to Anchorage. It was snowing like silt in a summer river and I'd been standing out on the highway for an hour with no car coming by. Just then a raven flew past.

"Chulyen!" I called out, laughing. "Good morning! Are you going to bring me luck today?"

He flew on his way, and I chuckled for about five minutes in the snowstorm.

That was when Bob Gordon picked me up and drove me to Anchorage. He gave me a $20 bill, fed me a steak dinner and told me I could work as chore boy in his hunting camp for the rest of the season. That was how I got my start guiding.

I always say good morning to ravens. It is kind of a nice old way of doing things. And it doesn't hurt.

I could have used some of Raven's confidence that night, but I didn't find any. The underlying beat of Anchorage didn't help any, either. Not with a boy from the Bush who just wanted to smell the smoke from his own stovepipe and hear nothing but the soft popping of the dried birch chunks in the heater. I thought about my dogs. I thought about hunting camp. I thought about the sweetness of Ravel's music, I thought of Betsy then and smiled and dozed a bit until the light made it too embarrassing to stay in bed.

CHAPTER 7

Betsy phoned about seven with the messages of the evening before. Buck wanted to know if we were going for a little ride in his Super Cub any time soon. Three hunters had called wanting to know how much I charge and did I guarantee the hunt (too much and no, of course not). And Red Tanner had called and said maybe it was nothing, but would I give him a call?

"Thank you," I said. "And how are you this morning, Miss Kelley?"

"I've been listening to the radio and they haven't caught that guy yet," she said. "How do you think I feel?"

"It'll be all right, Bets."

"Yeah, great."

"Look outside. It's raining. Every day of rain is good. Rain will slow him down and make him leave tracks, nice deep tracks. If he's smart, this will slow him down even more because he'll try to stay to rocks and hard ground to avoid leaving those tracks. We don't know how much food he has with him, and you know how hard it is to get a decent fire going in one of these cold Alaska rains.

"Put yourself in his place. He's living like a coyote out there, and each rainstorm makes it harder on him. Each cold night, each morning when he wears soggy clothes, he'll be thinking about how nice it would be to have warm dry clothes on, have his belly full of scrambled eggs and ham, and be able to watch game shows on TV, even if he has to do it from a cell."

"So you're saying every day that goes by is in society's favor on this creep?"

"Well, yes and no. Yes, he is more likely to give himself up or go nuts and make a fatal mistake. No, because the nights are getting longer and he can travel farther."

"Flip a coin?"

"Something like that."

"You know what's wrong?" she said. "You aren't laughing. You aren't happy. You're a sourdough. You're an Alaskan, for Pete's sake. You're supposed to celebrate life and greet each day with the enthusiasm of knowing you made it through another hazardous twenty-four hours up here in God's country. You're not smiling now, are you? Over the phone I can tell."

I smiled. "Wrong again, woman of Chicago-born instincts. But I know what you mean, and I promise to do better before very much longer."

"When are you going?"

"We'll see. Tomorrow, maybe."

There was silence on the other end of the phone for awhile. "Any further orders, Captain?" she said. No smile in her voice either.

"Can't think of a thing," I said. "Steer a straight course and I'll see you in safe harbor."

"Okay, Jeep."

"See ya," I said, hoping it would be true.

"Take care," she said, and hung up.

Red was home. "Jeep," he said, "this may be something just dumb, you know, but you asked if I could remember anything about the guy to let you know. I figure it was worth a phone call."

"Sure, Red. Glad you called."

"It's just this. There were two things about Lee you might want to know. He asked me if he could guide something besides sheep. I thought that was strange, because you know how guides like to go after sheep. Not Lee, though. I asked him why and he just said he didn't like sheep. Jeep, I think that it was the steep country he didn't like. Like a fear of heights, maybe."

"Sounds reasonable to me," I said.

"Well, that was the only thing I could figure. Funny, isn't it? You take a big guy like that, you'd think he wouldn't be afraid of anything, especially after that moose episode, but there you have it, right?"

"What's this moose episode?"

"That's the second thing I wanted to tell you. As I think I told you before, I pulled him off bear duty and stuck him in moose camp for the most part. On one hunt, he had one of those hunters in there I told you about—loud and rich and knows everything. It seems this hunter already had his moose, and Lee decided it was time to get his own moose for winter meat. He took the hunter along for fun, since it would be a day or so before the plane came in to take the hunter out.

"What the hunter told me later was that Lee spotted this big bull taking his nap down in some tall berry brush. He and the hunter got down about fifty yards away from the moose and then Hendrix whispers to this guy that he'll bet him a hundred bucks he can walk up and kick the moose in the butt."

"What?"

"Yeah, I know. The hunter thought it was nuts, too, but he agreed to the bet. Lee spent about fifteen minutes putting a sneak on that bull, and he did kick him in the butt. The bull jumped up and spun around, and Lee shot him in the head there at about three feet. Then he laughed.

"This hunter told me later in main camp, and this was one of those macho loud jerks, mind you, that he paid Hendrix off and just wanted out of there. He said the man was spooky."

"Sounds as if he can put a sneak on game, Red."

"Or a man."

"I'm sure you're right. Red, you said Hendrix mentioned a fishing boat. You wouldn't remember the name of it, would you?"

"Sure. The *Crab Cove*. Used to talk about it all the time. Drove me crazy, him talking about it on and on. I used to wonder if he talked about hunting when he was on the boat, you know? Like that old cowboy joke, about them riding broncs in the whorehouse and chasing women back on the ranch."

"Would you know where that boat is?"

"Sorry, Jeep. He might've told us . . . probably did, but I forgot. It's name was the *Crab Cove*, I do remember that."

"Thanks, Red. That's a big help."

"It's not much, son, but I want to do what I can. You sure I don't have anything you need?"

"Sure. You have about forty years' experience I could really use right now."

"You don't need anything from me. You just remember this guy will be worse than any bear you've ever met. Grizzlies make sense."

"Thanks, Red. I'll remember that."

"And you come back and tell me about it when you get home, right?"

"It's a promise."

"Stay downwind."

"You do the same."

A phone call to trooper headquarters got me the information I wanted about the boat. "We checked out the *Crab Cove*," Jim said, "but that went no place. It was lost at sea during a storm late last winter. There doesn't seem to be any connection between the incident and Hendrix. He wasn't around for the trip. The skipper and one crewman were lost with it."

"You get the name of the skipper, Jim?"

"Pete Hansen. Out of Cordova."

"Thanks."

"That's it? Thanks?"

I smiled. "Want me to sing you a song or something?"

"Spare me, Jepsen my lad. It's just that I thought you were going to keep me informed on what you found out."

I thought a minute.

"Jeep? You still there?"

"I'm trying to think of something I've learned that you haven't. Every place I've gone, your men have been there first, for the most part."

"We always get our man."

"You're on the wrong side of the border for that catchy little phrase, Captain Strickland. How about 'If we don't get 'em, the bears will'?"

"Doesn't work too well in winter's the only thing."

"How about 'If we can't catch 'em, they aren't worth catching'?"

"That one has possibilities."

"Hey, Jim, I've thought of something I learned that maybe you didn't know."

"Shoot."

"He once sneaked up on a bull moose, kicked him in the butt and then shot him point blank in the face while laughing."

"Our boy is a million laughs, isn't he?"

"This was strictly business. Hendrix won a hundred bucks betting on that prank."

"I don't mind telling you, Jeepers my man, that I'm having a hard time figuring this guy out. I don't know if he's a lunatic or a cold-blooded killer, or both or neither."

"Maybe part-time this and part-time that," I suggested.

"It will be interesting to find out, won't it? We might have a difficult time getting our boy onto the shrink's couch, though."

"I don't think he's the couch type, Jimbo."

"That doesn't seem to fit his image very well, does it?"

"Can you fill me in a little on what you're doing to catch him?"

"God, Jeep, it's so frustrating. I'd like to send some men in after him and maybe surround him if we could, but the powers that be are telling us to wait him out. We're patrolling the Glenn and Richardson highways about twice as much as normal. We've evacuated every cabin and fish camp we know about in an awfully big portion of Alaska—and you can imagine how popular that was with the fishermen—and we have a few men scattered along the highways."

"At roadhouses?"

"And villages, yes. It's to protect the people at the roadhouses more than it is to catch Hendrix. If he doesn't want to be caught . . . "

"Yeah," I said. "I know."

"Say, Jeep, just to pick your mind a little, what would you do if you were in my place?"

"I'm not a cop, Jim. I don't know your business."

"Tell me anyway."

"I'd send a tracker to locate him and then go in with some men and get him."

"Any particular tracker in mind?"

"You have several good ones on the force, Jim. There's Elias John and Bobby Block, for two. I know they're good men in the woods."

"Good enough?"

"I see what you mean. I'd hate to bet their lives on it."

"Anyone else you can think of?"

"Maybe."

"Anyone I know?"

"Maybe."

"Maybe . . . is this the silent Indian treatment again?"

"There's nothing silent about the Indians in Alaska, Jim. You have to put gags on us to shut us up."

"Jeep, are you thinking of doing anything stupid in the general vicinity of the Talkeetna Mountains?"

"I never do stupid things. But you know, that is real pretty country up there, and I've always wanted to take a little hike up there and see some new horizons."

"Don't do it."

"Anybody fence it off?"

"No."

"Any law says I can't go for a walk up there? You know, observe wildlife? Watch the streaming herds of caribou grace the undulating tundra with their stately dance?"

"Don't do it."

"Say, Jim, would you have one of those little radio things you guys play with? You know, those walkie-talkie things? I thought maybe I might get a little lonely up there and call you up, just to say hi."

"I can't let you have one."

"It'll be tough trying to visit with you."

"Look, I'm serious about this, Jeep. There are some things you'd best leave to the professionals, and this is certainly one of them. This guy has done enough damage already. I don't want you added to the list."

"I won't get added to the list so easily," I said.

"That's the truth . . . but Jeep, I can't do anything to help you. No planes, no ground help, nothing. Not until they change their minds about what to do on this guy. You understand?"

"Perfectly."

"So what are you going to do if you accidentally meet this guy out there?"

"I thought maybe we could come back to town together so you could get him the tender psychiatric care he so richly deserves."

"Bull."

"That's what I have in mind."

"Don't kill him, Jeep."

"I'm not a killer, Jim."

"You sure I can't talk you out of this?"

"Hendrix is going to kill whoever he comes across next, and you know it. I'm not a vigilante, but if somebody doesn't go and at least figure out where he's headed, how are your men going to arrest him, or shoot him, or whatever they plan to do with him? And to tell you the truth I don't care which they do as long as they do it.

"Hendrix is good in the woods. Good enough to make it to wherever he's going. Just in that little bit I followed his trail up at Murder Lake, I could see determination. This was not some nut who had done something terrible and wandered around in the woods trying to fathom what he'd done. He knew what he'd done, and he knew someplace to go, and he's going there right now, or I miss my guess. And he has to get there before snowfall, or he can be tracked from a gosh-darned satellite, and he knows it."

"I agree."

"But you can't do anything about it."

"But I can't do anything about it until we know where he is."

"And I can't borrow a walkie-talkie."

"And I can't lend trooper equipment to civilians."

I was quiet for a moment.

"Jim, before I go, I want you to understand something. Bill Turner was a very close friend. I've kissed his heart-broken children while they slept, and one of them is named for me. I've held his wife in my arms as she cried. She's so pale you wouldn't know it was Karen. It was like she was the one who was dead. This does not make me very happy about Lee Hendrix, and I admit I resent every breath he takes."

"I can understand that."

"But I'm not going out there for revenge. You and I drove the trail together, so you will probably understand. Revenge will not bring Bill or those other men back. Revenge won't even make the widows and their children feel better. Revenge would only boil the blood and cloud the thinking and probably get me killed."

"That's true."

"Revenge, in other words, is a luxury I can't afford. I'm going to follow this man's trail because I'm an Alaskan. I'm a member of a society that tries to protect its members, and this man, in anybody's book, is a menace. My tracking him will be no more or less passionate than dropping what I'm doing to stack sandbags during a flood or cut down trees to stop a forest fire. It's a part of the price we pay for living here."

"And you think the state troopers should do it."

"Don't you?"

"Yes. Of course."

"Want to come along for a little hike and bring your handcuffs?"

"I'd love to."

"But you can't."

"It's not my decision."

"I realize that, Jim."

"Going to get a little lonely out there."

"Oh, I don't know. There's bound to be some weather, and some animals and perhaps a homicidal nut or two."

"Nothing I can say to change your mind?"

"No, but I'd like to hear you say you understand why I'm doing this. I'd like to hear you say you won't feel guilty if anything happens to me."

"I can agree to half of that."

"You work on that other half, too. One more thing, Jim. Where exactly was the float plane when it caught a bullet from that cannon?"

"On a ridge north of the Talkeetna River opposite the head of Kosina Creek."

"Thanks. That makes sense."

"Jeep?"

"Yeah?"

"You be sure to take your rifle along on this hike of yours."

"Sure thing, Jim," I said. "Grizzlies up in that high tundra, you know."

CHAPTER 8

There are nights when it's impossible to be alone, and I had run headlong into one. The rain had gone east toward Canada, leaving one of those delicious evenings when the long pink twilight of summer in Alaska hangs forever in the sky, shrouding the Chugach Range in mystery and giving stark old-fashioned lacy dignity to the silhouettes of the jack spruce along Anchorage's edges.

A drive in the pickup didn't do any good. I knew the laughter of a bar wouldn't do it, either. I needed a friend, someone I could talk to.

After an hour of driving around and debating, I stopped at a phone booth, dropped a quarter, and she picked it up on the second ring.

"Good evening. Jepsen George Guide Service. May I help you?"

"Sorry it's so late, Bets."

"You all right?"

"Sure. I was just wondering . . . have you had anything to eat this evening?"

"You worried about my health now?"

I laughed. "No. Just wondered if you might want to get something to eat."

"Business or pleasure?"

"Which answer do I need to give to get you interested?"

"Well, it's after ten, and I don't conduct business after ten."

"How about pleasure, then?"

"You mean like a—dare I breathe the word—date?"

"Yes, Miss Kelley, just like a date."

"Just like, or a date?"

"Mr. Jepsen George requests the pleasure of your company for a dinner date this evening at a restaurant of your choice."

"Wow! I choose the place, huh? Do you have a necktie in town?"

"Choice of blue or brown."

"Blue. Captain Cook dining room?"

"You're on."

"Pick me up in half an hour, okay?"

"I'll go change and be there. I'll be the one with the blue tie on, looking for a date."

"In that case, I think I can eat a pretty good-sized meal. See you."

I smiled and shook my head and drove back to the office. I jumped in the shower for a quick rinse and picked out some city clothes and squirted myself with aftershave.

I wanted this evening and I wasn't really sure why. I had never really thought seriously about a date with Betsy before, but now that we were going to have one, I was nervous.

When she opened the door of her apartment, I gasped. She was dressed in one of those simple black dresses that clung to everything she owned. She wore some of those long-handled white cloth gloves that fashion models and old church ladies like to wear, too. How could she know how attractive I've always found women who wear them?

And her hair . . . the light from the lamp in the living room made it shine the way the waterfalls of soft brown river water shine.

She was beautiful.

"Did I forget to tell you I'm a woman?"

"Wow, Bets," was all I could muster.

"I take that as a compliment," she said. She reached out and straightened my tie with an efficient and friendly tug. "You clean up pretty well yourself. Let's go eat."

People who make a habit of eating dinner in the Captain Cook Hotel's dining room make more money than I do. This is for special times only, but I was glad she'd picked it because this was one of those special times.

I kept looking at her and shaking my head slightly and smiling a little, because I was on a date with a beautiful woman and it had turned out to be someone I knew and actually liked a lot. This takes some getting used to. I was willing.

When we were seated at a booth along one far wall and had ordered, I excused myself. I went back to the lobby and found the florist still open. She quickly put together a small corsage of two white carnations and I took it back in.

"Here," I said awkwardly. "I want you to have them."

She started to say something smart-aleck, which was certainly due me, I suppose, but she stopped and smiled at me instead.

"It's really pretty, Jeep," she said softly. "You pin it on."

Well, this was even more awkward, because her dress was cut low in front, and the place where the flowers go was dangerously close to some pretty great-looking flesh. I started it, but my hands were shaking so badly she probably feared for her life; she finished it for me.

I looked around a bit self-consciously to see if any other diners had noticed my clumsiness, but the dining room kept humming along, each table with its own share of dreams and plans.

Betsy and I didn't say much through the crab legs and salad. It wasn't until coffee that we said anything much except for pleasantries.

"Maybe," Betsy said, "well, I might have been a bit unfair, Jeep."

"Unfair?"

"On the phone. You know. I mean about this being a date? I just happened to think that maybe you had something to tell me about business, and then I talked you into taking me out, and I wanted you to know that if there is something about business you need to talk about, well, I'm happy to listen."

I had to laugh at her. "No business. Not one single damn thing, Bets."

"Just hungry, huh?"

"I'm beginning to think so," I said, and then wondered why I'd said it, then I realized why I'd said it, and then I saw she realized it too.

I thought it might be safer to change the subject.

"So what does Betsy Kelley do when she isn't running my business or looking beautiful in a fancy restaurant?"

She looked shocked. "Beautiful?"

"You have any idea how pretty you are?"

She smiled and reached over and squeezed my hand. "Thank you," she whispered. She sipped her coffee and straightened up in the booth and thought for a minute.

"What do I do? You really want to know?"

I nodded.

"Well, I've spent a lot of time with my friend Janice the last few days, Jeep. She and Tim are getting a divorce. You know them? Well, I guess she's my closest friend, and I have to tell you I don't get it. Of course, all I hear is her side of things, and I sometimes think it should be my job to go get Tim and kinda corner him and get his side, and then go back and talk to Janice, and then go to Tim and, you know, play Henry Kissinger in the Middle East.

"She says it's because he's gone so often on business and stays away for sometimes a week at a time. Well, a week at a time? I always thought that would give two people a little appreciation of each other and then, when he gets home . . . hey, dress up in something sexy, you know, like Saran Wrap? Then you stick a long-stemmed rose in your teeth and the miles and the days magically melt away in moments of pure passion. Know what I mean?"

"You get very interesting ideas, Betsy. You ever think of writing a marriage manual?"

"You're making fun of me, Jeep. I was serious."

"Really? Sorry. Actually, I always thought that was how a marriage was supposed to be, too. Full of . . . surprises . . . surprises and fun. I like the Saran Wrap idea, by the way."

"I think most men would."

"I think you're right.

"Your friends?" I asked. "Can't they make this up? Figure this out? It doesn't seem too serious a thing. There are sailors who are gone for months, you know."

"Yes, there's that. I guess it just depends on the kind of woman you are. Some women need that constant kind of marriage where the guy comes home every day at half past five, you know?"

"Alaska is the kind of place where men are gone a lot, I guess."

"You think Alaska is to blame for their problems?"

"Hey, I don't know. I don't know your friends. I do know that Alaska has a way of coming between men and women."

"You talk like Alaska's another woman."

She was leaning over toward me and I could smell her perfume and it made me feel a little dizzy. To make matters worse—or better—her leaning over made the front of her dress pooch out a little, and I kept asking myself, in the way stupid people do in cases like this, if this were from the weight of the carnations or just the way the fabric bent. Whatever may have caused it, I seemed to be staring darned hard down the left side of her dress. She noticed it, and I could feel myself flushing red, but she just leaned more and oh God! I wasn't sure what was going on here, but it was sure having several emotional and physiological effects on me.

I just wanted to put my arms around her and crush those carnations to death against my chest and I discovered I didn't really care if there were thirty other people in the room or if we were in Dodger Stadium, or—

"Jeep? I said you were talking as if Alaska is a woman."

"Oh . . . yeah."

I took a deep breath and stared into my coffee cup. It was safer.

"In a way I suppose I think of it that way. Alaska can't cook or bear children or keep a man warm at night, but there is a kind of comparison, I guess."

I turned and stared safely into her green eyes. Stare at the eyes. The eyes.

"You see," I continued, "besides sex and conversation and cooking and sharing children, a woman should be someone a man can look at and see a future in her eyes. Promise. Hope for the future. She should be someone who is a bit mysterious. Someone he never really gets to know thoroughly. She should always hold the scent of intrigue about her to tempt him. To keep him there. To keep him fascinated. He should wake up every morning and realize how lucky he is that she is here in his life."

I sipped the coffee. It was cold. I turned back to her eyes. God, they were deep.

"And in that way, Alaska is like a woman. Why do you think there are three men for every woman in this state? Most women can't handle the north. Oh, Anchorage, maybe. But when you get out there past electricity, you find an awful lot of single men. Most of them have been married before, too. With some, the time came when they had to choose between their wives and Alaska and Alaska won. In that way, Alaska is like a woman.

"Alaska is a forever type of temptress, luring a man out of his cabin to explore her and find her riches. Sometimes she rewards the man and sometimes she kills him."

I laughed. "I'm sorry. Seem to be giving you a sermon here."

"Don't apologize," she said in a soft voice. "Don't ever apologize for telling me your feelings. And, if it makes any difference to you, I can see where Alaska could be like a woman."

"Not as much of a woman as you are."

I expected a smart remark from her, but she must have realized I meant it. She just smiled and suddenly got up and scooted around next to me. She took hold of my left hand, and we just sat that way, holding hands and trying to look unconcernedly out at the rest of the dining room and the world.

"I think Janice is a fool," she whispered.

"Why?"

"Because when you make vows, marriage vows, that should be it, forever." She laughed. "Old-fashioned idea, I guess."

"Maybe it is," I told her. "But I think it's nice you feel that way."

"You're very old-fashioned, aren't you, Jeep?"

"More than I like to admit, I think. Never been much of a playboy."

"I think that's nice."

"Vows, though," I said. "Pretty scary."

"Making the commitment?"

"No. No, not that."

I gave her hand a little squeeze and she leaned closer. The perfume was driving me dangerously close to making a public fool of myself, and when I checked out the view—this time it was even closer—I gasped a little.

Right then, right at that time in that restaurant, at midnight on a clear summer night, I wanted to do nothing less than carry her off in my arms and hold her all night and ask her to marry me and arrange to have several kids by morning and take out life insurance and put an indoor bathroom in the Kahiltna cabin, and just touch that soft hair that was hanging so close to my left shoulder.

"Then what?"

"What?"

"Well," she whispered, moving just enough to make me berserk, "you said it isn't the commitment, so what is it?"

"It's . . . respect? Maybe respect." Concentrate on the conversation. Don't look down.

"Respect?"

"Respect for the woman, you see. A guy wouldn't want to get her hopes up. Some of us live a kind of life that . . . "

"Yes?" Betsy said.

"Uh, well, life gets hard in the Bush, you know, and . . . "

She was quiet, then squeezed my hand again and smiled a little sadly.

"You want to take me home now, don't you?"

"No, but maybe I'd better."

"Thank you for saying no first," she said, smiling. "I had a great time."

"It's more special than you could . . . "

I couldn't think of anything to say.

She smiled and scooted out. "Come on," she said, quietly.

Twenty minutes later, Betsy was delivered to her door by a man with his mind spinning between the cold miles reaching toward the Talkeetna Mountains and the warmth shimmering in her walnut hair. Twenty minutes after that, that same man was lying in a sleeping bag on the couch of his office and feeling lonelier than he ever had in his life.

There's so much to lose now. So much.

CHAPTER 9

The operator found a listing in Cordova for Pete Hansen, and Mrs. Hansen answered on the fourth ring. She sounded semi-old but very nice.

"Mrs. Hansen, my name in Jepsen George, and I wonder if I could ask you a few questions?"

"I never buy anything over the phone."

I smiled. "No, ma'am. It's about Lee Hendrix."

"Are you a police officer?"

"I'm a friend of one of the men who was killed."

"I'm sorry, Mr. George. How terrible for you."

"It's very hard on his family."

"Which man was your friend?"

"Bill Turner."

"I remember the name. I've been reading about it a lot and listening on the radio for more news. They haven't caught him yet, you know."

"Yes, I know."

"I used to know him, you know. Lee Hendrix, that is. He worked for my husband for a while."

"That's really why I called you, Mrs. Hansen. I'm trying to learn everything I can about the man."

"I'm afraid I can't tell you much about him, except that he scared my husband, and nothing much scared my husband."

"How did he scare your husband?"

"Just used to look at him. That's what Pete always said. That's the funny part. Pete used to tell me that this Hendrix was a very hard worker, but he'd look at him strangely, like a wild animal, maybe, or someone who is very curious about something. Pete said it made him feel funny. Uncomfortable, you know?"

"Yes."

"I just met him the one time, when Pete was paying him off on the last trip they made together. He was very nice to me. Courteous. A gentleman, you know? I couldn't believe this was the same man Pete felt so uncomfortable around. He took his hat off in the house. Wiped his feet well, you know? I didn't find him the kind of man to be afraid of, but Pete didn't like him at all."

"Why did your husband let him go?"

"They had gone out to check the pots, and there just weren't many crabs on that trip. Sometimes there aren't, you know, and nobody knows why that is. So you just make certain the pots are baited and set them back down again and hope for better luck next time.

"Well, it was raining a lot that trip, and it got on everyone's nerves."

"Who was there?"

"There was just my husband, and Mr. Hendrix, and a young man from Seattle named Chip Browning. He was just learning, but he was a nice young man. Pete liked him.

"At any rate, the fishing wasn't going well, and it was raining and so I guess people's nerves got on edge. I'm sure you understand how it can get sometimes."

"Of course."

"Pete said Mr. Hendrix began telling Pete how to do things on his own boat. Well, my Pete wasn't a big man, physically, but no one told him what to do on that boat. He used to tease me that he had to wipe his feet and his nose in my house, but he did as he pleased on his boat."

I could hear her voice breaking.

"Mrs. Hansen, if you'd rather not talk about this . . . "

"No, that's all right, Mr. George. I'm still trying to find my way, if you know what I mean, and thank God for my friends here in Cordova. They keep me going.

"Now Pete and Mr. Hendrix were arguing. Evidently, Mr. Hendrix thought my husband was too conservative. Told him he ought to get more pots, work longer hours, and go farther out. You see, Pete had been captain of his own boat for more than thirty-five years. It would have been thirty-six years this summer. Well . . . right about now, actually.

"He always said he didn't get to be an old skipper by taking stupid chances. If the weather looked bad, he'd head for shore and ride it out. I never really worried about him."

"And they argued about that?"

"Yes. Mr. Hendrix as much as called my husband a coward and said they could make a lot more money if he weren't afraid of a little weather. Pete then told him it might be a good idea if he got his own fishing boat so he could go fool around in hurricanes if he wanted to. That's just how he said it. Fool around in hurricanes."

"So they agreed to go their separate ways?"

"Yes. When they got back in on that trip."

"When was that, do you remember?"

"Last fall. November, I think."

"And when did you lose your husband?"

"February. Some time between the third and the fifth, as near as we can figure. There was never an SOS, you know."

"I didn't know."

"And they never found any sign of the boat or my husband or Chip. Isn't that strange? There should have been something. I've been a fisherman's wife a long time, and I know there's usually something found floating around out there that tells them where the boat might have gone down. But not this time. And there's something else that doesn't make sense, either."

"What's that?"

"That wasn't much of a storm. Pete had ridden rougher ones than that out at sea with no trouble. And don't try to tell me he hit a rock out there. He knew them all by name."

"Yes, ma'am."

"I'm sorry I haven't been much help, Mr. George."

"You've been a lot of help, Mrs. Hansen. Thank you. Could I ask one more question?"

"Certainly."

"How did your husband come to name his boat the *Crab Cove*?"

"Oh, that was just a name he had for a little cove he'd sometimes duck into in a storm. You won't find it on the maps."

"Do you know about where it is, ma'am?"

"Near Simpson Bay, I think. He's mentioned it before. He liked it there. Used to say it was so pretty there, with the mountains going straight up and this little waterfall pouring right into the sea. He said it would be a great place for a retirement cabin."

Her voice was shaky.

"Thank you, Mrs. Hansen. I'm sorry if my call upset you, but you've been a great help to me."

"They think he killed all those men."

"Yes."

"I wouldn't believe it, knowing how polite he was with me, but my husband would believe it, I think. Mr. Hendrix used to scare him a lot. It was very strange."

"Yes, ma'am. Thank you."

I needed a hill to sit on. I needed a place to think. I needed to sit where the spruces made black silhouettes against a semi-dark sky and stare into the embers of a small fire. I needed to try to sort some of these ideas out, to put some order to this crazy kaleidoscope of actions and timing and personalities. It was like being in a library with everyone yelling facts at me and everyone expecting me to remember all of them.

It was coming in bits and pieces and chunks and clots—flotsam and minuscule trivia that I had to piece together. I couldn't do it in Anchorage. So I bought three hundred pounds of dog food, threw it in the pickup and drove to Kahiltna.

CHAPTER 10

I t was good to eat lunch in my own home for a change, even if the buzz of the city hadn't left yet. That would take a solid dose of the wild country, and by this time I was looking forward to it.

After lunch, I walked out under the hot sun to the dog lot and laughed as the eight members of my team leaped and squalled in happiness.

I raked and shoveled for about fifteen minutes, then sat with each one.

Fade was first, of course. My best leader. Being first was his due. When he was born, Tanya had six beautiful black-and-white masked Malamutes, then she had Fade, almost as an afterthought. He emerged tan and white, so I called him the faded pup, as though Tanya had run out of ink. From that, his name became just Fade. The first time he was put in harness, he tried to run over his mother, who was in the lead, so I gave him a chance at it. He was five months old then. He's been in the lead ever since.

Fade's feet aren't the best for long-distance races, like the Iditarod, or anything over a hundred miles, so he has to be run in booties. But if I boot him up when I take him out of the truck, he'll take me around the world.

Fade always sits quietly next to me, leaning against me in a friendly way, but he's not as demonstrative as some of the others. I reached up quietly and scratched him under the chin and he grinned at me. We're pals.

A-Bob is Fade's father and the father of most of my dogs. A beautiful Malamute, he is at one time a very close friend of mine and my nemesis. A guy I knew moved to Alaska from the Ozarks and had A-Bob for a few months before giving him to me as a pup. He named him after a cousin of his.

A-Bob can be a royal pain in the butt, especially during the first few runs of the season. A-Bob can drive a musher to madness.

He can take voice commands with any leader in the state, but often I'll run him in swing, just behind the leaders, to try to keep him in line. I don't know how many times over the years now—several dozen I guess— A-Bob has been leading the team at a run down a snowy trail and suddenly swung the team around in a big arc and taken everybody right past me, all the way back to the cabin, with me screaming and shaking my fist at him.

I also have to remember to hold tight to the sled, as it snaps violently around when eight dogs going twenty miles an hour in the wrong direction tighten that gangline. It's like playing crack the whip. Sometimes I make the turn with them and sometimes I don't.

It's tricks like this that make A-Bob think his full name is A-Bob-U-Something-or-Other. I don't practice profanity, but the most pious dog driver who ever lived will tell you all bets are off when you drive a team. The only cure for A-Bob's tricks is to take him out of the team and tie him to a tree while the rest of us have a run for an hour or so. No sled dog can stand being left behind. When we pick him up again, he's usually pretty good for several weeks. Not everyone can drive this dog, but I am very fond of him. We've had thousands of miles together.

King is a cuddler. Fade's littermate brother, this giant wheel dog is the engine of the team. It is his strength, right in front of the sled, and that of littermate Joe, that hoists the sled and me over logs and up creek banks. I helped a bush neighbor sled a cast-iron cookstove to his cabin once and King pulled it in by himself, his back low, his belly nearly touching the snow. I could have put more dogs to work on it, but then it would have moved too fast for us to steady the load.

King is one stout dog and he demands a healthy dose of snuggling every time I go out to the dog lot.

Joe is a four-year-old dog, like his brothers Fade and King, and I've had him all his life, but I've never been able to figure him out. Never ouchy or mean, still Joe's always been a shy standoffish dog. One rumple of his ears is about all he needs or wants. But he can always be counted on for a long hard day's work.

Cider is a smallish forty-five-pound husky of Indian dog extraction. She's fast and runs in swing with A-Bob most of the time. Swing is the place for the speed dogs. Let them put the speed on the team and take some of the pulling pressure off the leaders, who need to be free to do some thinking. Leaders are a bit like the quarterbacks on football teams. They call the shots for the team. Swing dogs are a bit like the running backs.

Cider has another job, too. Each evening, shortly after everyone has eaten, she leads the singing. This is not barking, but a concerted lonely howl with muzzles pointed to heaven that sways in and out of key in minor chords and brings back primordial memories that even the dogs don't understand.

Mushers usually hate gratuitous barking, but most of them love to listen to the evening serenade. It lasts only a few minutes, but it's a song of love and joy and thanksgiving and it touches the soul.

Cider will stick her nose in the air and give one tiny quavering wail and in seconds the entire team has joined her. It is her job. Everyone knows it. No one knows why.

I like her.

Charlene is another of Tanya's and A-Bob's offspring, but she is a year younger than Fade and King and Joe. She's a big fluffy sweetheart of a dog, and when it's her turn to come into the cabin for special attention (what I call "cabin loving") she takes a more than usual measure of delight from the visit.

When Charlene was a pup, she tangled with a porcupine on a summer hike. All huskies do, of course, which is why I always carry needle-nosed pliers with me on these jaunts. Unfortunately, once in a while—once in a great while—I'll miss a quill. Maybe it's just so short it buries itself completely under the skin.

In Charlene's case, it was probably lost in all that long fluffy coat of hers. When that happens, it is never good. The tiny barbs in the quill make it dig deeper with each move the dog makes. Sometimes the quill goes completely through the dog and out the other side without hitting anything vital. Sometimes the quill hits the heart or liver and kills the dog. However Charlene acquired her quill, the quill worked its way through her and emerged through her right eye, blinding it.

It is hard to imagine the guilt I felt when this happened. But it sometimes happens.

That's why Charlene runs in second wheel, just ahead of the wheel dogs and just behind the swing dogs, on the left side . . . so her good eye is to the outside. This way she can dodge trees.

Her team partner, Me Too, was a gift from another musher who didn't believe she'd be a good sled dog with only one eye. Her left eye was destroyed in a fight when she was a pup, and she runs opposite Charlene so her good eye is on the outside, too. Fortunately, the two girls get along wonderfully. Each dog has its place where it does its best work, and each dog has other dogs it works well with and dogs it can't stand. In addition to this, some dogs work well only on the left side of the central gangline, while others work well only on the right.

I can teach a neophyte how to drive a dog team in minutes, but it can take months of trial and error for a new musher to discover the best combination of dogs, team partners and team positions. It's the equivalent of a finely adjusted timing chain on a car engine.

Me Too got her name from her enthusiasm. Walk into the dog lot with a harness in my hand and I'm met with excitement by all of them, of course, but Me Too goes berserk, jerking herself over backwards when she hits the end of the chain and screaming something that sounds a lot like "Me Too!"

If I had eight dogs like Me Too, and if they had sixteen eyes among them, I might win a lot more races. I get a kick out of her.

I always save Tanya for last on my dog lot visits. Tanya is the soul of the team, the heart of the team. For the most part, too, she's the mother of the team.

I found Tanya in the Anchorage dog pound. She was a "military dog" there, which has nothing to do with war dogs or patrol dogs. That means simply that when young soldiers or airmen are stationed at either Elmendorf or Fort Richardson, many of them want to immerse themselves in the true spirit of the north and they buy a husky pup for a pet.

This is a lot of fun until the pup weighs eighty pounds and takes up half the small apartment. Then the dog ends up either being given to dog mushers or put in the pound for adoption or, worse, abandoned.

Tanya's folks cared enough about her to put her in the pound for adoption. A pal of mine at the pound got word to me that there was a gorgeous big freight dog available, and I paid her hotel bill and took her home.

I've loved her ever since.

She normally runs in a double lead with her son, Fade. When the mental pressure gets too much for her, I put her back in the team for half a day for a little rest and let her mate, A-Bob, share the lead with Fade. But after a few hours, Tanya will get truculent with the other dogs and want her royal position back.

It's hard to talk about Tanya without sounding maudlin, because this dog has saved my life several times. If she hadn't quit pulling and started digging in the snow that time in the Brooks Range, I wouldn't have been prepared for the three-day gale that hit us twenty minutes later. I would have perished.

If she hadn't swerved off the ice of the Sagavanirktok River another time, I would today be at the bottom of that river, fallen through the ice that would have supported the dogs but not me or the sled.

Tanya has a regal bearing at all times except when the two of us are alone. At those times, she puts her head in my lap and is all love and adoration. I feel the same.

I save Tanya for last on my visits because she epitomizes what is good and brave and special about a dog team. I could drive the team without her, and I've had to from time to time, such as when she has new pups. But even though the other dogs and I still go down the trail, there is something missing from the team, a spark, a reason for being. A soul.

She represents the finest in dog mushing tradition—not the fastest, not even the perfect command leader like Fade, but the best of this ancient means of travel. I'm nuts about her.

Not all families have to be people.

After making arrangements to have the dogs tended for an extended time, I took the .30-06 down from above the door and wiped it clean inside and out. I loaded the magazine, careful to see that one wasn't "up the pipe," meaning in the chamber, then I took it for a walk up the river toward old Charlie Nickolai's cabin. He was sitting outside leaning against the cabin, reading an outdoor magazine.

"What you doing, Charlie?"

Charlie was about as old as his cabin and about the same color. They had both aged well. With us both coming from this tiny mixed-race village, he was bound to be some kind of cousin or uncle of mine. He is also descended from Chief Wasilla Stephan I know, but then I think all the Indian folks around here are. But although we once sat down and tried to figure it out, we never did it, completely. Our families, a generation ago even, weren't famous for keeping family records. In Alaska, if another fellow is from the same village, you just treat him like family because he undoubtedly is.

"We gonna hunt black bear, Jeep?"

"Not today, Charlie."

"I want to get some black bear, Jeep. I didn't get one yet, you know."

"If I get one, I'll send you some meat, Charlie."

Charlie is pretty old now, but he used to be the greatest black bear hunter anywhere around. He knew where to find them, and how to get them. He knew where they wintered. He could just about go out for a walk and tell you where to go and what to do, right then, to get a bear. He trained me on black bear, me and a number of other people, including my father.

Charlie loved to hunt black bear and looked on winter as a nuisance because its snow and cold made the black bears go to ground for six or seven months each year. Most of all, Charlie loved to eat black bear. Black bear meat, if it is cooked thoroughly, is wonderful if the bear has been taken in early summer.

"I think it's too late for black bear now anyway, Charlie," I told him. "They've been eating fish for a month."

He grinned and cackled through his leathery face.

"I don't care no more, Jeep. I guess I'm getting old or something, but I can eat them black bears when they're in fish now. You get one, you bring me some meat, okay?"

"Okay, Charlie. I'm going up the river and shoot a little."

"Okay."

Several hundred yards upstream from old Charlie's, the hills move back away from the river, making room for some large cottonwoods. I went up to one that stood against a steep bank and took a legal-sized envelope from my pocket. I wedged it in some bark about chest high, then turned and paced off fifty good steps. Resting my left hand against an alder, I set the rifle on my thumb, threw the bolt, and shot the envelope four times.

I walked back a hundred paces this time, looked through the peep and shot four more times. Again all four hit the envelope. Then I stuck the envelope in my pocket and walked back toward home.

Telescopic sights are much easier to knock out of kilter, which is why every guide has his hunter sight in the rifle the minute he reaches camp, but even a good solid peep sight like my Williams can be knocked out of zero a bit if the rifle is dropped hard, so I always check it before a season or a special occasion.

I considered this a special occasion.

Most hunters sight in for a hundred yards, or maybe even a hundred and fifty yards. That is, their rifles will be dead-on at that distance. With today's super flat-shooting magnum calibers, it is quite possible to hold on a Dall ram's vitals with one of those rifles from fifty yards to two hundred and fifty yards and still make a clean kill. But those longer distances aren't what we need for a back-up rifle. Most guides don't use scopes because it's too easy to fog them or knock them out of true, but mainly because that isn't the kind of shooting we're called upon to do.

If the guide has to swing his back-up rifle into action, it's generally in poor light and close quarters at a moving—sometimes rapidly moving—target.

One guide I knew had a scoped seven-millimeter Remington Magnum that he was awfully fond of. On the second hunter he had out, he was faced with an angry black bear at twelve yards. He looked through the scope and all he could see was black. He had no idea which part of the bear he was shooting, but he had to pull the trigger anyway. Fortunately for him, the rifle was pointed at the right part of the bear.

That fancy scope had been cranked up to nine power, inadvertently, but he solved the problem by simply taking it off.

My rifle enjoys digesting a certain diet, in this case over-the-counter ammunition with 180-grain bullets. I have nothing against other ammunition. It's all good. It's just that each rifle barrel will have its favorite bullet weight, powder charge and type of bullet. Mine likes these 180-grain bullets. It will group them very tightly from a bench rest. If I shoot 150-grain bullets or 220-grain bullets, the groups open up considerably down there at the target, so I just stick to what my rifle tells me is best.

The strange thing is, you can take the very next barrel off the assembly line, supposedly identical in every way, and it might stick those 220-grain bullets all in one hole and not like the one-eighties.

I don't understand the mechanics of things in life, so I happily throw my hands in the air, say that it's all magic, and go on living my life. If you spend too much time trying to think about things you shouldn't, it just burns up all your circuits and you'll have to go to wild country to get them back.

Old Charlie was still sitting there reading his magazine when I came back by.

"You're going to have that magazine memorized," I told him.

"Hard to see it any more. The print's too little," he said, folding it up and setting it next to him on the firewood. "You want a coffee or tea?"

"Maybe next time, Charlie. I have to go to Anchorage yet today."

"Big city," he said. "It don't move fast."

I got the picture. "I take some sugar in my tea," I said.

I sat on the firewood and he went in the cabin and I heard the slight whooshing of a gas stove. Pretty soon he brought out two mugs of tea. The tea was as dark as coffee and had the aroma of the woods in it.

"I put some spruces in it," he said. "Keeps you from catching cold or something like that."

"Thank you, Charlie."

Young spruce needles are loaded with vitamin C. When boiled, they make a tea that tastes exactly like boiled spruce needles, but when you mix them with some Lipton and sugar (and everyone does), it's not half bad. Had the old timers bothered to ask the Indians about spruce tea, they wouldn't have been so sick with scurvy. Jack London might have stayed two or even three winters in the north, rather than spending one miserable winter lying sick in bed on the Fortymile.

In summer, wild roses are everywhere in the north, and they have the second-highest jolt of vitamin C in the plant world. But spruce trees are always there, winter and summer.

"Rained yesterday," Charlie said.

"Looks nice today."

"Good one today," he said. "You sighting in, or hunting trees?"

"Hunting trees."

"You get one?"

"Great big one. Cottonwood."

"Don't taste so good as birch."

"But birches scream so bad when you shoot them."

"Nobody ever taught you where to shoot a tree?"

"I guess you should have done it, Charlie."

He laughed and laughed at the joke. "I think I'm too old now, Jeep. My eyes aren't so good, you know."

"How about moose this fall, Charlie?"

All guides have their "meat lists," those people who happen to be wonderful and deserving and for some reason can't go into the field any more with a rifle. There is always meat left over when hunting camp shuts down, and it all has to go to good homes, according to law. The worst sin in Alaska is wasting good meat.

Charlie drew himself up straight and put down his cup. He said, very seriously, "I ain't on the moose list yet, Jeep. I can still hunt my own moose."

"Well, sure," I said. "I just thought, well, a moose is more meat than I'll need all winter, and you'd do me a favor by eating some of it."

He thought about it for a while. "Well, if you need some help with it . . . "

"I'll bring some by."

"You get a wife and kids to eat that moose with you, Jeep George."

I smiled. "I guess I'm too ugly."

He shook his head and looked straight at me. "I knew your grandfather all my life, you know that?"

I nodded.

"And I knew your father all his life. I took him in the woods when he was a little boy about this big. I taught him how to make a marten set, you know that?"

I nodded.

"So I'm going to tell you something, Jeep George. You get a wife and kids to eat that moose with you. Living alone, like an old wolverine, isn't no good, Jeep."

"Why didn't you get married, then, Charlie?"

"I did, once. Oh, it was a long time before you were even born, I guess. She was a white woman. She didn't stay very long."

"I'm sorry to hear that."

"It was fun for a while, you know. Then she said she needed culture and she went back to her home."

"Culture?"

"Operas, concerts, theater plays. She said that was culture."

"That kind of culture."

He nodded. "You marry an Indian girl, Jeep. You remember that."

"I'll remember that, Charlie, and thanks for the tea."

Marry an Indian girl. Maybe that would have worked for old Charlie. The sad thing is, he'll never know now, and he probably never remarried because he still considered himself married to the woman who went off to watch the operas. Life's little tricks and turns.

Being a half-and-half the way I am, it's hard to know who I could be happy with. Even dating has always been something of a problem. For the most part, the women I'd known so far had come in two categories: what I'd call the Hillarys and the Meades.

The Hillarys I named for Sir Edmund Hillary, by the way. You know the type. They can climb Everest or the corporate ladder without a single boost from mere man. They come up here on vacation because there are three men to every woman in Alaska. Most of them go home empty-handed, though, because there might be a lot of lonely men up here, but there are reasons why they are here and not in Chicago or New York.

The Meades are more fun. They are named for Margaret Meade, the student of native cultures. These women come to Alaska hoping to find a Native man so they can be let in on the Big Secret.

The Big Secret is, of course, that anyone of Native ancestry in Alaska is automatically born this intensely spiritual person who communes with nature almost obsessively and can be found divining the essence of spruce trees at the drop of a phrase in our Native language.

It would come as a big shock to them to learn that most Native people probably don't actually understand the term spiritual, that there may be a few cultural events, like potlatches, during the year, but that only a few of the older folks can really sit down and explain to you how they work and what they're for.

Few of the younger people have time for any of Grandma's stories and omens and history any more, unfortunately. They are too busy, like other American young people, trying to learn how to score on the opposite sex, go to the moon, or buy a fast car.

Things have changed some for the better, in my mind, since the early 1970s. When the Alaska Native Land Claims Settlement Act went through Congress, it brought not only money and title to land but a resurgence of pride to all of Alaska's Native people. When that happened, Native graduate students from the university armed themselves with tape recorders and went back to the village to ask Grandma to tell the story of how Raven created the Aleutian Islands one more time, please. All of a sudden, grant money was found for fixing up some totem poles the Tlingit and Tsimshian had down there in Southeast.

It came in time to save a lot of Native culture—Eskimo, Athabascan,

Aleut, Tlingit—but it was a close shave.

Consider this. When a group of young Tlingit men decided they'd like to learn how to carve totem poles as their ancestors did, they could find only one man in the state to teach them: a very elderly man of Norwegian ancestry who had married a Tlingit woman and wanted to help her people keep this alive.

But it was in time.

The Tlingit language was written down by two white schoolteachers, and in many Native villages in the state, the children learn words in their own tongue only from their white teachers. But they're learning, and that's good.

There's something about how some white people perceive Native people that makes us downright irresistible. It is easy to take advantage of a Meade woman. If you have dark skin and dark hair, she'll believe any story you give her about the sanctity of Wolf, the cunning of Raven or how The People came into the world.

Do we have these stories? Of course. Do we believe them? Sure, along with the stories of creation of whichever church we attend, along with what our science teacher told us in high school about Darwinian theory. It's an easygoing kind of belief. It doesn't require a great deal of fanaticism or self-sacrifice, only one part of it has a collection plate, and any pressure to subscribe only to one third of that can send us scuttling to the other two thirds pretty quickly, so nobody pushes much. If any possible conflicts in belief arise, we can smile and shrug them off, chalk them up to magic and mystery, and go on with our lives. It's an easygoing kind of belief, but it works, and there are never any arguments.

The Scopes trial would never have been held in Alaska. Native people just don't get that excited about what they consider nit-picking differences.

Perhaps it's the difference in attitude. A number of the Meades have come up here and interviewed people and have written down the Raven stories and others. But they make one critical mistake in interpreting these stories. Where the stories of the Bible and the Koran and the Book of Mormon and others are best whispered about in hushed halls with organ music encompassing you and some terrible sword of blasphemy hanging over you if you say the wrong thing, Alaska Natives have more fun with their legends.

Raven, you see, is often laughed at. Jesus is never laughed at.

Maybe it's because the Jesus stories and the Moses stories and the Buddha stories haven't been around long enough. Two thousand years, maybe three thousand, tops. When the Raven saved the Tlingits from The Savages (that was us, the Athabascans), it was roughly when the last ice age shoved everybody together, about 10,000 years ago. Maybe what Raven did back then wasn't funny but was really religious. But that was 10,000 years ago, and who can keep from lightening up a story a bit here and there along the way to make it easier to understand?

Give Christianity, Islam and Judaism another 15,000 years or so, and who knows? There are some characters in the Bible who have some real potential.

But the Meade ladies come and tape record and go back and write and get master's degrees and doctorates. On the walls of their apartments in Chicago and New York are dancing masks from the Eskimo people. They have a few Tlingit carvings here and there. A pair of Athabascan moosehide moccasins with the beaded roses on them are next to their beds. And maybe, if they really got close to their subjects, they keep the memories of a night or six with a real Alaskan Native man and how they felt close to nature for a little while there.

The Native men, on the other hand, usually think of how they were close to a woman and what a nice experience that was.

I used to date a Meade lady from time to time. It's a strong temptation. But I got tired of thinking she was taking notes any time we talked.

Some of them are serious and some are just silly. There are the ones who come up here trying to get closer to the planet Venus, or live in a log cabin full of healing crystals, or hold seances to accomplish various things.

On one jaunt, when I was spending a week with some friends at a ski resort near Anchorage, I attended a seance where this medium from California, in my honor, tried to sing back the buffalo to Alaska. I was good. I waited almost a full hour until I was outside before I collapsed in the snow, laughing. Buffalo haven't been native to Alaska since a couple of ice ages ago, and the ones we have now were borrowed from Montana or somewhere about fifty years ago.

There are times when it is really a lot of fun being Native, or even half-Native, as in my case. It makes you want to trade in that marten-skin cap for one of those great Sioux warbonnets so you really get the feel of being an Indian.

Not that there aren't those among us—full blood, half blood, and a few of no Native blood at all—who wish to learn the legends, who want to take into their hearts the essence of history about the land and its peoples.

I am one of these.

Perhaps my not having parents as a young man had something to do with it. Maybe that's why I learned so much from my grandparents—both sets of grandparents. I was always the kid who paid attention. I was always the kid who wanted to learn the old songs and what they meant. I was always the kid who wanted to learn words and phrases in the Dena'ina language, and a few words in Norwegian as well from my Gramps Jepsen.

There are still a few shamans around. I've met a couple. For the most part, they frighten me.

Here you have the people who might have the answers to some of those Boston doctoral thesis questions, but they keep most of that to themselves. Being a shaman means to become weird and dedicate your life to being strange. No thanks. I'll content myself with being a hunting guide who doesn't easily dismiss the legends of his people. I can be satisfied with calling on the help of Raven, my personal pal in the forest, for a little help when I need it.

Superstition? Maybe. I don't know. But I don't think it has ever harmed anyone, and it's more fun than not believing in omens.

These thoughts kept my mind occupied almost all the way home from Charlie's place. When I rounded the bend of the river and returned to my cabin, I cleaned the rifle out again and placed a piece of Scotch tape over the muzzle. The tape keeps crud out of the barrel, and you can shoot right through it. In fact, the bullet doesn't even touch it. The air pushed ahead of the bullet blows the tape out of the way.

I oiled the sling and thought some more about old Charlie. No, I didn't. I oiled the sling and thought some more about Jeep George. I wondered if someday I'd be sitting out in front by the woodpile on warm days and reading outdoor magazines alone. It wasn't nice to think about.

I went through my stampeder's pack right at the doorway to make certain I had everything I needed: matches, hidden everywhere, of every shape and description; toilet paper, sleeping bag, plastic tube tent for rainy nights (and for a ground cloth in good weather); several knives, ammunition, monocular, a large tin can for cooking, and two rolls of aluminum foil. Besides for cooking, foil can be used in an emergency for signaling aircraft or even keeping warm. I liked to use it as a reflector oven for piroshkis, when I have time for that.

My fanny pack is extra and holds more emergency gear, including three of those cheap plastic disposable lighters (I'm not that much of a traditionalist when it comes to staying alive) and some fishing gear.

The stampeder's pack got its name back around a hundred years ago when the white men went to the Yukon Territory looking for gold. When one guy would come into the saloon and say he'd found gold on such-and-such creek, everyone ran home, grabbed a pack, and stampeded to the new area. So a pack that's kept in readiness for travel has come to be known as a stampeder's pack ever since. When you go for an airplane ride in Alaska (well, not on the big jets), you take your pack (or at least your sleeping bag) and your rifle.

What to put in the stampeder's pack has always been a subject for hot controversy in any bar, cafe, barber shop, gun shop or sourdough's cabin. It occasionally becomes the Alaskan's answer to reading the paper and talking politics. For every item one old timer says is as necessary as teats on a boar grizzly, there's another curmudgeon there who can quote chapter and verse on when the lack of that item cost someone his life, or when having it saved a life.

Truth be known, if all the items that were deemed necessary—absolutely dog-ribbed essential—for basic survival in the Bush were gathered up for one pack, you'd have to haul it around on a large truck.

In my opinion, there is absolutely no way of knowing what will be needed on any Bush jaunt, no matter how short or how long. You plan the best you can. You use the wisest judgment you can bring to bear on the subject. You make your selections and hope you're right, because your life may depend on it. The Bush is this huge killing factory, with about thirty ways to die on any given day. You get on through that day, and maybe make some progress toward your goal, and you've really accomplished something.

It's the Great Game, you see. Like Groucho Marx's old television show, it's called "You Bet Your Life," only sometimes it's harder to say the magic word and divide that hundred dollars.

I threw in about ten pounds of caribou jerky and tied the drawstring shut. Then I opened it again and grabbed an old pair of comfortable moccasins and tossed them in. A guide's ankle-fit hip boots, the kind that don't wiggle around and rub sores, are fine for walking all day, but they don't let your feet breathe. At night, it's nice to switch over to dry socks and soft moccasins. Sometimes on the trail, the little comforts mean a lot.

I found myself throwing this pack together a bit frantically, and several times I forced myself to slow down and breathe deeply and think carefully about what I was doing. The jangled nerves were just Anchorage. I knew that, and I knew what it would take to wear that off.

It's my opinion and philosophy that the body builds up protective layers of nerve armor to defend you from maladies like Anchorage. It's like white blood cells or antibodies to keep you from going nuts in town. Unfortunately, these protective layers make you think strangely, act very quickly and sometimes say things you wish you hadn't. It takes a strong dose of Bush to wear away the layers so a guy can get back to normal.

I put my rifle and pack in the truck, then walked back to the cabin and listened to some soothing Ella Fitzgerald on the oversized sound system I keep there. It helped, but it wasn't doing the job. Solitude brought on thoughts, and thinking wasn't what I was best at today. There was Hendrix, out there asleep in the sunshine, tucked back in some hollow where airplanes couldn't find him, waiting for the dark. There was old Charlie, living year after year in that little trapper's cabin of his. There were Karen and the kids. There was Danny and Mary and the hunters. There was Betsy.

So I took off the camouflage Jones cap I normally wear in camp and reached for the bright red wool crusher that has become the trademark of the men of Kahiltna. In truth, they are popular all over the state, but here in this little village where the rivers meet, it's joked about as being formal attire. Then I followed the trail through the birch trees, walked across the railroad tracks and into the little village of Kahiltna.

The South Seas roadhouse was in its usual fine form. I walked in and Hem Jones fished around in the cooler and brought out an orange drink. Around the big U-shaped bar were several centuries of experience in bush Alaska. Almost all of the men wore the red hats today, and they were all laughing.

I moved two sled dogs and an obese Labrador enough to get a bar stool pulled out and sat two stools down from John Thompson. Hemingway brought me the orange drink.

"I missed the joke, John."

"The joke's on me, I'm afraid," he grumbled, then started laughing again, which set off Frank Granger, the unofficial owner of the South Seas road-house, at his table next to the door, and the other patrons. Frank is the unofficial owner of the bar-with-rooms-upstairs because officially it doesn't exist. Half of it is on a surveyed city lot, half is on a dedicated dirt street and none of it is on paper down in Palmer—the seat of the Matanuska-Susitna Borough—where they pay a couple of guys to worry about things like this.

The only two men in the village old enough to know something about the bar's ownership come in for free beer a lot. When they are asked who owns the South Seas, they always say Frank does.

"You see," John said, twanging his red suspenders and leaning back with his beer, "it was about a week ago, I guess. Wasn't it about a week ago, Doc?"

"Well," said Doc Evans, who wasn't a doctor of any sort, "it was the day after that big Army helicopter landed."

"That helicopter landed on a Wednesday," Hemingway Jones, the bar-tender, said. "I remember because that's the night I drive to Anchorage, and . . . "

There was dead silence in the bar. The sourdoughs looked at the rather naive would-be writer (hence his nickname) as though they were a pack of wolves who had spotted a steak dinner. Even Frank Granger put his paper down and took his pipe out of his mouth. "You drive to town on Wednes-days? Every Wednesday?"

"It's my day off . . . "

"What's in Anchorage on Wednesdays, Hem?" John asked.

"Oh, just something." Hem blushed. "Hey, anyone ready for a beer?"

"Don't try to change the subject," Doc said, leaning forward. "You go to Anchorage every Wednesday night. We have to know what it is, Jones lad. A woman?"

"A woman! A woman!" John Thompson echoed.

"No," Hem said, trying to wipe glasses quickly.

"Then what?" Frank said.

"I know," said John. "It's quilting. I know the poor boy has been cold in the winter. By his own admission he isn't seeing a woman, so the only chance he has of staying warm this coming winter is to make quilts. I'll bet he's meeting with some old ladies down there and making a quilt."

"That's not true!"

"Maybe it's one of those writers' meetings, son?" suggested Frank more kindly.

"No," he said. "Look, it's just a hobby thing. For fun, that's all."

"Like what?" John said, his eyes twinkling. "Better tell us, Mr. Jones. We'll make your life so wretched if you don't that you'll wish you never came to this village. Next Wednesday, we'll follow you all the way to town and see for ourselves where it is you go. We'll pay people down there to spy on you. We'll put microphones in your suits so—"

"Dance lessons," Hem said quietly, looking at the floor.

"What's that?" Doc said from the other side of the U-shaped bar. "I didn't quite catch that."

"I take some country-western dance lessons on Wednesday nights, that's all," Hemingway said.

"Dance lessons! Well, hot dog, now we're talking!" Doc said. "Come and show us, Hem."

"Aw, Doc, I can't do that. Not here."

"Here? Why not? There's a jukebox in the corner that works about twice a week, there's room on the floor. We'll even move some tables around."

"I can't."

"Why not!"

"Well, for one thing, there's no women here."

Every sourdough looked around the room very carefully. Doc checked under his bar napkin.

"He's right, you know," said Frank.

"Yep," said Doc. "Not a girl in sight."

"Where's a woman when you need one?" John said.

"Well, Mr. Jones," Doc said, standing up and stretching, "who needs a woman? I'll dance with you."

"Oh no, Doc!"

"Come on, Hem," Doc said, "you need the exercise."

"No way."

"Look around you," Doc said. "Look at these faces. Are these the faces of cultured gentlemen? Are these the faces that once graced the grand ballrooms of history? Of course not. These, dear boy, are the culturally starved men of southcentral Alaska. These are the very people who can benefit by those dance lessons of yours. Now come out here and show me what to do."

Frank went over to the juke box and put in a quarter. Country music began playing loudly. The men were clapping and laughing, and so was I. But while Hemingway Jones came out from behind the bar and tried to teach the Texas two-step to a man old enough and kind enough to be his father, I was able to step back away from it a minute.

Oh, I still had the bottle of orange drink, and still sat right on the same stool I usually use, two down from John on the north side next to the Labrador retriever who didn't have a name, but then there was a strange feeling of being aloof, too. Here were two men in red hats, dancing together while a half-dozen more clapped and sang along with the music. On the walls hung the antlers of a record-book moose that had been shot just out the front door one night and the pelt of a black bear so old and musty and grungy it looked like a caricature of itself.

And while I watched and listened, I pulled back, drawn by something like Raven himself, perhaps drawn back to look down at the fun and laughter that is rural Alaska. The giant slam of contrast and emotion. The full-hearted laughter of rugged men. The quick slices of a crazy man that can end lives before they have a chance to bloom.

The dance ended and Frank put another coin in the machine, and this time it was Arizona John who wanted to learn the dance step. Doc bowed politely to old Frank and got him out of his chair, and began teaching him the dance.

Most of the men in this room were men of legend up here, as are the men in most rural roadhouses in Alaska. In this room were two men who were born with different names than they carry now, I knew. We never ask what those other names were or why they were changed.

It is at a time like this that I feel so tugged between the white-man laughter and the Native silence of the forest. Somewhere in there is where I belong. Someplace in the middle—this time verging toward the white man, the next time tending toward the Native.

On a date one time, the tourist girl I had taken out for the evening had finally had enough alcohol to bring her to ask:

"Well, are you an Indian or a white man or what?"

I had thought about it a lot, just that particular morning, and hadn't come to any solid conclusion on how that question should or even could be answered. But I turned to her that night and said, "I guess I'm an Alaskan."

I guess that's true enough, too. I'm an Alaskan, just like the men in this room, no matter what color or where they were born. Just like old Charlie. Just like Buck. Just like Doc and John and Hemingway and Frank. No more Alaskan than an Anchorage building contractor and no less Alaskan than old Chief Stephan himself.

I've known some young people who became more Alaskan in one year than a lot of folks I've known who lived in Anchorage for many years.

It's a mind set, I guess. It's a way of ordering your life so you come to the same general conclusion as other Alaskans: namely, life is fantastic, Alaska is the best place in which to live it, and no one should be able to tell anyone else what to do.

What trails, roads and freeways lead a man to find this conclusion are as varied as the people who live here in the Bush areas. And they don't matter. I can recall reading the obituary of an old-timer who had befriended me when I was a boy. He was a great bearded giant of a man who lived about a mile south of Kahiltna. It wasn't until he died that any of us learned he'd been a general in the army.

But the great land itself weaves threads between us, gently at first and later stronger and stronger yet, until we are all tied together in this vast place that gets so cold in winter and so heaven-blushed with beauty all year.

"The joke," said John, a little out of breath from the dancing, "was really on me. Well, I was just heading over this way from the cabin, isn't that right, Frank?"

"Well," said Frank, "I thought you were coming more from Dorothy's—from up this way."

"Couldn't be," John said. "I always do my shopping on Monday."

Doc looked at him. "John, you run out of pipe tobacco every other day. Like Tuesday and Thursday and Saturday."

Frank nodded. "That's true."

"Well, anyway, that was the day after the big army helicopter landed."

"Which was on a Wednesday," said Hemingway.

"That's right," said Doc, "because Hem always gets his ballet lessons on Wednesday, see, and so the next day is Thursday, because that's when he gets tutu chafe and has to powder himself. . . . "

I laid a buck down on the bar during the laughter and walked back outside into the late afternoon. Clouds were sifting in slowly from the direction of the Nelchina, and I hoped they wouldn't hurt the flight Buck and I had to make tomorrow.

From the warm, dense, almost tropical lushness of the hot day into the cloudiness of a long, slow evening. I liked it. It suited my moods today. Sometimes, weather and moods balance well and things become harmonious. This was one of those days.

I got in my pickup and drove the more than two hours back into Anchorage. I had to pick up the piroshkis, and I very much wanted to eat a steak someone else had cooked.

CHAPTER 11

A nchorage was in one of its charming moods.

Good. That's the way I'd like to remember it when I'm out in the boonies. For some reason, this evening seemed to pull together nicely. The weather, maybe. It was another starting-to-rain evening with just a little mistiness around, just enough to make the town smell salty and sweet and a little fishy, like Seattle.

The soft rains seem to lull everyone into being a little slower to anger. Even cab drivers forget there are horns on the cars.

In honor of the boys at the South Seas in Kahiltna, I wore my red crusher on a nice long walk out to where I knew I could get a thick steak and crisp salad without having to listen to some piano player from Outside butchering show tunes.

When I left, after a few lazy cups of coffee and some casual conversation with a tourist couple, I started back to the office in the misting rain. Perhaps by now Danny would have brought my piroshkis to the office.

The conversation I'd had was so similar to other tourist talks that they tend to herd together in my mind. I can recall the faces pretty well, especially if they laugh. I love hearing tourists laugh. So many just complain about how expensive everything is. But the actual conversations seem to run on straight rails toward the identical conclusion. You see, they come from Duluth and Brooklyn and Sacramento and Dallas and Topeka and El Monte and Columbus and Bakersfield. Most of them are retired now. Unlike the Japanese, who send their young people off on the big jets to be tourists, we Americans wait until we're gray and a little stove up before we set out to see the world.

Women lose interest in the Bush when they learn there are no flush toilets, but the men . . .

These fellows may have spent thirty years putting pipes together or running a drill press or selling advertising, but the country gets them, right away.

It can be seen in their faces. Their faces say, "Why didn't I come here?"

Sometimes, if his wife is a good sport, or excuses herself to go to the powder room, he'll lean toward me and whisper, "Son, if I were just twenty years younger . . . "

And I nod, because I know what he means.

We each make our decisions in life, I guess. So far, mine have been all right. Not perfect, but all right. I couldn't picture myself not guiding hunters. There's too much in it I need. There is the country itself, and that feeling of being out there with nothing but a .30-06 between me and God. There are the animals, and the constant education they give me. There is the weather, ever changing, ever adamant in whatever it does, and always spectacular. There are the hunters. Most of all, I guess, there are the hunters.

These men and women Danny and I take back into the fortresses of the Dall sheep and the barrens where the big bears roll along are what make all the really hard physical work worthwhile.

We take only those hunters we know, or those who come recommended by those we know. No exceptions. You learn early on in a career of guiding that there are plenty of hunters with the money necessary for a top guided hunt. You also learn that maybe nine out of ten are the best people in the world.

This seeming snobbery of mine is just my way of insuring myself against that one jerk in ten. I'd rather guide for free than have to tolerate someone like that. And it's not so much that he's an irritant (it's never a woman; women who hunt always seem to be nice) but more that he has been given a special look at a special part of my life and doesn't find in it the same awe I do.

The hunters I want in my camp are the ones who want to know the names of every berry growing in the tundra (even if I don't know all of them) and which are safe to eat. My hunters are the ones who want endless hours of stories about the animals they pursue. They realize inside themselves that by learning all they can before the hunt, they honor the animal they are going to take. My hunters are the ones who pitch in and help with the dishes in a spike camp, even if they are chairmen of the boards of huge corporations.

And some of them are.

My hunters are the ones who enjoy laughing at a good joke, and exchanging Christmas cards and every couple of years sending along a photograph of their families.

Because they know that when they get their moose, it's really our moose. Maybe I didn't make the shot, but I was with them, and helped a bit, and so that moose forever gets filed away as a very special event in the lives of both of us.

So each season is a little like a reunion and a little like expanding one's family. Each has a closeness with you that can only come from sharing some really special moments together, be they joyful or the occasional one that's tinged with terror.

The life works for me, anyway.

When I got back to the office, I found a note from Betsy to phone her, and no piroshkis. I phoned her.

"I'm glad you're in," she said. "Stay there, I've got your piroshkis and I'll bring them right over." Then she hung up.

I made some coffee and looked out across Knik Arm in the rainy twilight at the spruce on the distant shore. Right there, I knew, was Bush. No roads. No cabins. Nothing. Maybe four miles from the largest city in the state and it was as wild as anything the state had to offer. I always thought that to be strange, and I also wanted to go there some day.

I heard Betsy coming up the stairs, so I met her halfway and helped her with the paper bags she carried. She set them down on the desk.

"Piroshki Delivery Service!" she said. "I guess you're going out tomorrow morning? Well, these piroshkis, please notice, are sealed tight by some newfangled plastic sealer machine that Danny's mom has. I don't know, maybe she borrowed it from a friend. Anyway, she tells me it takes all the air out, so you can dunk these in the river, bury them in the yard for fifty years, do whatever you like to them and they'll still be good to eat as long as you don't break the seal on them.

"Now to open them, please observe, you just take a knife and cut right—"

"Hello, Bets," I said, smiling. I tried to turn my head so I could look into her face. She hadn't really looked at me yet.

"—well, you just cut these babies open, and then I guess you can heat them by a fire, or just . . . hey . . . eat those suckers the way they are, since they've already been cooked. Some have ham and cheese in them. Some have moose and broccoli."

"Betsy? You there, Bets?"

"Yes, I'm here. Of course I'm here. There weren't any phone messages that I couldn't handle. No, your friend the cop didn't call. Have you listened to the radio today? No, of course not. Well, they haven't caught him yet, but the radio news commentators, those experts on all Bush situations, are beginning to speculate he has perished in the wilderness by now. They can't imagine anyone going without chocolate puffies for breakfast and hair spray before work being able to survive."

"You do talk an awful lot sometimes, Betsy."

"Do I, Jeep? Maybe I do. Maybe I talk too much sometimes."

"Don't apologize. I shouldn't have said anything. It's just that you seem upset tonight."

"Oh well, don't let me be upset or anything. Hey, it's just the rain, maybe. What do you think? Or maybe it's just the ways of an inscrutable girl from Chicago."

I laughed.

"And Danny's mother won't take any money for the piroshkis and that's that, she says."

"Let's buy her a canned ham or something, what do you think?"

"I sent her two canned hams and a couple of large blocks of cheese with a card that has your name on it."

"Thanks."

"Did I say there were five dozen piroshkis? Sixty little plastic-coated mini-meals? Nourishment like Davy Crockett and Daniel Boone were never lucky enough to—"

"I don't understand Danny, though," I said. "I mean, he has a key to this place, and I asked him to just leave the piroshkis here. Is there some reason why he would make you come out in the rain on a night like this to deliver these?"

"Well," Betsy said, "it wasn't exactly Danny's idea."

Then she turned around slowly and reached for me and we held each other, in that soft way people do when it's the first time they hold each other.

I could feel her breathe, feel the curves of her, feel her breath warm against my neck. Then she pulled back a few inches and we just held there, our lips a few inches apart, and looked into each other's eyes. The green in her eyes had never been as deep and drowning as it was then. I could smell her skin, washed by the rain outside.

When we kissed, it was a combination of all the world and one sweet girl, and excitement and a comfort I'd never known before. Her lips parted slowly under mine and we both just held on to what we had there until I didn't think I could stand any more of it.

She pulled away, put her lips near my right ear and whispered, "Did you like that?"

"Oh God, yes," I managed to say between breaths.

"Would you like," she whispered, "to do it some more?"

"Oh yes," I said. "Yes."

She pulled back, looked me square in the eyes, and I saw for the first time the tears rolling down her cheeks.

"Then you better come back, dammit," she said, and walked out the door and down the stairs.

For a long time I stood there, trying to understand what had happened, and knowing now how much some things could cost. I didn't give a damn at that moment about someone named Lee Hendrix.

Then I heard the throaty call of a raven outside on the roof of the movie theater and I began to hear again the rain on the roof and the slow but constant song of responsibility.

CHAPTER 12

The Super Cub rose through the wet morning like a droning bird, lifting over the forests and climbing toward the Talkeetna Mountains. One minute it was clear, then rain would sweep the Plexiglas windshield, bringing with it some running streaks and a wash of grief as well.

After a few minutes, the tiny rinsed-clean trucks and houses below gave up their assault on the vast Bush and left the rest of the forest below, for hundreds of miles, to the moose and bear and raven.

As I did my best to hold onto the struts in the Super Cub's back seat (as a passenger, I've always considered that a vital job), I recalled how Buck and I had gone over the maps that morning at Peggy's Airport Cafe.

"It's been six days," Buck had said. "He could be completely out of the Talkeetnas by now and into the Nelchina Basin."

"Except for one thing," I had said. "He won't be taking any chances. He won't travel in daylight unless he's in deep timber, and he won't hit anything that looks like that in the direction he's going until he gets over to the Prince William Sound drainage."

"You think he's heading that way?" Buck asked, pushing some cups aside and opening the map wider.

"I think there's a good chance," I'd said. "He likes boats. Boats live in the water. I think there's a better than even chance, anyway. But this guy's some kind of nuts, right? So he could be walking back to Anchorage to get a beer. It would be a crazy thing to do, but there you are."

"You've been asking around about him. What do you think he'll do?"

I had to consider that for a minute.

"I'm not sure I think anything at all. Maybe I don't feel anything about it yet, either. But now if a hunch is worth anything to you, I have a hunch he will head deliberately for someplace or other. He will have a goal and he's going there right now. I felt it that day I checked out his tracks up there at the lake. There was a deliberation in them, a goal. Some idea of direction. But I don't know how smart this guy is, or how seriously his mental problems interfere with what brains he's been given."

"Sounds dangerous," Buck said.

"You bet," I said. "I don't mind telling you this guy Hendrix has me worried. I'd like to be able to count on him to react in a certain way to a certain stimulus. About the only thing I can deduce about Lee Hendrix is that after he kills me, he'll feed my dogs well."

"That should be quite a comfort to you."

"Right."

"Where do you think he is now?" Buck asked.

"Well, you figure a maximum of about four hours' travel each night, and a maximum speed in those mountains of maybe two miles an hour, and maybe a lot less, that could put him as much as forty miles from Murder Lake. If he kept going in the same direction he started from at the lake, he would be somewhere in here . . . over the crest of the Talkeetnas and heading down one of those canyons toward the Nelchina."

I looked at Buck and shrugged. "Or not. . . . "

"Yeah. Well, where do you want to go?"

"To get out of the mountains, he'd have to pick one of those canyons. I need to learn which one he used. Can you set me down somewhere near the crest of the Talkeetnas? I'd like to start checking up there."

"I know a couple of places up in the tundra there, close to sheep country."

"On the east slope?"

He nodded.

"Sounds fine to me."

"You don't want to try and get ahead of this guy and cut him off?"

"You mean, like the state troopers are doing? Cut him off where? Patrol hundreds of miles of highway? If you had thirty troopers—good Bush troopers—they could each wait at the mouth of those canyons to try and catch him before he gets out onto the Nelchina. Maybe they would. But he's moving at night, and despite being nuts, there's no sign he can't get along very nicely in the woods."

"I don't like it, Jeep," Buck said. "It just seems there's got to be an easier way of doing this."

"I'm all ears."

"Yeah. I know. That's the trouble. I can't think of anything else to do, either."

"My only chance, I think, is to come up behind him and find out where he's going. If he makes a mistake, maybe I can arrest him. If not, then I can tell the cops which way he's heading and they can get him."

Buck Davis looked at me, raising an eyebrow.

"You wouldn't want to sorta take a shot at this guy? He's armed and crazy. You know it would be self-defense."

"I'm sure that's what the courts would say, Buck, but I don't want to have to do that. Seriously. That would wreck my life, too, and he's done enough damage already. I haven't forgotten Bill, believe me, but I can't let those feelings get hold of me or I won't be able to do this."

"Fair enough. You see this ridge right here?" He pointed to a fairly level spot on the topo map. "If the rain doesn't close us out, I can put us down there easy enough. That about right?"

"Let's go."

So now below us was the giant sponge that is Alaska . . . the muskeg swamps that can swallow cars and even houses . . . the thick green undergrowth in the heavy birch-spruce forest, or taiga . . . the golf course-like undulating tundra that reaches up to the rocks where the sheep live. All of it designed to soak up the ample rains Alaska is given. It takes the water and grows plants, moose and bugs down there below us.

And now the forest seems to be climbing toward us and the trees become the sparse alder clumps in the transition zone, and then it's open tundra that is the sponge, drawing into itself not only the juices of the life around it but sometimes the secrets of the Bush itself.

Somewhere out there was one man, probably far down to the right of us now as we neared the high country. One man, and I had to find him before I could be free to paint my face black as the old ones had done and sing the ancient farewell songs for my friend.

I became lost in thought until the flaps descended, and then the engine slowed way down the way it does, almost coughing in its hesitation, barely keeping us in the air.

I tried to look down at the ridge ahead and could see nothing that looked anything at all like an airstrip. But Buck was going in, and he knows his business.

Then the plane touched and bounced and settled into that funny little waddle it makes when it's on rough ground, and then we were stopped and out of the plane.

"How'd you like that landing, Jeep?"

"Smooth as a baby's buttocks," I said.

"No extra charge," said the bush pilot who had been my lifelong friend. We got the Super Cub turned around, pointing into the wind.

"Got your pack?"

"Yep."

"Lots of matches?"

"I could burn down this whole mountain range."

"Food?"

"Lord, yes."

"Enough ammunition?"

"I could overthrow a medium-sized Central American country."

"Well then, you take care of yourself, Jeep."

"I'm just going for a hike, Buck, and that is truly what I plan to do. If I learn something on the hike, all the better."

"Got your red crusher?"

"In my pack."

"On the off chance you should hear the sound of an airplane engine on this little jaunt of yours, you take that camo cap off and put that red hat on, OK?"

I knew it wouldn't do any good to argue, so I just agreed. Then we shook hands, and the Cub roared along the tundra, headed downhill. One little rock outcropping looked as though it would give him some trouble, but he just tipped the Super Cub up on its left tire and avoided it. When Buck reached the dropoff, he sucked back on the flaps, making the light plane leap into the air. It then started falling steadily toward a creek a half mile away. Before the plane had fallen half the distance, it had picked up enough airspeed to pull out and fly away. He wagged at me as he crossed the ridge toward Kahiltna and home. In less than a minute, the only sound on that barren stretch of ridge was the wind blowing up from Cook Inlet, a hundred miles away.

I carried the rifle and pack to a rock outcropping and sat down to eat a piroshki. I made a last check through my pack for the things I needed, although at this point, if I'd forgotten anything, I don't know what I'd have done. It's just a habit. When you're in the Bush, you check and check again.

Then I opened the bolt of the rifle, stuck my little finger into the empty chamber to check it, and put four cartridges into the magazine. I pushed them down and gently closed the bolt on an empty chamber. At the same time, I squeezed the trigger, so there would not be any tension on the firing pin spring. Enough of that, over time, and the spring can weaken. My Scotch tape was still firmly across the muzzle.

The breeze was ghostly as I sat there and looked down on the world.

This is the point where a man is supposed to feel the onset of loneliness. All I felt was relief. To me, there is no lonelier place on earth if you're by yourself than a city. Perhaps it's simply because there are so many other things going on, and my own business of perhaps getting a meal or a cup of coffee or loading the truck with groceries or dog food just doesn't seem very important.

But I permitted myself the memory of last night as I sat there on that rock in the quiet little Alaska breeze. I could, once again, feel how soft her hands were on the back of my neck, the imprint of each finger burning the memory of itself into my skin like friendly fire. I could, if I tried, still smell the skin on her cheeks, taste the texture of her mouth.

But there was more than the physical feelings to this. Having her so close was a sensual delight, but it was the look in her eyes, too. It was seeing those deep green eyes through the depth of her tears that moved me, as well. It was the kind of memory to fog a man's brain and make him lose concentration. So I told myself to ration these memories. They were too dangerous to dwell upon, but too sweet to forget. I was going to treat myself to a remembrance of that kiss when I could, though. I would do it just before going to sleep each night, when it was just me and the sleeping bag and the funny little half-darkness that comes in early August. It would, I thought, be my treat, a little game to play. No one else would ever need to know what it meant to me. I'd keep it tucked away and only bring it out and dust it off and polish it when my work was finished and I could afford the luxury of the remembrance.

And I sat there, on a rock, thinking and looking and listening for the country to say something. Listening for the wind to tell me things. I couldn't hear anything, yet. There was too much Anchorage in me, of course. There was even too much Kahiltna in me.

Civilization, as we know it, covers a man like the layers of clothing on a hard winter day. He listens to the radio and a layer goes around him to protect his inner core from any harm from the radio. Then there's the sound of aircraft, and a man needs another layer to protect him from that. When people argue, this needs a thick layer. So it goes, it seems.

Well, it seems like that to me as I sit here up on this rock, looking out across a magnificent chunk of Alaska. It seems like that to me, with my own inner core protected from assault by all those layers of sensory long johns. The only trouble is, those layers also muffle the real sounds of life, too. They keep me from hearing what the wind says. They keep me from feeling what the mountains feel. Sometimes, I know, you can't get rid of enough layers to do any good when you need it.

It is that way with most of my hunters. They come up from their cities muffled in layers, and we really don't have time to get rid of them. We get a ten-day or fifteen-day hunt, and usually that's not enough. With some people, they can never get rid of the layers because their thinking keeps the layers in place. They think of solid objects. They think only of what they can touch and see.

Some of them live very happy lives, I'm told, but it must be a little like touching someone you love while wearing boxing gloves.

What I had to do on this day was use the things I could see and touch to get me started the right way after Lee Hendrix. It must be the physical way, too, because the layers Anchorage put on me have silenced the wind and muzzled the mountains. Nothing is talking to me now but my mind, and all it will say is danger. Danger. Danger the way it felt when I first saw a grizzly sow and two half-grown cubs in the tundra along the Swift Fork of the Kuskokwim and realized there was nothing between me and death but wind and tundra. Danger. And I had nothing to use against it but the practical Norwegian side of me.

Despite the rifle, I felt unarmed.

CHAPTER 13

Below me, canyons were born in tiny creases that deepened and grew down into the heart of the earth. They crept, one by one, across this eastern face of the Talkeetna Mountains.

When Lee Hendrix crossed this ridge, it would have been in the dim light that passes for night this time of year. He would have known which direction he wanted to go the minute he crossed the divide. It wasn't that easy for me.

Toward the north was Fairbanks and the multitude of small cabins that circle any city. To the south was Anchorage, a really big city and one in which the net might be loose enough to let one man slip through. To the northeast was the Alaska Highway, with its way out of Alaska and into Canada, and to the southeast was the Copper River Basin, roaming around between the sheep-heaven spikes of the Wrangells on the north and the Chugach Mountains to the south. He knew exactly where he was going by the time he got this far from Murder Lake, probably three days ago.

I had no clue at all.

Starting at the northernmost crease I thought he might have used, I walked down into it slowly. The tundra swells, rolling like tanned breasts on the land, hold no tracks. They spring back from anything lighter or blunter than the razor-sharp hooves of a one-ton moose. The only chances for tracks would be down in the little creases that would become creek beds farther down. Up here at the top they were tundra gravel, and chances weren't good anything lasting would be found in them. Lower, though, where the wind has had a chance to sift some sand down from the high perches, that's where tracks . . . or at least the hint of tracks . . . might be found. Of course, Hendrix might have gone down the tops of the swells, but I didn't think so. Even though the walking would be a little easier on the crests, I didn't think he'd take the chance of being seen that way. Down in the little secret wrinkles of the tundra, he'd have a better chance of concealment.

So I went down the first crease until I got to an area where some sand had blown across the gravel and checked it carefully for several hundred yards, looking for the little disturbances that might have been made by boots. There were none.

I climbed slowly out of this crease and, sidehilling, headed across the next swell until I came to the next crease to the south. This required careful checking, because if I overlooked tracks here, it could throw me off far enough that I would never be able to make up the time on Hendrix. As it was, I wasn't sure how bad the footing would be down in the far-off valley I could see in canyon breaks and, when I topped the tundra rises, the Nelchina Basin.

If there was good footing down there, or if Hendrix had found a solid trail through that mass of shallow lakes and muskeg swamps, he could have made some time. If that had happened, my looking for signs of him up on this windy ridge was academic. I'd have a nice long walk and maybe see some wildlife, but that was all.

On the other hand, I couldn't dawdle on this part of the hunt for the same reason. Hunt? Was this really a hunt? It felt like it, up there where only the sheep graze and the eagles fly.

My pack was on my back, my Jones cap pulled down tight against the wind. My green army jacket was anchored in place by the rifle hanging muzzle down and trigger guard forward from my left shoulder. If I need my rifle in a hurry, that is the fastest way to carry it. I'm right-handed, so my left hand is hanging next to the rifle's fore-end. If I want it, I grab the fore-end with my left hand, swinging the rifle up to my right shoulder. At the same time, my left elbow has remained within the sling to give the rifle a three-cornered brace for a steady shot.

It's a lot easier to just show someone.

This particular rifle and leather sling had become so used to hanging in that position on my shoulder that the part of the stock that rubbed against my jacket was polished like a gem. Only being against my body kept it from being detrimental to hunting, sending flashes to game the way the Apaches did in Jeff Chandler movies. I'd often thought of sanding it there, just enough to take the shine off, but I'd become fond of it, and it really wasn't much of a problem. The sling had set in a way to match every bulge and bump of my left shoulder, too. All in all, the rifle had become like a favorite pair of slippers, but these slippers could save my life and earn my living.

There's magic up here in the tundra. Magic in the way the weather plays on it. Magic in its animals . . . in the rolling of the bear, the ballet of the caribou, the scuttling up of the Dall sheep. The tundra has secrets, and that's the way it should be. There are holes in the tundra. Some are small, others the size of army foxholes. A guide's knowledge of these can be invaluable. During the times of the caribou migration, the holes can be valued ambush spots, and knowing where a deep one was has saved the life of more than one guide when a bear was around. Geologists can probably explain why those holes are there, but it's just tundra magic.

That's the way it should be.

On a day like this, when the afternoon brings the clouds down low, it is almost scary to be walking in rubber boots in this golden-textured landscape wrapped in fog. There's the rifle, but the tundra has secrets that can't be handled with a rifle. At times like these, a man alone in the high berry pastures of Alaska wants only to drop down into the more comfortable taiga zone, get in among the birch and spruce and nest up for a while.

I found what I was looking for in the fourth crease. They were down about a half mile from the crest, around the bend of the crease, which was beginning to become a canyon. A tiny rivulet of water trickled down through it, and in the mud next to a wide spot were Hendrix's tracks. The sight of them made me stand up quickly and look around. Being on the tundra is a little like what being on the moon must be like, and to see any signs of another human is startling. To see the familiar tracks of this killer, burned in my mind since Murder Lake, was a shock.

The tracks were old. Several days, anyway. The rain had worn down the crisp sides of the tracks and erased the manufacturer's name and logo raised on the boots' instep. That was fine with me. I didn't want to run across this guy until after I'd been in the Bush a bit longer. I was suffering from that overdose of Anchorage, and I needed some time.

The tracks started down the defile, went up the left bank for a while into tundra, and then he evidently decided to tough it out down along the tiny creek bed, because he came back to the creek later.

Had he heard an airplane engine? Or maybe, just maybe, had the mind of Lee Hendrix come back to logical long enough to bring him down out of the open? As long as he was walking down this canyon toward the forest far below, I didn't care. Just so I knew where he was going.

Finding these tracks had taken most of the day. I sat and ate another piroshki and celebrated. This was more like it. Now there was something solid to go on. Now there was at least a direction, southeast, to go by.

It was thrilling for me, and made me ask myself those questions again. Was I really out here to help the police with their work? Was I out here to try to settle a score for my buddy? Or, as I preferred to think, was I really just out here as a volunteer Alaskan chasing a rabid fox for the public good? No more, no less?

It shouldn't have made any difference, I knew, but in a way it did. For whatever motive, self-gratifying or altruistic, I was hunting a man. I needed to locate him and follow him and see if I could help the troopers catch him before he could kill again. In a hunt, I knew, you must be certain that what you're doing is the right thing. This was not the time to question why I doing it or if it should be my job. To be successful, I had to be confident and with full faculties, and be able to think more like an animal than an animal does. For better or worse, I had made this hunt my job. I was going after Lee Hendrix with all the skills I could muster, and blast the motives. There couldn't be a speck of self-doubt in a hunt like this. Hendrix was a dangerous man. Hendrix was dangerous game, without a doubt.

Three more miles down the canyon and I broke out to where I could see ahead. Below me, and still in that southeasterly direction, was a small lake. I left the canyon and dropped straight down the hogback ridge until I came cautiously to the edge of the lake. I got some water, then backed up about a hundred yards from it to some alder hells. I crawled into the middle of the toughest thicket I could find and made a fireless camp.

It was just the funny dusk of summer, but Hendrix would be out and walking now, and it was my turn to lie low. I curled up in the bag, spent a few smiling thoughts on Betsy, and slept.

CHAPTER 14

I had spent too much time in Anchorage.

I felt the trembling when it was almost too late. Like a nightmarish premonition, that trembling, the tiny shaking ran from my right hip to my brain, and to my adrenal glands. I opened my eyes slowly and they focussed on the leaves of a blueberry bush inches away. The breeze fluttered them, but there was something else, too. There was this tiny shudder they gave every few seconds, and it was this that made me instantly awake.

I didn't move and let my brain come fully awake and take in the situation. I had spent too much time in Anchorage, I kept telling myself. How else could the bear have gotten that close without my knowing it?

It was full light, of course, some six hours after I went to sleep, and the first proof I had it was a bear was from the whuffing sound I heard coming from the bear trail off to my left.

There he was, or maybe she; maybe it was a sow. There's really no way to tell until after they're dead, unless one has cubs along. But this bear was snuffling around where my trail had crossed his yesterday. I lay there without moving. The soft breeze on my left cheek told me the wind was blowing from the bear to me, so all I really had to worry about was making noise or moving. A bear is quick to see movement, but his eyes aren't the best otherwise. Their noses and ears work just fine, however, and this one was about twenty-five yards away and making me nervous. He was getting a bit worked up at the smell of my tracks the night before. This is another good reason for wearing rubber hip boots. Leather boots often leave a trail that smells good enough to be investigated, especially late in the fall when a bear's getting desperate for food. But this bear was evidently just trying to figure out what this rubber-boot scent was. All he really knew was that it didn't belong on his own familiar trail through these alders.

My rifle was handy, but I was in a sleeping bag and hardly in a position to do much about it if he found me and decided I'd do as breakfast.

What a lot of people don't realize is that bears, like this six-hundred-pound grizzly, despite their clumsy-looking rolling gait, can outrun the fastest racehorse that ever lived. They've been clocked at forty-five miles an hour. That twenty-five yards through the alders wouldn't have taken the bear very long to cover.

I tried to think myself invisible, the way my grandfather had taught me, but I had too much Anchorage in me. For this situation, I was going to have to rely on the bear's own ineptitude to get me through. I lay there and watched, but I watched with the corner of my eye. It may be superstition, but some old-time hunters believe that if you stare at an animal, it will feel the stare and turn to face you. Maybe. Maybe not. This was one hunter who wasn't going to tempt fate.

From time to time I could smell the rankness of the bear: a mixture of raw earth, dead fish, and a musty smell all its own that always reminds me of raw deadly power.

In a few minutes, the bear grew tired of trying to figure out the scent and ambled away down toward the lake. It wasn't until then I felt something banging on me and realized my heart was trying to beat my collarbone to death. Bears are a very frightening business. They are not too bright, but they are big and fast and ugly-tempered when pushed.

Needless to say, I was wide awake by this time. In a few minutes I was packed up and eating a piroshki on a rise behind the alder thicket. I watched that bear through the monocular until he disappeared around the left flank of Big Bones Ridge, ahead of me. Then I started off around the right side.

So had Hendrix, I discovered. He had stopped for water at one of the feeder creeks into the lake, and his tracks led off toward a saddle about five miles away.

It was strange to think, too, that Hendrix might be many times more dangerous than that grizzly. After all, a grizzly is a fairly predictable animal. When he attacks, it is usually for a reason. He either feels threatened, is wounded, or just feels like whatthehell and knocks someone down the mountain. Grizzlies are big and they live up in the tundra, where they can be seen for miles. Running into them isn't unusual.

Hendrix was a much more unusual animal. As I followed his tracks through the mud, then the sand, then just through instinct when he hit the tundra, I couldn't help remembering the first hunter I'd guided for grizzly.

This was when I was an assistant guide, of course, and was working for Bob Gordon not far from where my Alaska Range camp is today. He had a lot of patience with me, and I can recall him telling especially appropriate stories at the dinner table in main camp. They had a two-fold purpose: they entertained the hunters, which they did very well, and they were also to teach young assistant guides how to guide hunters. I've never forgotten any of those lessons.

That first season had gone along well. My hunters had taken a couple of moose, one nice Dall ram and later two black bears. It was at this point the boss gave me the worst hunter in camp to guide for a grizzly.

This hunter knew everything. He had read every book on hunting everything in Alaska and really didn't need a guide, but the stupid laws of Alaska required nonresident hunters to have a guide for sheep and grizzly. He knew all about ammunition, too. He had handloads for his magnum rifle that would knock a Sherman tank on its butt at half a mile, he told me. This rifle was one of those fancy jobs that cost about what a new car does and it had ebony inlays in the stock. Guides call them "whorehouse guns" but not when the hunter is around.

This same rifle also had a mirror polish on every piece of its action, barrel and stock. He could have stood on a mesa and signaled John Wayne and the cavalry . . . on a cloudy day. In fact, that's where we first locked horns, because after I told him to take the shell out of the chamber until he was ready to kill something, I crumbled up some soot from the fire and turned all that pretty gloss into a very homely (but much less noticeable) rifle.

I'd enjoy thinking it was the hunter's fault for getting me so angry that day. The trouble is, that responsibility always comes home to roost. I was the guide. It is always the guide's responsibility.

The truth is, neither of us was killed that day, so it turned out all right. But it almost wasn't like that.

I'd seen a beautiful chocolate-colored grizzly in the area for a week or so.

He had been going from one moose-gut pile to the next and feeding, and I thought that might be a good place to look for him. We started across some muskeg flats and heard the deep rut grunt of a bull moose.

This hunter had already taken a moose, so I grunted that deep, coughing grunt that is so much fun to imitate. It is one of the few animal calls I can duplicate with just my human voice, without all the woofers and tweeters they sell to lure in everything from coyotes to curmudgeons. Just reach deep from the diaphragm or islets of Langerhans and bring up this one great HUMPF!

Bull moose, during the rut, just mosey around occasionally going HUMPF! in a deep, guttural voice and hope some cow falls in love with them. It works for moose, and they need all the help they can get.

In a few grunts, we had that big bull, with a full sixty-five-inch width across his antlers, to within about fifteen yards. A moose is not only the dumbest member of the deer family, with barely enough brains to feed himself, he has lousy vision. To him, someone standing still is probably a tree. We took his picture.

We spoke to him then, and he trotted off. We cut across another big flat of blueberry brush, and all along we could hear that big bull grunting his loneliness through the middle of a stand of blueblack spruce trees off to our left.

About midmorning, we were having a candy bar in the trees when we heard him approaching us again, so we grunted him in and took his picture again. He didn't seem to mind being duped twice.

Then we cut across yet another flat of blueberries and were coming close to a moose-gut pile that was only a week old. Bears like things old and rank and ripe before they eat them. A week old, I later learned, is just marginal. Two weeks is getting about prime. When a grizzly makes a kill, or claims a gut pile, he tears down brush and small trees for twenty to thirty yards around and covers his prize to keep the birds from eating it. Then, if he is feeding, he will camp right there, feeding sometimes for days, until his food is gone. Grizzlies are very territorial.

This particular gut pile was in the center of a strip of spruce maybe fifty yards wide and dense as winter fur. As we started into the trees, perhaps thirty yards from the gut pile, I glanced up and saw two camp robbers—that's Alaskans' pet name for gray jays—sitting in the tops of the spruce trees. Then we heard that same bull moose coming toward us from our left. I grinned at the hunter and he grinned back.

Then the bear killed the moose.

That bull had reached the gut pile just ahead of us, and the bear killed him. This was a huge bull, and the surprising thing was that it took no time at all. There wasn't much of a struggle; it was over in maybe ten seconds. We could see nothing of the action, but I could picture the bear's swift grab, taking that huge bull around the neck just behind the antlers, and then the swift crunch as his teeth found the spine right behind the ears . . . Then all there was in the air was the flapping of the ravens, and the camp robbers, too, had taken to the air, leery of the violence even from their safe perches in the tops of those trees.

Then the bear whooshed, but by that time, that hunter and I had set the world's record for backing up a hundred yards with loaded rifles.

So now, with a gut pile and a fresh dead moose, that bear would stay around the spruce stand for several weeks. We went back day after day, waiting to see if he'd come out, but he just stayed in there. If the wind changed and blew our scent to him, he just whooshed but didn't come out of that morass of thick timber. In there, he was as safe as in the zoo. You couldn't get the 82nd Airborne to go into that copse of trees after that bear.

When grizzlies get angry or alarmed, they whoosh. Some say it is the evil coming from them. Whatever it is called, it is one of those sounds you never forget, like the sudden crack of breaking river ice or the slide on a pump shotgun. Grizzlies growl mostly in the movies. In real life, they moan and whuff and whoosh or they clack their teeth, except when they are talking to themselves or to their cubs. But before they charge, or just after they make a kill, or when something frightens them, they whoosh. A whoosh is a very loud blowing out of air from the bear's lungs. It is done suddenly, and the bear is always serious when he does it. I've never known a human who could come close to imitating a bear whoosh.

That autumn day, in that copse of spruce where the Kuskokwim Valley meets the Alaska Range, I almost got one obnoxious hunter and one young foolish guide killed real dead. If that bear had come after us instead of the moose, we would have had no more than a ten-foot notice, and that isn't enough. As we sat, a hundred yards away from the bear's thicket a few moments later, we both found it hard to control muscle spasms in our legs. It was difficult to talk because of the raw fear. We had come that close to death, and we knew it.

Alaska isn't a very forgiving place. There are many ways to die if you are careful. If you are foolish, there are many more ways to die and generally you'll find many more opportunities.

But if the Good Father is kind, and if the raven flies happily across your trail in the morning, you might get a second chance. You might learn from it.

I learned that day, years ago, about birds. If the birds are in the tops of the trees rather than scavenging the kill, it might be because there is something much larger than a bird already on the kill.

I watch for birds now. Sometimes you can find game that way. It's a little like how the astronomers found the planet Pluto. For a long time they couldn't see it, but they knew it had to be out there somewhere by its effect on the other planets. They knew where it was before they saw it.

In the forest, nothing lives alone. When we move, it's like a canoe going across a lake. An area around us is affected by our passage. Maybe the animals are quiet, or they run away, or they stop feeding. Maybe they stand on their hind legs and try to see, like the bear and the wolverine. As we continue through the forest, life returns to a sameness gently behind us, just as the lake clears away again after the canoe has gone.

The predators cause the biggest fuss, stir the biggest wake. The wolf, the wolverine, the bear and man. We are all predators. We all have eyes in front to see our prey. The animals we eat all have eyes on the sides of their heads for peripheral vision. It is the way the Good Father made us, and not a bad way to be.

So we make a mistake but no one is killed, and we go on from there: the hunter to go back home and tell everyone how bravely he stood there while the cowardly guide backed up, no doubt; and the guide who was just thankful to be able to learn.

I went back to that kill a month later. There was nothing left but bones, of course, but I found that moose's antlers about thirty yards away in some brush. I took my pack saw out and sawed off a small tip of one antler tine and put it in my pouch, which remains in my fanny pack most of the time.

Medicine? Who knows? This is where the dividing line becomes awfully hazy between Athabascan and white man. I like to think of it as just taking along a piece of that bull as a show of gratitude. He saved my life. If putting a tiny piece of antler in a little buckskin pouch honors his memory a little, so be it.

That is how guides learn, by surviving and remembering. And by listening to others who have survived, and remembering.

It was midday before I topped the last ridge between me and the hundred-and-fifty-mile width of the Nelchina Basin. It lay below as a massive maze of lakes and rivers and swamp systems and forest. Marking the basin's eastern border, the sheep fortress they call the Wrangell Mountains loomed up from the valley floor, breathtakingly dominating everything below. To the south, the Chugach Range separates the Nelchina from the ocean . . . particularly that gem of a piece of placid ocean known as Prince William Sound, with its hundreds of mostly uninhabited islands and its fiords.

I knew if Hendrix went almost to the base of the Chugach Range, he'd come across the Richardson Highway, which affects this huge basin about as much as stretching a string across it affects a football field. Far across to the east, where the little town of Glennallen lies, the trans-Alaska oil pipeline also comes along, pumping crude toward the mammoth tankers waiting in Valdez.

The basin is an awesome sight in a land full of such things.

Down there, somewhere, was a man I wanted to meet . . . on my own terms, of course. He would be sleeping right now, or lying low and eating and waiting for dusk. He could have been in any one of a thousand tiny forests out there that separate a thousand lakes and five times that many ponds, and rivers that show up here and there.

The Nelchina is one of those places where a man can get lost easily if the visibility is poor, but he won't really mind too much because it's so beautiful. He won't mind until he dies, that is—starved, frozen, eaten or drained of blood by the untold billions of mosquitoes that live there.

I decided it was time to gamble.

CHAPTER 15

No one ever won anything in Alaska by going fast unless it was a dogsled race. I was at a disadvantage here: Hendrix knew where he was going, and I didn't. So I pulled out some jerky and sat and looked down at the vast land below me and did some thinking.

Below me and almost due east were the twin lake systems of Lake Susitna and Lake Louise, which draw upon all the thousands of swamps and ponds of this high plateau and organize them into the headwaters of the Susitna River and eventually see the waters empty into Cook Inlet, about six hundred miles downstream and only about a rifle shot away from downtown Anchorage.

A sharp breeze came up and some clouds began boiling around the summits of Mount Drum and Mount Sanford in the Wrangells. Rain coming. I pulled on a jacket and drank a little water and looked down there and tried to figure out the mind of a killer.

Between the tracks at Murder Lake and the tracks I'd found here in the Talkeetnas, Hendrix had been traveling southeast. And he was traveling a pretty straightforward course, with no serious attempt to hide himself. He was smart enough not to walk out on open ridges in daylight, of course, but he had expected no pursuit on the ground and had made no attempt to hide his tracks.

If he continued this way, he would cross the road that links Lake Louise to the Glenn Highway. Or maybe he already had. That road was maybe three days away through these swamp systems, straight the way he was going. If he crossed it, he would more than likely leave tracks.

In that morass of muskeg swamp and taiga forest between here and there, it would be nearly impossible to track this man. The ground wouldn't hold tracks. There may be a tracker somewhere who can look at a broken twig and tell you, with no other evidence, that a man broke it, but this hunting guide can't.

There is something else about that muskeg, too. A man on foot, even with hip boots, just isn't going to travel very fast through it. A strong man who can give you a good three miles an hour on tundra will be lucky to struggle five miles in a day through this syrupy mass that sucks at your legs until you want to drop with exhaustion but leaves you no dry place to sit.

If Hendrix had the big advantage over me in knowing exactly where he was going, I had a couple of smaller things going my way, too: I figured, rightly or wrongly, that I would be able to think more rationally than a crazed killer, and he couldn't know anyone was following him. If this would make him take a few more chances than he otherwise might, that was all in my favor.

The weather had been pretty good, and he couldn't help noticing no search planes were after him. Did he realize this was because he had shot one, or did he think they really didn't know in which direction to look? How would Hendrix's mind run?

It was while I was finishing a meal that another thought came to me. Hendrix would have to slog it out through the muskeg, but I didn't have to. If I headed straight south for the rest of this day and the night, I had a good chance of hitting the Glenn Highway before noon the next day. I could hitch a ride to the Lake Louise road and check for his tracks there. By heading straight south, I could stay in these comparatively dry uplands that are the eastern foothills of the Talkeetnas. I could make up a lot of time on Hendrix that way.

If it worked, if I had Hendrix figured right, if Hendrix was headed in a straight line southeast toward . . . toward what? Glennallen? Unlikely. That road junction would have state troopers all over it. Copper Center? Tonsina? Chitina? There wouldn't be anything there for him. Valdez? Cordova? Two little fishing ports like that? Well, he liked fishing boats, didn't he?

There was always the odd chance that Hendrix would try to sneak into Canada, but I didn't think he would. For one thing, the way he was going led only to a massive wall of mountains at the head of the Chitina River. Only sheep and eagles lived up there, and I recalled Red Tanner saying

Hendrix hadn't liked sheep duty on the high cliffs.

So, tidewater? I wasn't ready to guess that far. At that moment, I was willing to gamble that he'd cross the fifteen-mile-long road that connects the summer cabins at Lake Louise with the main highway. If I were wrong there, I'd have to refigure, but I really had a lot riding on this.

Hendrix would have to stay in the forest. He couldn't walk out on open ridges as I could. He sure couldn't go to the Glenn Highway and hitch a ride. Alaska is the world's largest small town and by this time even tourists would know about the maniac out there carrying a rifle large enough to knock down a grocery store. He'd have to stay in the woods and walk at night, but I wouldn't.

I finished my lunch, ambled off down the tundra ridge and when I found a comfortable elevation for walking, began sidehilling south toward the backdrop of the Chugach Mountains.

I stopped for another snack about nine that night, rested for an hour and then started on south again, each hour putting me just that much closer to the highway.

The rain hit about three in the morning. It came from the east, along with a stiff wind, and it was only the wind that made the rain tolerable, because mosquito bites hurt worse when they happen in a cold rain.

I hated to admit it, but the rain gave me a good excuse to lie up for a while. Down below where I was, some alder thickets teased the higher tundra areas, and I ducked down into a nice think tangle and sat a while to think things out.

Then it occurred to me there was no way Hendrix could see a fire here or smell the smoke, because he was probably twenty miles away upwind by this time. So I treated myself to a cheery fire in the sodden, chilling rain. I took out my cooking can and fixed hot soup, then rinsed it and made coffee, and it tasted better than what I made at home.

But the rain continued to fall. This wasn't a quick summer thunderstorm. Those are over in twenty minutes. This was a steady soaker, the first of the autumn rains.

The combination of rain and wind so soaks and freezes a man that some don't survive. I had my jacket on, my cap pulled down with the ear flaps lowered and the plastic tube tent wrapped around the whole shooting match. For exercise I had been feeding the fire from the little bundle of sticks I kept to the right of me, tucked beneath the tube tent.

If there's anything colder than the rain in Alaska, I don't know what it is. That may be because, in winter, we know the weather will be cold and dress for it. When the first snow hits in October, we all bundle up in subzero clothes until our bodies adjust. By spring, we can go out and cut wood in a T-shirt in fifteen degrees above zero if the wind is still and the sun is shining.

But when your body has been telling itself it's summer, and you're in light clothes, and you're caught miles from home, the rain is almost painful. When a stray drop touches the back of your neck, it burns almost like a brand. You develop violent shivers until you get yourself settled. So I dress warmly, get a fire going, wrap up in something waterproof like this tube tent, and turn my back on and my mind away from the cold. I keep busy cooking, or keeping the little fire going. I was either confident or foolhardy at this point, so I allowed my mind to rest also—took it off the important things of the day and gave it to Chulyen. But first I got some fresh water, shaved some jerky into it and boiled up some more soup. I didn't realize how thirsty I'd become until I started drinking.

Then I leaned back against an alder and stared into the small fire. In the embers, in the glow that comes after any good fire, my eyes look for things. They look for patterns, they look for designs of life. They look for answers to why a man who has a comfortable tent camp, a more comfortable log home and even an office-cum-bedroom in downtown Anchorage is out here leaning against an alder and feeling every little bump and roughness of it in his back.

But there was something else, too. My belly was full of soup and coffee. I was in the rain, but I was warm. I had built a fire and was keeping it going in the rain. I didn't owe anything to anyone—in money, that is. And I was on the hunt.

This whole business of hunting can always spark very interesting conversations at cocktail parties. When someone introduces me to his friends as a hunting guide, there are usually two reactions: most men envy me and most women think I'm a monster.

For some reason, too, the people who don't hunt always have to bring the conversation around to hunting just so they can spout off. Most of them are pitifully ignorant of what hunting actually is, but seem to be adamant in their ignorance. It's as though they would be disloyal to some animal they loved as children if they didn't comment on the cruelty of the hunt.

There are generally two types of people who don't hunt: those who have a genuine interest in saving the planet, whatever that may mean to them, and those who think taking any life is cruel.

No argument can satisfy the latter. Everyone is entitled to an opinion on the sanctity of life. It just bothers me when I find one of these preaching to me while eating a steak and wearing a suede jacket.

If the first type of person who doesn't hunt, however, thinks hunting is harmful to the animal populations, then there is something we can calmly and rationally discuss. Most of them simply don't realize that hunting seasons exist only when there is a surplus of game and the herds must be thinned to keep them healthy. If there were just the right number of animals, the biologists would close the season and make the hunters wait for another surplus.

Many of these people, when told the facts, will say, "Well, I guess that makes sense. As long as they take the meat and aren't just trophy hunters."

At this point, I usually nod and we shake hands. But the truth is, most trophy hunters want to take only a few pounds of meat back to Germany or Japan or Texas. It's just too expensive to fly a moose that far.

Which is all right with me. You see, trophy hunters are the greatest boon to game management Alaska ever had. A trophy hunter comes up here, drops $15,000 or more into the local economy and kills a big, nasty, tough old bull moose or caribou or Dall ram, one that is probably well past his breeding prime and is just eating forage the younger animals can use. Then he leaves the lion's share of the meat behind to be distributed free to Alaskans like my pal old Charlie, who need it and sure can use it. And the hunter heads for home with a trophy and several boxes of slides to remember his special hunt up north.

All in all, a pretty good deal for everybody.

Not all people who hunt—or all the people who guide them, either—cooperate with this nice little plan. One by one, though, they get thinned down by the game officers, and they should. Alaska's game is a treasure, exactly like its timber or salmon. It's just more fun to go after. If people don't want to play by the rules and work to take an animal, let them go somewhere else and be someone else's headache.

The rest of us stay in our little remote camps and we play it straight even if the chances of our being caught cheating would be slim. We play it straight because that's the right way to play it. And we choose our hunters to play the same way.

One German industrialist spent more than a week with me in an early moose camp one year. It was hot every day, in the 80s. When it's hot, you won't see moose. Where they go, I don't know for sure. They must lie down in dense thickets. But in my moose country, the land is so open and the trees so sparse, it seemed as if the ground had swallowed the moose.

My hunter was discouraged, of course, but he was a good egg about it. He and I spent our hot days sitting on a high tundra ridge, glassing for moose we knew we wouldn't see, and talking about ourselves.

He had wanted to know about me, about my two cultures. I explained to him the best I could what it was like to be a blend and not know which side to pick in any circumstance. In turn, he told me what it had been like being a Nazi soldier, at the age of fourteen, in the final days of the war. He had resisted going to war until French soldiers had dragged his father, the village doctor, out into the street and shot him, along with nine other people from the village.

I had never thought of anyone on our side doing something like that, but I guess those things happen in war.

We got well acquainted, because it was hot and the moose were hiding, and Germans would rather hunt moose than anything else.

They have a little moose in the Black Forest, it turns out, with antlers about as big as your two hands together with the fingers fanned out. When German hunters get their first look at a bull that has an antler spread of five or even six feet, they have a hard time shooting for all the drool. You can keep all the sheep and bear, as far as Germans are concerned. If they get a decent moose, they fly home happy.

Finally, one morning, the weather turned cool. Clouds hurried in and even spat some snow for a while. Out came the moose. Now from our tundra lookout we could see seven or eight really good bulls and one that was outstanding. Two hours later, he killed the bull and we got ready to take its picture.

But first my hunter picked a green sprig of needles from a spruce, then walked back and sat down by the bull's head. He put the sprig into the corner of the dead animal's mouth, then pulled the massive head partly onto his lap and just sat there stroking it as you would a pet dog, while the tears came down his cheeks. I had to go fuss around in the pack for a few minutes. We took the pictures later.

Hunters, with few exceptions, don't hunt for meat. They love the meat. They eat the meat. But that isn't why they hunt.

I figured it out, once. The average deer hunter in the Lower Forty-eight spends $600 a year on his sport. You get maybe a hundred pounds of meat, cut and wrapped, from a big buck. Statistically, since a deer hunter is successful once every four years, that makes venison cost something like $24 a pound. My hunters will end up paying about $1,000 a pound for the meat they take home with them.

Hunters don't hunt for meat.

Everyone who hunts has his own reasons, I guess. Some of them are probably pretty foolish . . . at least I think so. I have my reasons, too. They are equally difficult to explain to the people who don't hunt. It has a lot to do with the challenge of returning to the earth and seeing how well we still match up. We are animals, too. We are predators. We aren't fast or fierce or strong. Our eyesight and hearing and smell are pitiful. But we're the smart ones.

We've also been given instincts that go back in time to when man first walked upright. Have you seen hound puppies? Even when tiny, they use their noses to find everything: the food dish, their mother, the water dish. And husky puppies start pulling whoever holds onto them as soon as they get their legs under them. It's instinct, and we have it, too.

As nearly as we can figure out, man became man around three million years ago. He began using agriculture for the first time only around 8,000 years ago.

To put this another way, if man arrived on the earth a year ago, he's been something other than a hunter for less than eighteen hours. Is it any wonder, then, that with some men the rustling of autumn leaves on the birches sends their minds wandering to the forests?

Out here, leaning against an alder tree and nodding off to sleep in the rain, it's a comfort to know we still have some of these instincts . . . that if we let them, they can surface and protect us, and I wondered if they'd work when a skilled killer found himself confronted by an Alaskan combination-plate-special hunting guide who probably should be home in bed.

But it wasn't going to happen tonight, so I let the soft pattering of the drops and the popping of the fire help me to sleep.

CHAPTER 16

The rain stopped five hours later, and I was up and on the trail in minutes. I had needed that sleep badly, I discovered. The soup, too.

With the misty ground clouds rising around me, obscuring all but the tallest peaks of the Chugach fifty miles ahead, I kept walking steadily south, moving at a brisk pace that should put me on the Glenn Highway before another long day was gone. I stopped to rest twice, once building a fire for coffee and soup, and both times I ate jerky and piroshkis. Just about when it began to be dusk, I came out of some willow brush suddenly onto the Glenn Highway.

I stuck out my thumb to the first car and it screamed to a stop and set the red lights flashing on its roof.

"Lay that rifle down very carefully," said the nervous voice from behind the open car door.

"Yes, sir."

"Now walk away from it. Okay. Open your jacket. Take off your pack and lay it on the ground."

"Yes, sir."

"What's your name?"

"Jepsen George."

"Are you carrying any identification?"

"Yes, sir,"

"Walk up this way real slow. Okay, now lay it down on the pavement and back up."

I did. He came slowly out from behind the car door and felt around for the driver's license and brought it up to where he could watch both me and the license at the same time. He asked me a few questions about what was on the license.

"Are you carrying any more guns?"

"No, sir."

Watching that revolver made my hair feel electric. Please don't let this guy get nervous, I thought. I was determined to stand as still as a statue until this officer had me stripped naked and had learned my entire family history, if that's what it took.

It didn't.

"Where are you heading?"

"Looking for a lift up to the Lake Louise road," I told him.

"Well, that would be a damnfool thing to do right now."

"I know that."

"Where are you from?"

"Kahiltna."

"Long way from home."

"It was nice weather for a hike."

He grinned at me. "You can't be dumb enough not to know we're looking for a guy who's about four inches taller than you, thirty pounds heavier and a whole lot blonder."

"Yes. I know that."

"Look," he said, "I can't stop you from going to Lake Louise. It's a free country. But if there is something else you can do for a week or two, that would be a smart move."

"Thanks," I said, "but I need to take a little stroll up the road there."

"Something going on here?" he said.

"Jim Strickland will vouch for me."

"Captain Strickland? Wait here."

He went back to the car and used the radio. Then he stuck his head out the window. "What you say your name was?"

"Tell him it's Jeep."

He ducked back inside. Then he popped back out again.

"Captain wants to talk to you."

I took the mike and told Jim what I'd learned and what I'd guessed and that I thought Hendrix might head for either Valdez or Cordova. Jim asked to talk to the officer again, so I stood outside a few minutes just watching the mountains rising out of the mist and feeling chilled without my jacket on.

"Captain says you're okay," he called. "Says if you need a ride to give you one. I can take you clear to Glennallen if you like."

"No thanks, but I'd sure appreciate a lift to the Lake Louise road."

"Just unload that rifle and get in, then."

In twenty-five minutes on that highway, I covered ground that would have taken long, arduous days on foot. The trooper gave me a cup of coffee as we drove and tried to pry out of me what my business was out here that his captain would have him give me a ride in the middle of a manhunt. It was almost funny, but I put on my Indian face—the stoic one, you know, 'carved of granite, with eyes mysterious as to the thoughts which lie behind them'—and just mumbled something about picking blueberries. He didn't believe it and I didn't expect him to. That's what made it so much fun.

He pulled over at the road junction. "Look, if you like I can drive you to Lake Louise. Save you a long walk."

I reached over and shook his hand. "Thanks, officer. I really appreciate the offer, but this is where I'm going."

"There isn't anything here at all."

"Yeah." I smiled. "Nature at her unfettered best, don't you think?"

Then I gathered my gear and watched him make a U-turn and head back down the highway. I applauded myself for being such a nice guy because that was one cop who wouldn't be bored with the rest of this patrol. He'd be trying to figure just where I fitted in, who I was, and why I'd wanted to be let out of the car twenty miles from the nearest cabin.

Ahead of me lay fifteen miles of unpaved road, so I started out to see how much of it I could cover before it got too dark to see bootprints.

The first thing that crossed my path was a raven, flying from west to east.

"Good evening, Chulyen," I said, smiling and doffing my cap. "Are you going to show me a certain man out here?"

About three hundred yards later, when the muskeg became a thick belt of timber, I found Lee Hendrix's tracks. He had evidently come down from the mountains into the swamps, then dropped lower until he could walk in the safety of these black spruce trees. He was still heading southeast, and paralleling the Glenn Highway by less than a quarter mile.

I wished I had that state trooper back right then. It would have been handy to have him run on up the road and let the good folks at Glennallen know they had a killer headed their way just out of sight among the trees.

I sat down next to his bootprints and ate some more.

All right, Lee. Where are you going? What do you want from the rest of us? Are you going to kill anyone else? And, the big question we all want to know . . . why? Why kill those men? Even a maniac must have some reason, real or imagined, tucked away. Even a demented mind must have some rationale for butchery. Things this big and traumatic don't just happen. Something must have set him off.

Would he be set off again the next time he met people? That was something to think about, too: what if I was the next person he met? Oh well, a walk in the woods wouldn't be much fun without a little excitement.

I studied his tracks. He wasn't limping and had a normal, longish stride across the road and down off the gravel bank into the timber on the other side. He wasn't hurt and he wasn't slowing down. This meant he was rational enough to eat and drink properly and rest sufficiently. If Hendrix continued to stay a rational woodsman, I could have some real trouble with him. If the guy was going to be nuts anyway, why couldn't he do something nutty like try to flag down a cop car on the highway, or bog down in some blackwater muskeg that would gradually suck him down until the only things left behind would be some newspaper clippings and the grief he left as a legacy? Why not?

But here were the same tracks I had seen going purposefully ahead around the mire side of Murder Lake, about a hundred hiking miles ago, and nothing had changed. The heels and soles of his boots didn't even appear to be worn any more than they had been. I could still read the brand of the boots where the raised lettering punched it into the mud. He hadn't crossed this way before the rain, or there wouldn't have been much left of the tracks but vague impressions, and it couldn't have been since the rain, or the tracks would have been much clearer. My guess was that Hendrix had crossed this road during the rain and during the darkest time of the night. So far, so good. That meant I'd made up days on him. He couldn't be too much more than about twelve hours ahead of me now.

This was fairly slow going, but the ground in this belt of spruce timber was much better for walking than open muskeg. Figure maybe a mile an hour.

Off to my right a quarter of a mile was the highway. I could have walked back out there, walked three miles an hour for a day, and maybe caught up to him. But what if he camped? What if he took a different route? What if he saw me out on the highway and prepared a little surprise for me?

As tempting as that solid footing was, I decided I'd better stick to the forest and tag along behind. Right then I was sure he didn't know he was being followed, and I wanted to keep it that way as long as I could.

So I followed the trail of branches he'd brushed clean of rain and of the odd bootprint on the forest floor, and I kept on until the light was getting too bad to see. I made a cold camp, this time laying the rifle alongside me in the tube tent. I slept fitfully for about four hours, until it started getting pretty light again, then gave it up and got back on the trail.

A lot of people who don't hunt think hunters track animals all the time. The truth is, we hardly ever track game animals at all. There is the odd time, of course, like the time my hunter and I deliberately tracked a bull caribou up a canyon to get a look at him.

Normally, you see, caribou are like Japanese tourists. They do everything in a herd. The caribou know that an animal that goes off by himself can get pulled down by wolves or a bear. Why the Japanese stick together is anyone's guess.

It is not uncommon to see fall migratory herds of several thousand head of caribou. They'll look at first like ants crawling on an anthill. Then you get out the monocular or spotting scope and there they are, one of the north's most magnificent creatures. They move like ballet dancers and have the soft muted colors of earth and snow and tundra. To me, the caribou bull's antlers are the most beautiful in the animal kingdom, and you can see them reaching up out of the massed herd like surrealistic fingers in a modern sculpture.

Finding caribou isn't the challenge in hunting season. Being able to penetrate that herd and get the bull you want is the challenge.

That's why my hunter and I decided to track this caribou bull one fall and see if we could understand what had drawn him to those high places alone. We had seen his solitary tracks many times and had dubbed him "Lonesome Pete."

So we followed his wanderings from one little tundra ridge to another, watching where he had apparently aimlessly crossed the river and made tracks in the sandbars. He kept working his way higher and higher in this canyon until he started up a side canyon with a tiny bowl at the very head of it where dwelt about seven of the largest Dall rams in the Alaska Range. I'd been trying to get a hunter on one of those rams for two years at that time, and I knew every rock. There was no other way out for the caribou, although the sheep could scuttle up a rock chimney behind them that would give nosebleeds to a sky diver.

That was where we found the bull.

He stood in that little tundra swale and looked at us as we crossed the ridge about two hundred yards away. This was a very old caribou. His antlers had lost their huge reach at this point and had become much smaller, but with many points. The way the Boone and Crockett Club scores caribou, this old bull might have made their book.

The caribou stood there, looking at us with no fear but with a kind of resignation in his eyes. I got the feeling we were intruding into something very private.

I asked my hunter if he wanted the bull. We looked at each other and just smiled.

"Let's just leave old Lonesome Pete alone," my hunter said. "What do you say?"

"Sounds about right to me."

So we fished around in the hunter's pack until we found his camera, and took old Pete home a different way that day.

As I said before, I hand-pick my hunters.

That was a very unusual case, though. The truth is, if we have to track an animal, it is almost always because someone didn't make a clean shot and we have to follow the animal and put it away. This is usually done by following a blood trail, which can get tricky in September when most of the tundra berry bushes are a flame red or pink.

So tracking is normally something we want to avoid, as it usually means failure. No one likes to have a wounded animal out there. I've known guides and hunters who had to wait from falling darkness until morning before resuming the tracking, and none of them could sleep a wink.

Bears are the worst to track. First, they can be hard to kill. If someone tells you he made a one-shot kill on a grizzly, look him straight in the eye. Four out of five will avoid a direct stare after they make a statement like that. A one-shot kill happens occasionally, but it's rare.

Normally, a guide will tell the hunter not to shoot unless the bear is within a hundred yards or so and is far enough from an alder thicket so hunter and guide can get three or four shots into him before he reaches those alders. A wounded bear in an alder thicket is a nightmare you don't even want to think about.

The guide will also tell the hunter to place that first shot well, and if the bear doesn't go down instantly, both rifles will go into action.

If a wounded bear runs away, there is another problem with tracking it: a bear is an obese animal, with thick layers of fat just beneath the hide. That fat can act just like one of these puncture-proof tires and keep most of the blood from running out of the bear. It doesn't stop the internal damage, of course, but can make following a blood trail a long and tedious process of finding two drops every thirty feet or so. And with bears, you usually find the blood on twigs where they brush against them, not on the ground.

Nothing else quite brings you to full alert like tracking a wounded grizzly. I'd rather take oboe lessons.

Perhaps it's the infrequency of tracking that makes me enjoy the pure sport of it. You see, it's part craft, part psychology, and part . . . mystical may be the closest word to what I'm looking for. It can be very satisfying to the tracker on all three levels. His observation and analyzing skills can carry him through the physical part of tracking. He knows what to look for and he looks for it. No animal, man included, can pass through an area without leaving some effect behind. It may be minuscule, but it is there.

It was on a walk one day with my Gramps Jepsen, he of the completely practical mind, that I started training to be a tracker.

We had been walking along together, and he had been teaching me some Norwegian song. I must have been about five or six, and Gramps would listen to me try to sing the foreign words in a loud, high voice and he'd laugh and slap me on the back and encourage me. I still have no idea what that song was about, probably either drinking or women, judging by how Gramps was laughing. Someday I'll corner one of my Norwegian relatives and ask.

But between songs, I would ask him about tracks we found. What animal made this one? Was it a big animal? Was the animal walking or running?

Gramps was a woodsman as well as a craftsman. He answered me to the best of his knowledge, although he didn't know what all the tracks were. But he knew something more valuable.

He motioned for me to sit down on a log. "Listen, son," he'd said. "I don't think this is the best way for you to learn about animal tracks. Maybe you should think about learning this on your own."

"On my own?"

"There are lots of things a boy can learn by himself," Gramps had told me. "Like these tracks. You don't need an old-timer like me to help you, or even a book. You just need to think things out, boy."

He always used to say that. Just think things out, boy, he'd say. If you sit down a minute and think, you can figure 'most anything out.

"You asked me about those wolf tracks and how fast that wolf was going, didn't you?" he had asked me. "Well, to tell you the truth, I'm not at all sure. But I know how you can find out. We have dogs around the village, don't we? Yes. And those dogs go down along the river and sometimes they walk and sometimes they trot, and sometimes they run. Seems to me all a smart boy would have to do is go down there where a dog had just been running and look at the tracks. That's what the tracks of a running wolf would look like, too. Except the wolf tracks are much bigger.

"When you are watching animals, go over to where they've just been and look at their tracks if you're really curious about this. When that beaver waddles back down into his pond, go over and see what his tracks look like. Then when you see them again, you'll know a beaver's been here. When you see a moose trot, go look at the tracks. Then you'll know."

And I did, and that's how I taught myself about animal tracks and how to tell the stories left behind for me in the mud or in the snow. There are fascinating stories there of flight, of fear, of play, of death. You just need to know how to read the book. And Gramps Jepsen taught me the common sense I needed to teach myself.

So much for the physical sign. The tracker must be a great deal more skilled to follow the psychological trail of the hunted. Most fine guides spend a lifetime in the Bush without knowing a thing about this. You could simplify it by asking, "If I were a caribou-bear-moose-killer-sheep, where would I go?" It's simpler with animals than with men. Animals will invariably follow the path of least resistance. Find that and you're halfway there. For instance, when faced with a maze of alder thickets at timberline, guides know to follow moose trails through them. Moose always know best. Follow your own instincts and you'll hit a dead end and have to backtrack to that moose trail eventually, anyway. There are things an intelligent man must trust the dumbest members of the deer family about. Strange, isn't it?

A guide must always know what to expect of an animal in certain situations. A wounded moose will go off into a thicket and lie down to die. A wounded black bear will usually run away in a straight line as far as he can. A wounded grizzly will either charge until someone is dead or run into an alder thicket, lie down next to the trail, and wait for you.

But Lee Hendrix. . . .

I'd gained a lot of time on Lee Hendrix. I'd gained so much time on him that I would have to be careful in the next few days so I didn't overtake him before I was ready. I could still travel twice the hours that he was likely to travel, but as the forest got thicker down toward the Copper River (and I was almost certain that's where he was heading) he'd be able to travel continuously.

I guessed he'd probably not risk detection at Glennallen or Chitina or Tonsina and would stay to the woods. If my guess was right, and if I were in his shoes, I'd cross over to the south side of the Glenn Highway and stay in the thick timber along the foothills of the Chugach Mountains on my right.

The only problem with this thinking was that I wasn't Lee Hendrix, and perhaps no one else in the world thought like Lee Hendrix. Not on some things, anyway. But so far, Hendrix had acted as if he had all his marbles and knew just where to take them.

The farther he went, the narrower the list of his possible destinations would be. He would be getting braver, too. After all, he had to know every cop in the state was looking for him and he hadn't seen even one. That they were waiting for him to make a mistake, or waiting for the Bush to kill him, he couldn't know. But covering all that ground undetected would have to be a confidence builder. It could make him do something stupid.

If, as I'd been picturing in my mind, those killings had been the result of a spurt of madness, what would happen if another such spurt hit him? He might walk out in the open in daytime. He might be foolish when crossing a river and not face upstream and sidestep it the way you're supposed to. He might even walk into Glennallen and kill some more people.

Or he could be killed by a bear or a cliff or a swamp.

Part of me wanted something like that to happen, but another part of me didn't, because I wanted to know why. So I decided to continue tracking him very slowly and cautiously and keep an eye ahead of me at all times for signs of him. I had one advantage, anyway: he didn't know I was here.

That wouldn't last long.

CHAPTER 17

D ays later, I saw where Hendrix had crossed the Glenn Highway
and started into the forest along the base of the Chugach
Mountains. Assuming he'd made the crossing at night (you could
tell he'd waited in the trees for hours before crossing), I couldn't be that
far behind him. Three hours? Five hours? Eight at the outside.

When trying to guess his destination, I had thought it was fairly safe to
rule out Glennallen. That wasn't much of a real option, anyway. It was an
open town of houses and businesses spread along both sides of the Glenn
Highway. All activity in Glennallen always seemed to be dedicated to fixing flat tires.

The main thing was, Hendrix was going into the Chugach Mountains,
and that suited me just fine.

Shortly after I crossed the Tazlina River, I heard the drone of a plane. It
flew north of the highway first, making several sweeps low over the trees
down there. Then it came across the highway and began hugging mountains. Long before it came close enough to see me, I recognized the silver
and green of Buck Davis' Cessna 185. I dug through the pack and put my
red crusher on and stepped out into a blueberry meadow.

In less than five minutes, Buck had the flaps down and was sweeping
low toward me. A cloth bag with a long streamer of toilet paper dropped
like a shot duck and bounced not six feet from me.

He wagged his wings once, banked and flew back toward the west. Buck
always prides himself on pinpoint airdrops. Most of us consider him a
frustrated bomber pilot. After dropping a canned ham through a front

porch a couple of years ago, he's backed off just a little.

In the bag were several dozen piroshkis, courtesy of Danny's mom, two recent newspapers, a pound of coffee and two notes. I read the one from Buck first.

> *Jeep:*
>
> *I'll be back over you in about a minute. You want more airdrops, raise two hands. You OK, just wave with one and I'll stay out of your hair. You get smart and want a ride home, wave two hands and I'll come back for you with the Super Cub. In either case, be careful, and I'll see you back at the South Seas.*
>
> *Buck*

He came low this time, skimming the timber, and I stood there waving one hand as he passed over. He wagged his wings again, banked and flew away once more. It was a little lonely when he'd gone, but the noise of that engine had jarred my senses. It was unpleasant. That was a good sign. Anchorage was all gone from me now. I had become a man of the Bush again, and that's the way I feel the most comfortable.

I packed the piroshkis, the papers and the wool crusher back in the pack and put the Jones cap back on. Then I sat down on a log in the sunshine and read Betsy's note.

> *Dear Jeep:*
>
> *Everything is fine here. Danny and Mary are in camp with the hunters. Mary says she'll skin you when you get back for going off like this. I think she's really worried, too.*
>
> *Jeep, I don't care if this guy gets away. He's not worth you getting hurt. I won't put anything more down on paper until I've had a chance to talk to you again.*
>
> *But you know.*
>
> *Betsy*

It was several minutes before I realized I was sitting still and being bitten by eight or ten mosquitoes at once. Then I smiled and slapped them. The sky was a much deeper blue than it had been a few minutes earlier. The outlines of Mount Sanford and Mount Drum stood with even more grandeur than normal. I celebrated by changing my socks in the middle of the day, then got back on the trail.

"But you know," she had said. Know what? Yes, I wasn't that dense, I knew. And I felt the same way. As I walked along, following the obvious trail Hendrix had left over the moose track, my mind went back to that last rainy evening and the way she smelled when our faces touched, and the way her lips tasted beneath mine. I knew, too, that it wasn't just the strong physical pounding it gave my nerves that made that moment so memorable, but it was the way I'd felt inside, too. That embrace had felt very normal and natural. I'd felt as though I'd come home.

The explosion knocked me to the left, with the right side of my face suddenly numbed. I rolled even as the sound of the explosion came from in front of me. My eyes and arms worked, and I lay behind the roots of a spruce with my rifle ready.

Then I felt, rather than saw, the blood running down my cheek, and I pulled the long slivers of wood out of it. The blood dripped on my rifle stock, but there was no helping that at the moment. Everything seemed to be working all right. I glanced over at the spruce tree that had been just to my right when all this happened. A large chunk of bark and cambium layer and the creamy white inner wood was gone, splintered and blown out as if by a bomb. And I could still hear the explosion echoing through the canyons above me. The attack had happened so swiftly, it took a few seconds to realize that I'd just been shot at by a very high-powered rifle. It didn't take a genius to guess the caliber of the rifle, either. I was at the same time the dumbest man in the mountains for losing my concentration and about six times luckier than I had a right to expect.

I stripped the pack from my back quickly, held onto it by a strap, and slithered along the ground, careful to make as little noise as possible as I dropped into a small creek bed and burrowed down in there, covered by the thorny branches of the devil's club plants above me. The huge, almost tropical leaves of the devil's club make good cover, but the thorns are so bad I'd almost rather take a chance on the bullets. Almost.

Another shot came from a hillock about a hundred yards away. It blew another chunk of bark out of another spruce, this time to the left.

He wasn't going to sucker me into a gunfight with these rifles at a hundred yards.

"Who are you?" he yelled, in a voice I found surprisingly high. It might have been just the tension, of course. I held my peace and quietly slipped a shell into the chamber, then put on the safety.

"I said who are you, dammit!"

His voice was lower this time. It must have been the tension.

From where I lay I could watch that hillock and I was pretty certain he couldn't circle back uphill without my seeing him. But the downhill side held more timber. A man who can move silently can get very close to his quarry in cover like that.

Holding the rifle in one hand and the pack in the other, I began to walk up the center of the little rivulet where I had taken refuge. I needed cover and time to think, and I needed a place where my rifle could cover all the approaches while I did that thinking.

The little rise between me and that open space to Hendrix's hillock offered less cover the higher I climbed. I was walking bent nearly in half by now, but I'd managed to put a good two hundred yards between me and where I'd been ambushed, and more than that between me and Hendrix's last known position.

Ahead was a thicket of alders, dark in the center and branched in a crazy quilt toward the edges. I cut around the back and went in to the center and lay down with a good view of everything and settled in to wait him out.

For two hours I waited, and silently squashed the mosquitoes without slapping them, and felt every little branch and stub stick me until my ribs and legs were sore. Two hours. And I didn't think of Betsy for two hours, or of hunting camp this year, or of how Mary's cooking tasted after a long day in the field. I didn't think of my dogs, or the music I had at the cabin. I thought of Lee Hendrix.

Lee Hendrix.

Lee Hendrix.

I had to get him in my mind. Lee Hendrix. What would he do? Would he just keep walking to get away from me as quickly as he could? Or would he circle around and come up behind my last position to see if I was dead?

I was pretty certain Hendrix hadn't seen me move. I'd pulled that move on bears and moose and even fooled a Dall ram or two with it.

If I read Hendrix right, he'd want to know who I was and if I were dead or not. It would be a challenge for him, and he'd almost have to come and see. I was counting on it.

I had a view of the general area where I'd been, down along the tiny creek and in those few spruces. He had to come, I decided. It would drive him crazy if he didn't. Which was a strange thought to have, if you think about it.

But it would be bothering him. For one thing, I hadn't fired back. If a man is fired on by another in Alaska, since it's almost always a mistake, he'll fire a shot in the air to show that dummy that this is a human and not a moose or squirrel or something in between. The fact that I hadn't shot would mean that either he'd injured me seriously enough that I couldn't shoot, or for some reason I didn't want to shoot. And it would be this last possibility that would drive him to circle around and come back.

Then he was there.

First I saw a stirring low in the devil's club leaves, then a blond and capped head rose and looked around quietly and slowly. He was about thirty feet from where I'd been. He had seen the blasted tree, of course, in his scope when he fired, and now he was only yards from it.

I got the impression of some primordial creature rising from the ooze. I fished out the monocular and focused it.

So that's what you look like, Lee.

Hendrix moved with the stealth of a cat. His head was all that was visible in the devil's club, and he moved those remaining feet very slowly. In summer jungle like that along the creek, you could pass within six feet of a man and not see him. If that same man is armed and has been shot at twice, it would make the guy who'd done the shooting move very cautiously. He did. His head seem to float toward where I'd lain. There were no jerky movements, no hesitations. He moved the way a snake moves when it feels its way along into unfamiliar territory. There is the feeling of controlled power there, and an immense sensation of stealth. Lee Hendrix was not going to be much fun to deal with.

Then he was there where I'd lain, and he quickly looked around. And for a moment he seemed to stare right at me. Then he looked back again and I knew he was studying tracks and the blood I'd left behind. He saw my tracks lead to the creek and disappear, and once again he looked up the hill and seemed to stare at me.

Then, just as quietly as he'd come, he sank back into the brush and trees. But at last I'd seen him and knew what I was up against. Every muscle in his face spoke of strength. Power. But more than that, too.

Maybe when a man's mind has gone to the extremes of murder and muti-lation, that makes some basic differences in the rest of him. Maybe it was just that Hendrix had always been a loner and lived in the wild places. Whatever it was, the air of wildness that I could sense even through a monocular at two hundred yards wasn't the same as it is in woods-wise but friendly old sourdoughs. Hendrix had about him a feral air, some-thing that was more than wild, more than dangerous. It was as if he was able to gather some of the better qualities of the animals and mountains around him and then turn them into a sickness looking for something to strike at.

This was not going to be a simple tracking job from here on in. Hendrix might not know who I was, but he must certainly know why I was there.

The shout came from the approximate area where he'd been when he'd fired at me.

"Leave me alone!" His voice carried off into the mountains. "Don't follow me! I'll kill you!"

I lay there for another two hours, eating piroshkis and wishing I'd holed up a little closer to a creek so I could get a drink.

Then it was dark, one of the first days of darkness of the coming winter. The darkness was helped by a wall of clouds that settled down on the basin like a mama goose on her eggs. It shut out Mount Sanford and Mount Drum and clogged the sky. You could smell the moisture. By full dark it was raining. I shrugged into my slicker and began walking uphill into a morass of alders. Up here was the one place I knew he wouldn't come. He couldn't see any more than I could, and he knew I had to be up here somewhere. And he could be pretty sure I carried a rifle and could probably still use it.

What he didn't know was how badly hurt I was, or just who I was. I was counting on that. He'd never expect the state troopers to have only one man after him, and he'd be right. So why was I back here and who was I?

I hoped the questions would give him sleepless nights, or days, rather . . . the way all my questions had kept me awake.

I slipped quietly and very slowly along the muddy moose trails through the alders in the rain. It was one of those cold Alaska rains again. I swear the rain comes down at below-freezing temperatures sometimes in sum-mer. Don't pester me with facts—I know.

Hendrix would be on the move now, too. Not only would he want to take full advantage of the dark but he wouldn't want to stop and camp in this rain, either. But he'd still be down the mountain, walking a course parallel to mine by maybe a quarter to half a mile. Hendrix would be in the thick forest. I was up here on moose freeway.

That got me to thinking.

The way we were heading now, we were both going to run smack into Tazlina Lake in the next day or two. I had only flown over Tazlina Lake before—this wasn't my home ground—but I recalled timber interspersed with berry flats, a whole valley full of them. If I could somehow beat Hendrix to the lake and find a nice lookout, I could keep an eye on him and follow his progress clear across the valley without being seen.

The more I walked through the rain that night, the more I liked the idea. Here was a way of tracking a man for maybe twenty miles with just my monocular. Even if he moved across the valley at night, he was bound to leave me some good sign to find.

When the daylight crept back, the rain slowed to a drizzle that lasted a full day and into the next night. I rested several times, taking time to eat and drink, but the weather kept me on the trail—the weather and the plan I had.

The stars came out that second night for an hour before it got light again, and the day began to dawn fresh and warm. The tundra up on the high hillocks where I walked oozed steam like a wet dog that has just come into the house. By the time I decided to make another rest stop and eat, I was topping a rise and there, lying several miles away below me, was Tazlina Lake, a huge shimmering gem in this wilderness of trees and bushes.

I stayed out of sight in alders, working my way slowly down the mountainside, measuring every step. This was no time to get careless. Whatever else Lee Hendrix might be, he was not going to be easy to sneak up on. His mind might be on some other planet, but there was nothing wrong with his survival instincts.

About halfway down the mountainside was an outcropping of car-sized rocks, set slablike into the mountain as if either just emerging or just going back inside. From these rocks I would be able to watch the valley and, probably, Hendrix as he crossed it.

Hendrix likely wouldn't expect me to make this kind of time and arrive at the lake ahead of him. After all, I still had a swollen cheek and a good-sized gash to remember him by. If I were smart, he'd think, I'd hotfoot it down the comparatively few miles to the Glenn Highway and safety. Maybe. But I hadn't fired that identifying shot, either, and that would have him plenty worried.

It took me a couple of hours to make it to the rocks. The last forty yards were in open country, just out of the tree belt, and I wormed my way to the rocks on my belly across the open space. I went in and found just what I needed: a slab to sit on leaning against another for a backrest. I made myself comfortable and looked around. It was a good place to be. For Hendrix to see me, he'd have to be directly in front of me, or on top of the rock behind my head.

I munched some piroshkis, washed them down with water from a spring nearby, and settled down for a long wait. I did a little housekeeping then, pulling off my hip boots and tucking them out of sight to my right where they could catch a breeze and dry out. I changed my socks and celebrated the clean socks by propping my feet up and just letting the warm air of morning wash around every toe, every curve of my feet. It was delicious.

Since I was going to be stationary, I checked the rifle first, then slipped a cartridge into the chamber and flipped on the safety. I'd unload it before walking anywhere, but it's always nice to know you have something lethal close at hand. This was prime bear country, and Lee Hendrix wasn't the only dangerous game in town.

Then I sat and thought about things. I looked out across this huge lake to the swelling forested ridges beyond, and reached a hand up to that swollen cheek. Hendrix would have to pay for that, I decided. But I couldn't afford the luxury of hating this guy. Not yet. Someday, maybe. Right now, I was just here to hunt.

CHAPTER 18

The quick march through the uplands for two days had been tiring, but I was at home now and feeling the world around me, and the push I'd made wasn't the worst thing that could happen to a man.

I like to think of the feeling part of tracking as the third or highest part, after and above the physical and psychological. At least it has been for me. It's a bit like being in tune with the mountains, so when the mountains strike a note that is a little out of harmony, I can hear it.

Like this morning. The mountain music came again, filling me with that awe at being privy to something few ever experience. When I mention the music of the mountains to people from the city, they look at me funny, so mostly I don't. It's inside my head, of course, but through a strange series of acoustical tricks, I can swear the flowing music comes from beneath my feet, swelling up from the tundra ridges until it seems every tree, every peak, every creek is an instrument in some primal fugue designed to taunt the sourdough who has been in wild country long enough to hear it.

The music is not a conscious tune that can repeat itself over and over in my head as though I just heard it on the car radio. The music is fresh and new, composed by someone with a greater knowledge of life and beauty than I have.

On stormy afternoons it can be a glorification of something Stravinsky might write; a gentle morning could be reminiscent of Ravel or Debussy or Franck. The violent storms of November outdo Beethoven at his bloody best.

It comes to the mountain people, the ones who live in wild country and earn their livings pretty much alone: the hunting guide, the trapper, the timber cruiser, the prospector. Psychiatrists would probably call it a way of compensating for the loneliness we feel out here, but we are seldom lonely, so that probably wouldn't wash. And no one cares what psychiatrists think, anyway.

The phantom music is not a general topic of conversation, either. Only when you know someone really well and know he or she has been there, alone, for a long time can you feel comfortable broaching the subject. There are usually just some mutual smiles and nodding, and then it is forgotten.

And that was a morning for music. A time, for me, that gave me a chance to let the soft breeze out of the Chugach Mountains sift through my beautiful fresh socks. A chance to fill leisurely up on food, to listen to a little music from the rock pile I sat on, a chance to look down on the beauty of Tazlina Lake and stick Lee Hendrix on the back burner for a short while.

I sat there and began practicing a relaxation technique I'd learned in college. Tighten the feet. Relax them. Tighten them again. Relax them. Tighten the calf muscles. Relax them. Tighten them again. Relax them. Work my way up the body, tightening and relaxing, and with each small segment of my body relaxing, feeling that warmth spread over me in the sun. Looking down. Watching the high-kneed trot of a moose coming down from the mountain behind me and disappearing into the trees below this little throne I had. The summer sun doing its best on my tired body. Tighten the belly. Relax it. Tighten it again. Relax it.

See the moose turn and look back up the mountain, then keep trotting, and tighten the chest muscles and . . .

The noise was off to my right and I spun that way with the safety off my rifle, rising out of my throne to face the challenge.

But the blow came from behind.

CHAPTER 19

My head exploded. I recall feeling stones scrape my body and I tried to reach something. But my arms and legs weren't there and when I hit the bottom of the rock pile I was beyond feeling it.

There was only Betsy, smiling, and then her smile turned into a dripping grimace and fear grabbed me when I saw her try to speak, but her mouth wouldn't work because it was melting, and I saw a sadness in her eyes and then it was Danny standing there, coming up from the bottom of a lake and he said why did I do it? I tried to think, and all I could think of was that I was tired of piroshkis, and that's why I did it, whatever it was, and he said I shouldn't have done it. Why? I tried to think, but I couldn't because someone wouldn't let me, and then I realized it was Chada, my grandfather. He had told me never to use the canoe alone.

His face was furious, and I thought he was dead, but here he was and he asked why did I do it, then leaned forward and shook me and said, "Who are you?"

"Jepsen," I tried to say, but my mouth had gone away, so he grabbed me again and shook me. "Who are you?" And I tried to tell him Jepsen but I couldn't so I said "Jeep" . . . a little. But it didn't sound like it. It sounded like "eep" or "eet."

"Who are you?" he said, and I opened my eyes and it wasn't my grandfather, but another man. I couldn't see him. I tried, but all I could see was some ghostly figure in front of me. I tried to touch my head, to hold it, to figure things out, but I couldn't. My hands didn't work. I tried and then discovered they were tied together and tied to my ankles. Then I rolled half over and was sick and tried to wipe my mouth off on grass. The man had a brightness to him that I hadn't seen before, flickering. Then I knew it was a fire, and as I tried to focus my eyes and deal with the worst hangover in history, he put coffee on the fire as if we were old friends.

"I told you I'd kill you, didn't I?" he said, walking toward me. "Why didn't you believe me? You think I like killing people?"

Lee Hendrix stood about five inches taller and forty pounds heavier than me. None of it appeared to be fat.

Without his cap on, I could see his blond hair was short-cropped and crowned a head like a bullet that sloped into massive shoulders. The way he moved suggested power, and that was borne out a minute later when he picked me up like a trussed puppy and carried me to the base of a spruce tree and propped me up.

"I'll cut you loose for a cup of coffee pretty soon," he said. "Don't bother looking for your knives. I have them both."

My eyes were going in and out of focus now, and I tried to turn my head to look around. When I did, a large lump on the right side of my head pressed against the bark of the tree and started me retching again, but this time with no ammunition.

"Did you shoot me?" I managed to ask.

He laughed in a friendly manner. "Just a little love tap with a rifle butt, pal. Not feeling too hot, eh?"

"Been better."

"You got a sense of humor," he said. "That's all right. I like a man with a sense of humor."

But there wasn't any humor on Hendrix's face despite the words he used.

So this is what it'll be like, I thought: trussed like a pork roast against a tree and sick, terribly sick. I wished I didn't have the indignity of being sick, anyway, but only suicides get to choose how they go.

I straightened up the best I could and tried to catch my breath, which wasn't easy. Across the fire from me, Hendrix had my rifle. He jacked the shells out of it, and in a moment of focus, I could see the fall had put a deep scratch in the stock on the right-hand side. I'll have to fix that, I thought. I'm not too good at things like that, but maybe old Charlie would know how. Old Charlie who would live to be older. And I kept thinking of that rifle, and how bad it was to have it scratched like that. It wasn't a fancy rifle, but I had spent a lot of time fixing it just the way I wanted it. Considering what I faced, I knew it was silly to be sore at someone handling my rifle without my consent, but that was my overriding feeling at the time, aside from a head that I was certain had split in two.

Hendrix looked at me and gave me another insincere smile. "I hate to do this. This is a nice rifle. You cared for it real good, didn't you?"

He walked up to the large rocks behind me and smashed the barrel again and again until it was bent. He smashed the stock, then, until the oiled walnut broke off in chunks and splinters and lay around the little camp. That rifle would never shoot again. He tossed it aside, and I felt a terrible depression overtake me. I wanted it to turn to anger, but I couldn't arrange it. Things were still too new. I kept remembering Betsy's face melting and the hurt it had showed.

Hendrix walked to the fire and poured me a cup of coffee and brought it over. He set it on a rock next to me and untied my hands, then tied my right hand back to my ankles. My left was free.

He tossed me one of the dirty socks I'd taken off when I got there. "Coffee's plenty hot. Don't burn yourself."

I drank it and watched him, and he watched me.

He set the contents of my pack out neatly next to him. I hoped he liked piroshkis, because there were enough over there to keep him going for weeks. No, I didn't hope that at all.

"It was the airdrop," he said, suddenly.

"What?"

"The airdrop. That's how I knew you were there."

I tried to nod.

"You're good. It was just the airdrop."

I sipped the coffee and pretended it didn't hit my stomach like fishing sinkers.

"You Native boys are hardheaded," Hendrix said, and I swear there was a tinge of genuine respect in his voice. "Thought I'd killed you, you know. Native boys got thick skulls like the colored people, must be. They got these real thick skulls . . . it's a fact . . . because of they got to fight lions and stuff in Africa. You Native boys got thicker skulls, too?"

I just looked at him without saying anything.

"Who are you?"

"Jepsen George." My voice sounded as if it came from someone else, but at least it worked.

"I didn't catch that."

I looked at him and my eyes went again. A wave of nausea hit me then, and I waited until it passed and I could see again. "Jepsen George. Jeep . . . Jeep George."

"You run the dogsled races, don't you?"

I nodded.

"I seen you at Rondy. You're not very good, are you?"

"Not very."

"You ever win?"

"Very seldom."

"Why do you do it?"

I tried to shrug, which wasn't easy in the ropes. "Fun, I guess."

"Fun and you don't win?"

"I like dogs."

He nodded. "Yeah. How many you got?"

"Eight, not counting pups."

He nodded and smiled, somewhat more sincerely this time. "Eight, not counting pups."

He looked at me strangely, as if trying to put things in place.

I thought I'd better speak. "Do you have dogs?"

He looked at me and the expression froze on my face.

"No."

"Never?"

"You know, don't you?"

No, I sure didn't, and I didn't know what to say either.

"Know what?"

"About Tagger."

"Tagger's a dog?"

"You know," he said, nodding coldly. "Look, I took care of him, didn't I? But they said it was their dog. Well, I'm the one who fed him and he slept in my room, but they always said it was their dog, and they weren't going to let me take him with me when they made me move. He was mine, though."

I nodded, thinking this might be the safest way to handle things.

"Did I do right?"

"Uh, sure . . . why not?"

He seemed to relax a little at that. But I didn't. I had no idea what had happened to Tagger or the family who thought they owned him.

"My name is Lee Hendrix," he said. "Pleased to meet you."

I think he meant it. He smiled, then took the empty cup from me and poured himself some coffee. He sat and sipped and watched me.

"I ate some of your biscuit things. What do you call them?"

"Piroshkis."

He smiled. "Just learned another Native word."

"Russian," I croaked.

"You talk Russian?"

"No. Piroshkis are Russian. From the old days."

"What do you know?" he said. "Russian. How do you know what's in one before you eat it?"

"You don't."

"Why not?"

"It doesn't matter."

"Is that one of those Native things nobody understands?"

I thought about that question for a minute, looking hopefully for anything that might resemble a crack in his armor.

"We don't talk about it, that's all."

He smiled as though he'd just guessed the answer on a quiz show.

"I knew it was something like that. Well, all that mumbo jumbo won't help you none now, will it? Look at you."

I was thankful I couldn't, but at least my mind was semi-functioning.

"Are you a cop?"

"No."

"But you're following me."

I stared right through him with no expression. I was going to give him the stoic Indian bit as much as I could.

"How long?"

I just looked at him.

"When did you start tracking me?" he said.

"Talkeetna Mountains."

"You found my trail there? Up there?" He had raised his voice in alarm, then stared at me and sucked at the cup of coffee.

"In the tundra? You found my trail in the tundra?"

I shrugged this time, as if there was nothing to it.

"Nobody can follow tracks in the tundra," he said.

"I'm here," I said, and smiled.

"Nobody's that good. Not even a Native tracker. Nobody's that good."

"Any chance of getting another cup of that coffee?"

"Sure." He brought me another one. "Why are you tracking me?"

"Guy named Bill Turner."

"Who?"

"Bill Turner. You remember him, Lee?"

"Don't think so."

"You killed him and cut him into pieces."

Hendrix screamed with some unseen terror, then leaped across the fire and held a knife to my throat. The look on his face let me know I was seconds away from death.

"Don't ever say that! Why would I kill someone and cut him into pieces? That's a devilment thing. That's a devilment thing, isn't it? Are you a devilment thing? A Native devilment thing?"

"I don't know what you mean."

"You know the Native guys that can be wizards and turn into things. I don't believe it for a minute, so if you tell me you are, I won't believe it for a minute."

"I'm not one of those."

He pulled away and sat back down across the fire. He fed some more sticks into the fire, never taking his eyes from me, and he wasn't looking at me in the same light he had before.

"If you were a devilment thing or a wizard, you wouldn't tell me anyway, though, would you? So how would I ever know?"

I nodded. "I guess it would be a problem."

I gave that sentence my best village voice, the accent of old Charlie I like to copy when I'm teasing him. I can do old Charlie pretty well.

"I'm not saying I am one, or even know about them," I said, in my trying-to-be-helpful voice, "but sometimes you hear stories."

"What stories?"

"Oh," I said, looking down sheepishly, or as sheepishly as I could muster, "just some silly old things, that's all."

He started to rise and his face became set with that rigor of fear or hate I'd just seen. I quickly continued. " . . . stories about owls."

He settled back down and seemed to relax a little.

"Owls?"

Think fast, I told myself.

"About the wizards, the spiritual people. Just that they sound like owls at night and can see in the dark. But that's probably just an old story."

"See in the dark? Maybe it's a story and maybe it isn't. Anyway, thanks for telling me. You want one of these pirosh-things?"

So I can die on a full belly. I shook my head.

"You're a strange guy," Hendrix said. He walked over and retied my left hand to my right. "I'm going to rustle up some wood. Don't run off."

He was back in five minutes with a big armload of dry spruce. It was getting dark by this time, and he built the fire up higher.

"Nobody's going to see us at night up here, anyway," he said.

I had to know some things, but I also knew I had to be very careful about how I found them out.

"You remember that camp up in the Talkeetnas?" I asked. "Where you were working?"

"Yes," he said, "but I had to leave."

"Why did you leave? I mean, if you don't mind my asking."

"There were some guys there . . . ," he said, in a faraway voice.

"Yes?"

He looked confused, then he shrugged. "Well, there were some guys there. I guess I didn't like them or something. Anyway, I had to go. You know how it is. Sometimes you find out something about someone and you know you have to go?"

"And you found out something about one of the men there?"

"I guess so. I don't remember."

"You thought I was a police officer. Why?"

He shrugged. "They're always looking for me to give me a bad time. Remember that time in Fairbanks?"

"What time in Fairbanks?"

He jumped up and screamed at me. "Don't lie! Don't lie! Don't think I don't know who you are! Don't think I don't know that you're one of those devilments and they sent you to get me! I know it! I know it! I'm not stupid, you know! Just because I'm not Native, I'm still not stupid!" He sat down and glared at me.

I sat as quiet and as dignified as a man hogtied into a figure eight can get. We stayed that way for at least a half hour, neither of us speaking.

"Bill Turner," he said, quietly. "Bill Turner?"

I nodded.

"Was he one of the men?"

I nodded again.

"So where do you come in?"

"He was one of my closest friends. We went to school together."

He nodded. "Want more coffee?"

I shook my head. "Do you remember Bill?" I asked.

"I don't think so. What did he look like?"

I described him.

He shrugged. "Doesn't sound like anyone I know. What happened to him?"

Looking at him in disbelief, I took a minute to think.

"He died," I said.

"Sorry to hear that. I lost a friend once, too."

"It's tough."

"Yeah. He was a good guy, too."

He sat for a minute, then looked at me with a puzzled expression.

"So what are you doing out here? You're his friend, but why are you here?"

"I just thought you might be able to tell me something about Bill . . . about what happened to him?"

"Sorry, pal. I don't know anything about that."

"Why are you angry with me for following you, then?"

"I thought you were a cop."

"Why would a cop want you?"

"It was when I left camp—I took the food, a lot of it, anyway. It was supposed to stay there. I needed it for my trip, see? My pack over there is full of food. I have to take it along with me. But it belonged to the company."

"And the company didn't want you to . . . ?"

"Don't ever talk to me like that again!"

I sat quietly while Hendrix paced, the firelight showing the face of a man so caught up in an unreal world that he might have killed four men . . . for what? A backpack full of food?

"What happened, Lee?"

"They didn't understand."

"Understand what?"

"That it was time to go." He looked at me. "You understand, don't you? I'd worked for that food. They had planes coming in and out all the time. I'd worked for that food. But they said it belonged to the company and I was going to be sent out on the next plane. Fired!"

"That must have been tough."

"I couldn't let them do that. You can see that. You see that. I needed the food."

So he was looking to me for absolution for killing four men to cover the theft of a backpack full of food? Me, who was trussed like a turkey and at the mercy of a madman? I tried to imagine what could take place in the mind of a man to bend rationality into something so ugly and evil.

I couldn't.

Then Hendrix brought out a stick and went to the fire and brushed out an area around it. He began to draw figures on the ground between us. He drew them slowly and carefully, and I watched each one in horror. I had seen these designs described before. By Jim Strickland, describing the way bloody clothes had been displayed in wall tents at a place called Murder Lake.

He finished, then looked at me and smiled. "I'm done with those now."

"What are they?"

"If you're a devilment, you'll know what they are. They're to keep you away. They stop devilments."

"Then you have nothing to worry about from me, do you?" I said. "If I were a devilment, it would stop me anyway, so you have nothing to worry about from me."

He had to stop and think about it for a minute.

"I don't know," he said, slowly. "I've heard devilments can do anything to fool a man, you know. They can turn into animals, even."

"You mean like owls?"

"Like owls? Why did you say that?"

He walked over and grabbed me and twisted my arms until I thought the skin would peel off the muscles. I'd never seen so much fear on a man's face.

"Why did you say that? Why? You know about owls, don't you? You Native guys can do things with owls, can't you?"

It was hard to know exactly what to say.

"We can't do anything with owls," I finally said. "It's just there are things the old ones talk about sometimes."

"What things? What things?"

I shrugged. "White people aren't interested," I said in my best village voice.

"What things!"

"It's just the things they say. Nobody pays any attention to them."

"What do they say?" he growled.

"Well . . . oh, you'll think this is just stupid and superstitious."

"No . . . no, really. I want to know. What do they say?"

"Just that owls know things."

"What things?"

"You'll think it's stupid."

"What things?"

I looked at him across the fire. He looked wound up tight enough to break.

"They say," I said in an embarrassed whisper, "that owls know when someone is going to die."

"What do they do?"

"They talk about it."

He was hooked.

"Is that all?"

"Yes. Well, almost all."

"What else?"

"They say the owl calls the spirit of death to the person who is going to die."

May my forebears forgive me the lies, but I was trussed up like a sandhill crane on the potlatch table, and I didn't see any forebears around helping at the moment.

"Calls it? How?"

"I don't know. They just say you'll know because of the owl and the spirit of death when it comes."

The firelight played on his face, and I could see he was sweating despite the cool night air. How strange this was, this night on the mountain above Tazlina Lake. The fire and the camp looked so similar to thousands of other camps in my life.

Didn't feel like them, though.

The new part of the fire burned brightly, and below it was the chunky golden hell of coals that could be counted on to last all night. Hendrix sat there, staring at me, the flickers making his strong face appear to move, giving his pale skin some hues it didn't really own. The nearest branches of the spruce flashed back in little flickers, while the rest of the trees behind stood like solid tall ghosts guarding the secrets of the night.

Was this to be my last camp? The others had had hunters, friends, or even members of my family sitting around laughing. Some had my Gramps Jepsen singing old Norwegian logging songs and laughing. Some had my Grandpa George, Chada, telling stories about the trickery and kindnesses of Chulyen. Some had a very nervous hunter sitting across from me on the eve of a bear hunt, and I was the one telling the stories, joking around with him, trying to loosen him up.

I wondered how long it would be before anyone else found this camp. Months, certainly. Maybe never. Bodies left uncovered, I knew, are cared for swiftly by the Alaska Sanitation Department in all its various sizes and employments. The officers and employees of the department work for free, and range in size from a thumb-size shrew to grizzlies as big as a compact car. They are all very efficient at what they do. Even Chulyen, the raven, would feed his children and help clean up camp.

"Hendrix," I finally said, "you don't look as if you belong here in the woods."

He looked at me curiously.

"I get along in the woods."

"But you're not the type, are you? You were born for something else, I can tell."

"You are just guessing," he said. "You're just guessing. You said you aren't a devilment. You don't know anything like that. You said that, didn't you?"

"Yes. I didn't mean a devilment thing, it's just that when I look at you, I can see you someplace else."

"Where else?"

"I can picture you smiling, and you seem to be surrounded by water."

He leaped forward. "What! What do you mean, surrounded by water?"

"Sorry, Hendrix. I didn't mean anything by it. Just a feeling I had, that's all."

He looked at me and smiled, and chills ran over my body like creek water. "I knew it about you Native boys. You know stuff, don't you?"

I shrugged. "Just a feeling, that's all."

"You got any more feelings?"

"I can see you being your own boss."

He laughed. "So can I, Native boy. So can I."

"It must have been hard, having to work for other people."

"They couldn't do anything to me. They thought they knew things, but I knew better. They think—why am I telling you this?"

"Because I'm interested?"

He shrugged and brought me another cup of coffee, untying my left hand again. I assumed this was some sign of buddy-buddy stuff again.

"You know how it is," he said, quietly. He sat down and pulled the rest of the things from my pack. "You have to have money, so you work for someone, but he doesn't have to know anything. There are a lot of stupid people out there, but some of them got money to pay you."

I nodded my head in agreement, but it hurt, so I said, "That's the truth."

He smiled. "Yes. I knew you'd see it. You're smart, Native boy. Are there dumb Native people, too?"

"You wouldn't believe how many."

"I knew it. I always knew it," he said, gloating. "You'd think people smart enough to get money would be smart enough to take care of themselves, don't you?"

"They don't take care of themselves?"

"They get stupid and then somebody smart has to finish up for them, even if they aren't around."

"Have you done that, Lee?"

"Done what?"

"Finished for them."

He screamed, "Finish for them! Don't ever say that!"

When he'd been quiet for a minute, I asked, "Why not?"

"I don't know. What do you mean?"

He seemed sincere, so I let it drop. Talking to this guy was like drilling for oil on a volcano. You never knew what you were going to hit.

By this time, he'd found something to do. Piece by piece, he tossed my clothes from the pack into the fire. All of them went in, including my red crusher and the Jones cap. He burned, or actually melted, my tube tent. It turned to stringy yellow blobs among the coals. My wool shirts took longer, and created a terrible smell. He cut the beaded moccasins in half, the ones my aunt had made for me, then burned them. I sat silently and waited.

In the course of another half hour, he'd gone completely through my stuff, burning what he could, stuffing what he couldn't burn into his own pack. He topped the huge pack off with piroshkis until it wouldn't hold another, then tossed the rest of them into the fire. I didn't like how this was going.

He carefully checked each pocket of the backpack, was satisfied that it was empty, and tossed it down the hill. He couldn't very well burn the backpack's aluminum frame, and now there was nothing on it to tie it to me. It was a pretty neat disappearing job I was about to pull.

It was hard to decide whether my fear took precedence over my curiosity. I believe they took turns alternating between my brain and my adrenal glands. At least the adrenal glands seemed to be working quite nicely at this point.

Then Hendrix came over and tied my left hand to my right again. He reached down and pulled each of my new fresh socks off and tossed them in the fire. I felt naked with my bare feet awash in the light of the fire. The cold breeze made them feel uncomfortably cold, and I recall thinking at the time, as if to cheer myself up with the joke, that Hendrix had been making me feel very uncomfortable ever since we met.

I said nothing. I gave it the stoic Indian treatment. It might not have been the best way to handle things, but it was easy, and at least I couldn't say the wrong thing to him, as I had been doing all afternoon.

Finally, his chores seemed to be done, and he looked at me and smiled, but in that strange way that made me think he might not realize where we were, who I was, or why he had me tied up. My stomach started churning again and my heart was beating rapidly. I could feel myself stick to the tree through the sweat in my shirt, despite the coolness of the night.

Hendrix walked over to a tree, shrugged into his pack, and slung that heavy-barreled .375 H & H Magnum rifle, muzzle down, over his left shoulder. This was a pro.

"Don't go nowhere," he said, laughing. "I mean, not for a while. You're gonna get out of those ropes, I know, but you'll have to go back to the highway, and it's gonna take you a long time with no boots, Native boy. I still think you're crazy."

"Crazy?"

He grinned. "You think it's fun to race dogs and you can't even win."

Then he was gone, laughing, into the blackness of the spruce timber. I could hear only the first few footfalls, then there was just the quiet crackling of the fire and nothing else.

CHAPTER 20

I was alive.

It took me a long time to decide I wasn't really going to die. Not tonight. There could be another fire like this someday. Maybe I'd have Betsy sit around a fire with me, someday. These thoughts occurred to me as I sat there with my head bursting with pain. It would be nice to share a fire with Betsy some day. We could maybe have a picnic, with Mary and Danny, or maybe it could just be a little quiet-talk fire for the two of us. I liked that idea.

I lay there, letting the fire get down to coals, before I moved. Ignoring the pain in my head the best I could, I hunched closer to the fire, wiping out some of Hendrix's symbols as I did so.

With my feet, and with great difficulty and many tries, I managed to push an unburned stick into the coals hard enough to pop an ember out of the fire. By holding the rope that connected my hands to my feet on this ember, I became a trussed-up hunting guide who could stretch out a bit. After another half hour of meticulous work, my hands and feet were free, if a bit scorched, and I carefully set the lash cord aside for my needs.

When I was tied, I was under the mistaken impression that if only I were cut loose, I would feel better. I was sick and sore and even though I knew I wouldn't be getting a quick blade or the smash of a three-hundred-grain bullet this night, the pain was still there. I tried to walk, but the ground kept meeting me halfway. I finally gave up and crawled down the hill to a small creek. I drank and drank, then got sick again. I fell asleep, then awoke and drank some more, feeling a bit better this time, then crawled back to the fire, piled on more wood, and slept.

When I woke up it was midday and drizzly. The fire had been out for ages. I tried standing and this time I made it. The muscles in my arms and legs hurt terribly, but I was apparently whole, except for a large lump on the right side of my head. The headache was still there, and it was still fairly difficult to balance myself while walking.

A thought had occurred to me during the night, but I had been too sick to check on it. Now I crawled up around the rock pile where I'd been ambushed and finally made it back to where I'd been sitting. I reached down behind the rock and grinned as I pulled up both my hip boots. In the melee, Hendrix had missed these. If he had been thinking more clearly, he would have realized I hadn't walked a hundred and fifty miles in those moccasins he'd burned.

I pulled the rubber boots on over my bare feet. I missed my dry socks.

I still had the clothes I wore, an empty backpack, and the cord he had used to tie me. Then I remembered something else. I walked down the hill until I found the broken rifle. I took off the leather sling and stashed it in the backpack, then I used the tongue of my belt buckle for a screwdriver and removed the butt plate from my rifle. The waterproof metal cylinder holding the matches was still there in the hole I'd drilled for it. I took the matches and reluctantly left the rifle there. I felt like burying the rifle, or covering it or something, but even the action was damaged. This one was gone.

I went very slowly down the hillside, using a long stick as a helper. I wanted to get near water. I wanted to get in some dark timber. I wanted to get well.

By the time I reached the edge of the Tazlina River, which was here a large stream, it was getting close to dark again. I made a lean-to of poles and spruce boughs and tossed as many of the large-leafed devil's clubs on top as I could. Then I gathered firewood, built a cozy little fire near the entrance to the lean-to, and lay there until I dozed off. I woke up several times, shivering in the cold, and kept the fire going. By daylight I was feeling a lot more like my old self. My eyesight was managing to stay pretty much in focus all the time now, my head was still sore but only on the outside, and the muscles in my body whimpered rather than screamed when I asked them to move.

It was time for some serious thought and planning. How close I'd come to death I knew only too well. Was all this worth it?

If I went downstream about a half mile, I'd hit Tazlina Lake. If I cut straight north from the lake, in a day or two I'd be back at the highway. I could even consider it my duty to report what I'd learned to Jim Strickland. He'd asked me to, hadn't he?

In two days, three at the most, I could be back in Anchorage checking my phone calls, eating in a good restaurant, and listening on the radio to hear when Hendrix ran into the state police. And he probably would, and I'd play a distant part in that, because at this point I had a pretty good idea where he was heading.

But there I sat with a sore head and an empty stomach, and no food, no coffee, no tea, no knife, no rifle, and thirty air miles from people.

I'd done things better before.

Hendrix was insane, of course. We'd all pretty much figured that out as soon as the camp at Murder Lake had been found. Our very intense chat up the hill there hadn't done anything to change my mind about him, either. But I had learned something. This wasn't just a guy who had gone Bushy and killed some men on a whim. This was a man who could be calculating and who would kill again without thinking about it if he had to. Or even if he didn't have to.

I guess I'd already decided to keep on after him even before the headaches subsided. This was disturbing to me, too, because I'd always considered myself a man who does what is best for society in general. I'm a courteous driver, I wave to old people, and take time to talk to children. If my schedule permits, I volunteer to do volunteer-type stuff. But here I was, deliberately planning to go against everything sane and rational and for-the-public-good and keep tracking this killer. Had he hurt my pride that much by ambushing me? Was that it?

There had to be some altruistic angle to this I could use to ease my conscience, but I hadn't found one yet. I'd keep looking.

Of course, if there was some way of stopping him before he could kill someone else, that would be a good thing to do. There was that.

I'd never seen anything more frightening than the look on Hendrix's face. In it there was a combination of madness, confusion, fear and a certain quality that I'd never seen before. Some might call it animalistic, but those would be people who didn't know animals. A bear will kill you, and very swiftly, too, if the circumstances are right. The difference between a grizzly and Hendrix, though, was that a grizzly would just as soon leave you alone and go fishing. The bear harbors no innate hatred for people, just a solid dislike and a fear that can make it dangerous.

Perhaps it's splitting hairs, since both will kill you, but Hendrix made me shudder as no bear ever would. Maybe there is such a thing as evil. Maybe a force called evil had chosen Lee Hendrix to be an instrument of some perverted wrath, something that had an aversion to good people or good places.

Hendrix would kill again, if he got away. I knew that. He had to be stopped by somebody, and I could justify dogging him until he could be stopped.

But the truth was, he had killed Bill Turner, and I wanted to paint my face black and sing the old song of farewell for my friend. That Hendrix was extremely dangerous game in the woods only added to my growing obsession to stop this man.

I had no idea what I could do to stop him, of course, but I knew I'd have plenty of time to think about it. In the meantime there were the immediate problems of everyday living, and those had to be taken care of first.

CHAPTER 21

Not having a rifle bothered me. In Alaska, you don't go past the outhouse without a rifle. Some men live more than eighty years in the Bush without ever once having to shoot to protect their lives. With others, the need arises the first day or two in the woods. But savvy men up here understand that if that need ever pops up, you'd better be armed and ready.

The rest of the problems I had were fairly manageable. You don't grow up in this country, where the supermarket is a hundred and fifty miles away, without learning how to improvise.

You certainly don't grow up with the two grandfathers I had without learning how to take care of yourself.

I looked around in the river until I found two fairly flat pieces of slate, and rubbed the two flat sides together. They foamed up as though they had soap in them, and then I rinsed them off and began again. In an hour, I had two perfectly flat whetstones. I left one sitting on a log near the fire. If another man found himself here someday, he could have a whetstone and wonder how it came to be here. With the other one, I began putting an edge on my belt buckle. In a couple of hours I had what would pass, in a pinch, for a very sharp brass knife.

And I was in a pinch.

Then I honed the tongue of that buckle until it was as sharp as a new nail. I put the belt and buckle in my pack and began thinking of food. It had been two days since I'd eaten, and it's hard to think properly when you're that hungry.

I found a stout four-foot stick and went hunting. In a twenty-minute walk I found what I needed. He was sitting on the branch of a spruce tree about fifty feet from me, looking as stupid as possible.

The books tell you he's a spruce grouse, but everyone in the woods calls him a spruce hen, regardless of gender. Some of the more roguish Athabascan people say the Great Father put spruce hens and porcupines on earth so white men wouldn't starve.

With my best Hank Aaron grip on the stick, I looked away from the hen and walked toward him obliquely, so that I'd pass within a few feet of him. I watched him out of the corner of my eye, and when I got to within about six feet of him, he decided to become invisible and closed his eyes. I stepped one stride closer and hit a home run.

Back in camp, the fire was ready about the same time he was, and I cooked him slowly with rocks and coals. I'm not sure I've ever eaten anything that tasted as good.

In late afternoon, I turned my attention to salmon. It was getting past time for the really prime salmon, but there were still latecomers straggling up those hundreds of miles from the ocean, looking for that one spot on that one sandbar where they had hatched four years ago. If scientists could ever understand and somehow harness the guidance system of anadromous fish, no one would ever get lost again.

As I looked at the reddish salmon hovering in the wide river, I marveled at them. These fish had been almost to Japan and who knows where else in the Pacific. Then something had flicked a switch in their minds, and they started for home, full of eggs or milt. These were the fish that had made it past the hundreds of miles of net the Japanese and North Korean trawlers put out across Unimak Pass and other places in the Aleutians. These are the fish that later made it past our own commercial fishermen.

They had gone unerringly to the mouth of the correct river and then began to swim against the current to find that one place they knew had to be there. They made it past the sport fishermen angling from the shore. They made it past the eagles and the bears. They jumped waterfalls, slithered over rocks, splashed through water so wide and shallow their backs were out of water. They did all this while rotting—literally. When a salmon enters fresh water, it stops eating. The flesh at its outer edges begins to die as it begins this Herculean task of going home. If it is lucky, there is still enough life left in the fish to spawn when it arrives. If the timing is bad, if heavy rains slow the fish down in its final odyssey, the fish dies without reproducing itself.

The fish who reach that sandbar, maybe six hundred miles up a series of rivers and streams from the ocean, and live to spawn, inspire awe in anyone who understands what happens. Of the eggs they lay in this river, only one in thousands will produce a fish that will return as an adult four years later and spawn. When you take these fish for your own use, especially when they are so close to spawning, you always apologize to them.

I did so, then waded very slowly and quietly to the center of the river. Ahead of me was a flotilla of very tired salmon, several dozen resting in the comparative calm of this pool before challenging the rapids waiting upstream.

I put both hands into the flesh-numbing water ahead of me and then began inching forward toward the rear of a red salmon who looked to be as fit as any. His ugly hooked jaw marked him as a male, a rooster salmon. Inch by inch I went, careful to stir no silt on the creek bottom. In ten minutes, my hands were on either side of him. I was wondering whether they would have enough feeling left in them to catch a fish.

I froze there and watched his movements. He'd swim forward about six inches, then drift slowly back, then swim forward again. I waited for him to repeat this five or six times until I learned his timing. Finally he swam forward, began drifting back, and I grabbed him and threw him well up into the trees with a single motion.

The other salmon panicked at the commotion, but salmon don't panic very seriously, and in less than a minute they were back to their routines. I started a stalk on another fish. I blew my sneak on three of the fish, but managed to get five more in the next couple of hours.

After cleaning and splitting them with my belt buckle, I trimmed away any brown meat I found on them. Fortunately these were pretty sound salmon and didn't have much brown meat. Brown meat is dead. Pink meat is what you want.

With a framework of sticks, I propped the fish up, open side toward the small fire, then piled on all the grass I could pull, along with some dead alder branches, and covered the framework with devil's club leaves. The smoke poured out the cracks and I let the fish cook and smoke for hours. I was still full of spruce hen, and I had picked pocketsful of blueberries to eat as a treat.

When darkness fell, I added more slow-burning fuel to the fire and then waded back across the Tazlina River and made myself as comfortable as I could.

The bear came in after full dark. I heard him whuffing and grousing over on the other side of the river, coming down along the riverside trail toward my smoke fire and my salmon. I was ready for him. It was dark and it was about thirty yards across the river to the fire, but I had a good supply of egg-size stones ready and I let loose a volley at that bear while yelling at the top of my lungs, and I could hear the brush crashing as he ran away up the hill. He didn't come back, and I was glad I'd made the decision not to sleep too close to those fish.

A man without a rifle has limited resources.

When the light came back to the world, I dined on smoked salmon and saw things with new eyes. By careful rationing, and by eating plenty of berries, I would have enough food now for a week, or maybe two.

What I missed, though, was a good cup of coffee. Unfortunately, if Alaska's plants have a substitute for coffee, I don't know what it is. But there is tea. My problem now was in not having a cooking vessel. Hendrix had taken my cooking can with him.

I'd hoped to come across a deserted tin can someplace, but I was just too far back in. So I decided to make a pot out of birch bark. I'd seen it done before, of course, and I'd seen it written up in books, but I'd never thought I'd ever need one so didn't pay much attention.

This was going to take time, I knew. Hendrix had three days' start on me now. Should I take the time and try to make one, or just get back on the trail?

I decided to make the pot. I didn't want to catch up to Hendrix now. If he found me on his trail now, I knew there would be no second chance, even if he did like dog mushers. Besides, I had a theory about our Mr. Hendrix, and proving it didn't include pushing him.

So I put the salmon in my pack and hoisted it with the cord that had bound me well above bear reach, in a tree that was well out of camp, and set about making a bowl out of birch bark.

It took me four tries. There are some things I can be very patient about, and others I just can't stand. When materials don't want to bend the way I want them to bend, and I know they're supposed to, I get filled with wrath. Finally, though, by late afternoon I had fashioned a bowl close to six inches across and about that deep, stitched together with split spruce roots and sealed with pitch.

For supper than evening, to go along with my salmon and berries, I heated some water and made spruce tea. I knew the birch bark wouldn't burn as long as the fire didn't reach above the water line. I scraped out a spot at the edge of the fire, pulled some coals into it, and braced the bowl of water about an inch above it. When the water was boiling, I crumbled in the new needles, the light blue needles at the very tips of the spruce branches.

It was the best spruce tea has ever tasted since the beginning of the world.

The bear came again that night, but this time the fish were hoisted way up in a tree and I was back across the river again. I let him be frustrated over there for about half an hour, then heard him shuffle off. I slept well that night, and the soreness was nearly gone from my body.

CHAPTER 22

For the next five days, I didn't break any land speed records. I made no attempt to find any physical evidence of Hendrix's passing. That would come later. I pretty much knew about where he was going. Or I thought I did. And all I needed was some occasional confirmation.

My lack of speed was not just due to my injuries; I'd pretty much recovered from them and had gained back the strength I'd lost from hunger, too. I was doing well on the salmon and berry diet, even if it was a bit boring, and my cups of spruce tea morning and evening gave me something to look forward to.

I knew Hendrix would still be moving only at night, or if he did move in the daytime, only in the thickest forest. I was perfectly willing to give him all the space he wanted. If he thought that I'd died there, trussed up next to those rocks, fine. If he wanted to think I'd spent the next five days limping painfully toward the highway, wonderful.

By this time, I thought I pretty well knew the man and the mountains and I seemed to know things I wasn't supposed to. When I came across two of his old camps, I wasn't even surprised, because I almost knew they would be there.

The tracking was changing. I didn't need the footprints. I didn't need the broken twigs or tiny threads on the devil's club thorns. The game had become mental now.

The bear and the moose proved it.

The bear came first. I was past the Klutina River, climbing a ridge and heading toward the Tonsina drainage, when I stopped. A bear was coming up the other side of the ridge. When I realized this I smiled, because now I knew. Now the city was gone. The bear was out of sight and out of hearing, but I knew he was there.

There was a bearness, if that's a word, to the place. I checked the wind, and moved downwind so the bear wouldn't smell the fish, gauged where I thought he'd cross the ridge, and waited. In about twenty minutes, the lord of the forest topped the rise just this side of the rock where I thought he'd appear, and wandered off down the mountain on his own business.

The moose, too. This was a cow and calf, and they were lying down in an alder thicket, and although they were out of sight, I knew they were in there as plainly as if they had been wearing flashing lights and a neon arrow.

It's a difficult experience to explain, but it was almost as though the mountains were an extension of my own skin, and I could feel them. This ability frightens a few hunters, so I often soft-pedal it and pretend I heard the animals I've felt or saw their tracks or something.

I can tell by the looks on the faces of some of my hunters that they've fallen prey to the old superstition that Native people are born with supernatural powers . . . second sight. They argue that, since we are supposedly only a few generations removed from a subsistence living in the Bush, the wild ways stay with us better than someone whose ancestors have been building cities for twenty generations.

Occasionally it's convenient to let someone believe that, but the reality is that people who spend all their time in the mountains, regardless of race or background, are liable to get a bit sensitive to what's going on around them. The truth is that no animal, no human, nothing at all, can move through the land without disrupting some balance the land enjoyed before.

When the bear travels, berries are crushed underfoot and disappear into his maw. Animals move back well away from his path. Once the bear begins eating salmon, his mere presence leaves behind a strong odor.

When the moose ambles through, his heavy hooves punch deep into the tundra or the mud, crushing plants that spring back very slowly, the tracks filling with water in an almost silent sucking oozing that goes nearly unnoticed by anything else.

Man, of course, leaves more of a disturbing wake behind than any other animal. Everyone else in the forest is afraid of him and will scatter at his approach. He often leaves harsh and unnatural scents behind him, marks on the country that don't heal soon, and sounds that don't fit anywhere in nature's repertoire.

So, if each animal leaves these myriad signs behind and shock waves ahead as it goes, and in the center of this activity is something that smells and sees and breathes and hears and makes sounds, is it so surprising that some animals, including man, can sometimes acknowledge this presence from a distance without understanding why?

It's all I can think of for an answer, at any rate. But it happens only when the frustration and rush of the traffic has been replaced by the music of the mountains. Sometimes the first we notice is a slight interruption in the music. Sometimes it's just knowing something is there that doesn't belong.

In tracking Hendrix, I was going out of my way to avoid him. I wanted him well ahead of me. By this time, I knew him well enough to be able to spot his camps long before I got to one of them. It became a game with me, as one day went into two and three and then five and six. I reveled in it the more attuned I became to Hendrix and to these Chugach Mountains we both traveled through. I knew just about where he'd stop for his day's rest, and at least half the time, I'd find his camp within a hundred feet or so of where I guessed.

When it rained, I'd sit under the densest spruce tree I could find with my pack over my head trying to keep as dry as I could. I missed my jacket. At night, I'd build a small fire in some large rocks or against a cutbank and stick myself between it and the fire as though I were some johnnycake in a reflector oven. When the trail was smooth, I took the hip boots off and hung them upside down from the pack and I walked barefooted. It was a good feeling, once I got used to it. It reminded me of the summer I bought a Popsicle just for old times' sake, to rekindle some childhood feelings.

As the days went by, my feet got tougher, and I spent more and more time each day out of the hip boots. In colder weather, when the sting of Alaska came through the single layer of rubber in the boots, I put some moss down in the bottom to help insulate my bare feet. It could never replace clean socks.

Twice I stopped for the entire afternoon and night, replenishing my supply of salmon with fresher fish. I wasn't out, but I'd rather carry a lot of food and not need it than need it and not have it.

I kept a close eye on the tracks Hendrix left on the ground, careful to note how fresh they were, dating them by the last rains, and backing off if I thought I was getting any closer than three days to Hendrix.

Once you get the hang of it, dating tracks isn't really that difficult. When a footprint is made in thin mud, such as one would have during a heavy rain, the water outside the track rushes back into the track, caving the track walls inward. If the track is made after a rain, when the ground has time to dry a bit but is still sticky, the impression of the boot will send the wall edges outward, as though the track were an explosion.

If the day after that is dry, the top edges of the track will dry and crumble. Two days of dry, and most of the wall will crumble.

Three days is a little harder to tell, depending on whether it has rained since the tracks were made. If it rains on the second day, for example, the edges of the track won't be of much use, but the condition of the tread marks can be.

The only way I know to learn this is to look at the tracks I made yesterday and see what they look like. When I camp for the night, I can always see what the night and the night's weather has done to the tracks I left at the edge of camp the day before. When I was learning, I would deliberately make tracks on different kinds of surface, gravel bars, mud, dry dirt, and so forth, then go back each day and look at them to see what had happened.

I was trying to stay three days behind Hendrix for several reasons. Another rendezvous with him would lead only to another fatality: mine. I didn't want that. Also, by staying far enough back from him, and watching the wind, I could have my fire every night. With no hat and no jacket, no sleeping bag or tent, the little fire was nearly as necessary to my survival as the food. Perhaps it was just as necessary.

He was traveling slowly, but of course I was, too. A man just doesn't walk around through the Alaska Bush as though he's lord of everything when he's armed with only a sharp belt buckle. I stayed in open areas, keeping note of the wind at all times, and avoided going through the denser forested parts where I might meet someone who had lived there longer and thought he had an exclusive lease on the place. Lee Hendrix wasn't the only dangerous animal in the mountains.

But mostly I avoided trouble just by traveling slowly and listening to the land for the things it could tell me. It said the right things, and so I just kept going, with my feet hardening more every day to the sharp rocks and roots. These long days took me along the northern slope of the Chugach Mountains, and was almost like a vacation because I didn't really have to worry about Hendrix for a while. That gave me the luxury of putting him on the back burner, and so I talked to birds and animals. No, I'm not Doctor Doolittle, and they didn't talk back . . . it's just sometimes fun to talk to animals.

A short-tailed weasel tagged along for two days to bum salmon scraps. At least I think it was the same weasel. He was his ordinary summer brown now, but I knew he'd turn a brilliant white in winter and become known as ermine, especially if a trapper caught him then.

Hendrix's trail led back into the secret places, the pretty places in the Chugach Mountains. He waded rivers up where few venture, and went through saddles in the mountains that led to even more remote canyons. I found Hendrix's tracks across the saddles, where the migrations of caribou had worn away the tundra grasses, leaving dirt instead. But mostly I kept track of him by knowing about where he was going and taking the easiest routes to get there. I located his camps, more by feel than by anything else at this point, until it became a game with me. I came to know Hendrix's methods in the woods pretty well.

One fact became clear; he certainly didn't expect any problems from me, or from behind. He made his camps where he could see the backtrail, but he also built a little fire every night. Each of these fires would be invisible to anyone ahead of him on the trail, which led me to believe he was concerned about what lay ahead, but not with what lay behind.

I tracked him down Stuart Creek to the Richardson Highway and the oil pipeline as they climbed toward Thompson Pass. Hendrix had come upon the highway in daylight, evidently, because I found a dry fireless camp about a hundred and fifty yards up in the trees on the west side of the pass. He had obviously waited here many hours, until full darkness had fallen. From the plastic wrappers he left in this camp, he was still enjoying Mrs. Manning's piroshkis. I'd have to tell her about it. If she ever sold them, she could use it as advertising.

"Mrs. Manning's Hermetically Sealed Piroshkis . . . the choice of mass murderers everywhere."

Catchy.

When Hendrix had crossed the highway and vanished into the timber on the other side, he had done it at a high lope. Since Valdez had become the terminus for the pipeline, traffic is pretty brisk, like one car every five or ten minutes or so. Enough so Hendrix wouldn't waste any time out in the open.

This was the place where I had to check tracks very carefully. If he was heading for Valdez, he would have stayed within sight of the highway, following it until he crossed Thompson Pass, a fairly easy route through the mountains and down to tidewater.

But after a long afternoon of checking and rechecking tracks, I was certain Hendrix planned to take the longer route by hugging the Copper River through its timber and canyons and tangles of cliff down to the sea. Following the river's valley would bring him out to the coast a ways east of Cordova. He would emerge in an uninhabited area of tidal mud flats, scarred bluffs and hunter's paradise.

I had to be certain, first. I checked for more than a mile, and Hendrix had stayed to deep timber and had moved slowly through the trees down the Tiekel River toward its confluence with the huge Copper. There was no mistake.

Cordova, then.

Cordova had been the home of Captain Pete Hansen. By this time, that almost had to be the answer. Cordova is approached only by air or by sea. A highway from the town up the old railroad route next to the Copper River was begun decades ago but ends at what locals call the million-dollar bridge to nowhere.

I found a moose trail on the side of the hill above the highway, hidden well in timber, and perched myself on a log slowly turning to shredded wheat.

It was time to think.

What was it Mrs. Hansen had said? *Crab Cove.* The name of the boat and the name of the place, a place somewhere west of Cordova near Simpson Bay, off the stunning waters of Prince William Sound.

If Hendrix continued to follow the Copper River down its channel, he'd be at least another week on the trail and then would have to bypass Cordova without being seen and make his way west of the fishing community to near Simpson Bay.

I'd never been there, but I'd checked it out on the map—a rugged sawtooth of fiords with serious glaciers backing them up. Dozens of tiny little coves and hideaways lay all along this coast. Hundreds, maybe. I remembered all too clearly the look in Hendrix's eyes when I mentioned the water, and that's when I began to think of what Mrs. Hansen had said. Good shelter in a storm. Mountains going straight up. A little waterfall pouring straight into the sea. A perfect place for a retirement cabin.

That description might help in some areas of the world, but in Prince William Sound, that could describe most of thousands of miles of spectacular coastline.

There was something else, too. Prince William Sound and southeast Alaska are the two most likely places I've seen for a man to live off the land fairly comfortably. Fish and crabs abound in the waters. Edible clams can be dug up on almost any beach. Blacktail deer and black bear live in the forests. Mountain goats live higher among the glaciers. And the huge timber along this stretch of coast is so tall and so dense that it wouldn't be impossible to hide a village in there, let alone a single cabin. If I were on the dodge, this would be a great place for me to hole up.

Somehow I knew this had to be the answer. Pete Hansen had been an old hand in the sound, and he hadn't taken chances. At the first sign of a storm, his widow had said, he'd head for cover, and his favorite cover had been this place he'd called Crab Cove near Simpson Bay . . . enough of a favorite that he'd named his boat for it.

Think for a minute, Jeep. You're Hendrix. If you wanted to find Hansen alone, where and when? In Crab Cove during a storm.

Maybe.

If that happened, how many storms must you wait through until the boat sought shelter there? Hendrix might have waited. Maybe.

But that was, I thought, a pretty strong maybe and at that point really all I had to go on. I had to gamble on where he was going, but I'd been gambling ever since I closed the door on that Super Cub up in the Talkeetnas, so it wasn't anything new.

What I wanted now was to reach the ocean before Hendrix did. Long before Hendrix did. By taking the Copper River Canyon, he was making it a lot easier for me. He had evidently elected to stay to the river bottoms, rather than try to cut over the tops of the peaks, and that was all to my good. Red had told me he'd pulled Hendrix off sheep duty because Hendrix seemed to be afraid of the high stuff.

Would he still be afraid? Sure. I didn't think he'd even have much reason to rush things. He certainly wasn't worried about me. So what if I'd made it back to the highway and told the police where he'd been? That was a long time and many miles from here, and there still hadn't been search planes looking for him. He had plenty of food and water. Why rush?

This all worked to my benefit now. I had no idea what I'd do with Hendrix when we'd meet again, but I knew I wanted to get to the ocean well before he did.

So it was up to me to frighten myself on the high cliffs. I figured if I hustled right along, I'd only have to spend maybe two nights in the barren lands, making the dense timber along the coast in three days. Hendrix would be at least a week getting to the same place. Those four extra days would give me some time to think. Some time to plan. Some time to look for Crab Cove.

CHAPTER 23

It took me more than a day to get to the Tasnuna River drainage and find a likely looking canyon to follow.

There was a lot of work to do first, however. I spent the day gathering berries and spruce needles, which I stuck away in the pack for food and tea. The rest of the day and part of the next morning I spent gathering the lightest, driest spruce firewood I could locate. I tied these in six-foot lengths to the pack, so they hung down to my knees and stuck up well above my head. I was a man traveling alone in the rainy season in the high country with neither hat nor jacket. One little bit of nasty weather with no shelter and no fire, and I'd die right there. It wasn't a pleasant thought, so I added some extra sticks to the already heavy pack.

Then I padded my hip boots with fresh moss, pulled them on, and started up a good-sized stream that flowed down from the Chugach Mountains. By lunch break, when I got into the salmon, I was just at the last fringe of alders. By the time I'd climbed all I wanted that day and stopped to make a fire, I was very high in the mountains in a long treeless tundra canyon that cut deeply back into the soul of the range. High above, ahead of me up the canyon, a band of Dall sheep skittered away. It made me wish I still had my monocular, to see just how big those two rams were. The hunter in me, I guess.

That night was unforgettable. It was clear and crisp and quiet. As it got dark I saw the moon would be full soon. That would help Hendrix, but I didn't care much, because I had this feeling that it didn't matter. What mattered was then and there, that night.

189

There was a little dry gully on the right flank of the watercourse, and I built my tiny fire there. It was a good place. Not a particularly scenic spot. I couldn't see back down the canyon or out onto the flats where the Copper River roamed. I couldn't see the peaks that I knew had to be at the head of the canyon, in this tiny portion of the world. But when you can see peaks, peaks can see you and blow their cold breath down upon you. In my condition, I'd leave the scenery for later and huddle tight to my small fire. It was enough.

As most other bush Alaskans would, I, too, wondered if I were the first to camp in this canyon. Since it had a pretty fair stream of water in it, prospectors had probably been here. But when? Sixty years ago? Eighty?

With something like twenty-five hundred acres for every Alaskan, this country up here isn't exactly overcrowded. And when you realize that half of Alaska's people live in or around Anchorage, that thins out the boonies even more.

So it is probably true to say that an outdoorsman up here has quite a few times stood where no one else in history has ever stood, has seen a particular view from a particular place that has never been focused on a human retina before.

The only way this country got properly mapped was with aerial photos first, and later, satellite photos. I wondered what this little canyon of mine would look like on a map. Just some velvety tundra ridges that would be translated by someone in a sterile room in a large building, with large drawing tables, into contour lines.

This night I wouldn't have the trees to hang the pack in, out of bear reach. If there were bears around, they could come into camp and eat that salmon in the pack, but I wasn't worried about that. I'd just keep a small fire going and trust that that would keep any bear out of mischief.

I can't sweat the bears tonight, I thought. Hey, the moon is nice and see how it makes black gashes in the other canyon wall where the little gullies are? Hear the creek bubbling on down through these barren uplands toward the hidden forest well below? This is a magic night, Jeep. Relax and enjoy it. Your body is strong now, stronger than it has been in months. Your mind is tuned to the mountains like a 440 A tuning fork. It's a good evening to brew up some of that noxious spruce-needle tea, spice it with some blueberries, and pretend it's a party and it tastes really good.

So I did, and I lay back against the dry tufty tundra and looked out at the moon and I could almost smell the ocean on the other side of the starry mountain peaks to my right.

The night was clear and special and worth remembering, for with each night that goes by, we lose a little of ourselves. We lose a second in the time span of our bodies. We come a bit closer to being old, to sitting in that lonely cabin like old Charlie and dreaming of black bear roasts. We come that much closer to joining Chulyen and the ones who have gone before us in the villages.

I'd doze and then wake up and toss some more small pieces of wood on the fire. Then I'd doze and the next time I woke it would be cold, so I'd build the fire up and make a cup of tea and walk out away from it for a minute to see the moonlight and the mountains, then I'd go back to the fire and look deep into the embers searching for whatever it is we all look for there.

It was morning too soon, and I ate and started onward.

There were two really big turns farther up the canyon, about five miles apart, before I saw the actual crest. It was hung with its glaciers and multiple peaks, demanding respect at the top of the canyon. One branch of the canyon went through a low glacial gap to the left of a central peak, the other to the right of it. I took the one to the right, knowing I needed to head in that general direction.

I spent that night, that very cold night, at the foot of a glacier just below the crest, and used the remainder of my wood trying to keep warm. That glacier was like some prehistoric beast, groaning and cracking in its bowels like a dinosaur whose time has come and gone. It was a spooky night, and I was glad to see the sun come back and to find myself still there.

I munched salmon on the trail that morning, climbing slowly but steadily up the right flank of the glacier, watching each step to avoid falling into the crevasses where the dirty ice met the mountain.

Dall sheep appeared above me and watched curiously, and I wondered if they'd ever seen a human before. It was unlikely. This was well away from any of the prime hunting areas.

Then, suddenly, I was in nearly vertical rocks, and I picked my way very carefully around one peak only to find it was the knee of a still taller and rougher one behind it.

I've never been a mountain climbing enthusiast. As far as I'm concerned, the only reason those sport climbers rope themselves together is to keep the smart ones from going home. There hasn't been a lot on those cliffs I needed, and I always believed if I couldn't get my hunter a shot on a ram without overly endangering his life, I didn't deserve my license.

I rested once, on a ledge, and turned around and looked back. The view took my breath away. There was Mount Billy Mitchell just across from me, and farther away to the north were the Wrangells. The peaks to the right just kept blending together off into the Yukon Territory of Canada. To the far north, turning hazy blue in the distance, were the peaks of the Talkeetna Mountains. Could I really have come this far in just . . . what was it? Two weeks? No. Three? Something like that. It didn't matter. It seemed a lifetime away by now.

Sitting high on that mountain in the wind, with no jacket and no more firewood, I did the only thing I could do to keep warm: I ate. I ate fish and berries until I couldn't hold any more. I wanted all the calories in me I could hold, and it didn't hurt my feelings that the pack was lighter with every meal, too. At least I didn't have to carry any more firewood.

I rested until I couldn't stand the bite of the wind any more, then rose and began climbing from rock to rock up a talus slope. I'd climb two or three rocks, then rest and breathe. Then climb two or three more and rest.

It went on and on and that's why I was so surprised when the next rock was level with the one I was on. I raised my head and found myself on the very roof of Alaska's coast, the crest of the Chugach Range.

Before me was a splendor of tiny green canyons and muddy blue glaciers, all mingling and carving their ways to the sea. And out there I could see pieces of Prince William Sound through breaks in the clouds. Mountains rising straight up from the ocean. A paradise by anyone's measure.

I hunkered down in the lee of some rocks and watched and planned. I could see a few fishing boats down there, and that's really why I knew where Cordova was. I couldn't see the town from there. I needed to find a way down that would put me off to the west of Cordova.

I found the way. By slowly working my way down a long rocky ridge to the right, I could drop into what looked to be a long canyon that had to end in the sea and not in another glacier.

I tried it. It worked.

By nightfall, I was sitting by a cheery fire down in a heavily forested canyon, and my pack was hanging in a tall spruce tree. There was no wind down here, no noises but those of the creek.

If this came out opposite a huge island, I'd know just where I was.

CHAPTER 24

t did.

I reached the ocean around noon the next day, and fell in love once again with the very different world of Alaska's rainforest. It is a world teeming with life and yet tells tales of long-dead cultures. Its monstrous trees are like the bones of ancient animals and the crux of life itself. They shut out the sun and are often covered so heavily in moss as to appear smothered. And there is water. Everywhere.

From the Kenai Peninsula all the way through Prince William Sound and on down to Ketchikan—more than a thousand miles—this rainforest belt is cut every hundred yards or so, it seems, by creeks, streams, rivers, rivulets, branches, seeps, springs, and waterfalls.

There is also the feel of the rainforest. The gray cloud cover almost always hangs between the offshore islands and the peaks of the coastal ranges to bring out the pungency of life that is always moving and search-ing and living, and yet smells constantly of decay. The mammoth spruce and hemlock trees fall quietly onto thick carpets of ferns and mosses, and in time they turn to shreds and add to the thick layer of organic padding that carpets the forest. It is a silent place to walk, with thick underbrush pretty well limited to the banks of streams, where the sunlight reaches in.

There are the smells, too.

From the forest itself the sweet smell of growth rises over the rich scents of decay, while along the shoreline, there is the sticky smell of miles and miles of mud flats. This is accentuated by the odors of rotting fish and the bathtub ring of stranded, decomposing kelp at the high tide line.

Other than the occasional scream of a bald eagle, there is little sound in this country except the sweet song of fresh mountain water plunging down the steep slopes through tiny thickets of devil's club and alders as it fans into the sea. At low tide, these little creeks carve meandering trails through the mud flats until they finally make it home, leaving behind lacelike patterns that are different each time the tide goes out.

Then there is the rain, which suddenly drops the clouds down to the water and hides the giant timber. These aren't the sudden thunderstorms of the Interior, but the slow and steady soaking rains that seem to penetrate to the bones of men and animals and the forest alike.

I loved it.

My shortcut through the mountains had brought me out about five miles or so west of Cordova, but out of sight of that community. A long headland was in the way.

A pass lay to the south between the mountainous island and the headland, and I could just see the flashing light from its buoy through the fog. If I was right, my course would go west from here, toward Simpson Bay, so I started off.

The rains caught me before I'd traveled an hour through the forest. Deep soaking rains. Rains that fell in sheets. Cold rains.

In less than a minute I was as wet as I was ever going to be. Even my feet inside the hip boots weren't spared, as the rain ran down my face and back and chest and into the tops of the boots. Twice I took them off and dumped them out.

With no hat and no jacket, I was in a tough spot. If I had had enough warning, I could have thrown together a lean-to and built a fire. Now I had a tough decision to make.

I was very cold and was shivering uncontrollably. The muscles in my back and shoulders were cramping severely. I could either try to set up a camp and get a fire going, or keep moving and hope to find a cabin or abandoned mine shack or an old dead cannery. Such things could be found along this coast occasionally, I knew, but I had no idea how far it might be before I found one.

I had a hunch I should keep moving, and I followed it. I needed shelter, and I would just have to hope my hunch was right. I bowed my head against the rain and hugged the coastline, staying just back in the trees and following what I knew to be an old bear trail. At least I wouldn't have to worry about bears today. When it rains, they stay home.

I kept on, shivering violently, and looking for anything that might be a clue to some habitation. As it was, I felt so miserable that when it came, I almost missed it. It was in the next small cove.

I'd been slogging along in the trees, following the bear trail, when the trail suddenly veered off to the right, heading inland. Bears don't give up a good route for nothing. If there are fish along the shore, they'll walk along that shore, fishing the creeks and rivers and watching for targets of opportunity at high tide.

From what I could see, there wasn't any obvious reason for the bears to swing inland. There was the trace of an old trail that branched off and hugged the shore, but it had been overgrown for many years.

I decided to follow it, and that's how I found the log cabin, about a hundred yards away. That it was empty was obvious: no smoke from the stovepipe, no light in the window despite the gathering darkness. I hurried across the clearing and went in quickly.

The cabin was dry, and it held groceries and books and everything a person would need. It hadn't been lived in for a very long time, though. A fire was laid in both the wood cookstove and the wood heater, and with violently shaking hands, I managed to get them going, although it took four matches to do it.

As soon as the chill started coming off the cabin, I stripped and wrapped myself in a blanket from the bunk. Before full darkness had set in, the spasms had relaxed to the point where I could light the kerosene lamp without breaking it.

I was glad this was the cabin of a single man. One single bunk. Almost everything within reach of that bunk. One small table that folded against the wall. Two chairs. The two chairs were the mark of an optimist. There were table settings for two in the cupboard, too. This was the habitation of a trapper or prospector who hoped he'd have company for dinner, but expected any visitor to leave before bedtime.

The cabin was about twelve by twelve feet inside, and because it was small, it heated quickly. I added more fuel to the fires, and in less than an hour, all the inborn chill that had had years to seep into the log walls had been run out by the vibrant heat of the two stoves. In about an hour and a half, I began to think my own body would survive its chilling and might actually function again. I had half a pot of real coffee inside me now, thanks to the stores of my unknown benefactor, and I was heating a large pot of canned lasagna.

My clothes were hung up to dry, my boots hung upside down, well away from the fire. I looked around and found some dry clothes my host had stuffed in a trunk beneath the bunk. Among them, much to my thrill, were a half-dozen pairs of clean socks. I took two out, put one pair on my cold feet, and tucked the other away in the pack.

Later, with the rain still pounding on the roof and the fires blasting away, and my belly full of lasagna and even more coffee, I sat down and wrote a long note to my host.

I needed some things from this cabin, things that I would take only if I knew this sourdough could do without them. There are some things that can never be borrowed. You never take a man's only ax, but borrowing a gun during an emergency is acceptable under the Unwritten Law. As long as it's returned promptly.

Cabins in the Bush aren't locked, just fastened. The only thing inhospitable about them is that Swede saw blade nailed along the outer edge of the door to keep bears from pulling it open.

I've met some of the nicest people through those who needed to use either my camp or my cabin in my absence. When I returned, here would be a few dollars, some extra firewood cut and brought in, a new fire laid, and a note from a new friend.

Alaska is a hard place, at times. You do what you can for the next guy.

In this case, it was my turn to borrow some items. In the past, I'd never borrowed more than warmth, light, and maybe some coffee, but this was life and death, and I was going to have to take advantage of my host's generosity well beyond the ordinary.

When I finished the letter, I rummaged around and explored the cabin and the two trunks on its false porch. There were no guns in the cabin, but I hadn't expected to find any: a man always carries his rifle and sleeping bag with him. But one of those trunks was more or less a tool box and inside it I found an old Marble's sheath knife from the 1920s, complete with a leather sheath that looked to be from the Jurassic Age. The knife was razor sharp, which I expected from a sourdough as well prepared as this one. There was also a small whetstone, which I borrowed. There was a decent set of black oilskins in the trunk under the bunk, and a black rain hat to go with it. Two sweaters and a light jacket were also added to the debt I owed my host. Some coffee and macaroni and sugar and pea-nut butter were stuffed in the pack, also.

When I lay back in the bunk beneath three blankets and watched the fire shadows from the stove lids flickering on the ceiling, listening to the cracks and pops of the fires, I finally relaxed and gave some thought to where I was and what I was doing.

I knew only too well how close a call it had been for me. Death had ridden my heels since the rain began, but I had outrun it, thanks to bears that didn't want to come close to a cabin. I owed the big black bears of Prince William Sound a solid debt.

As I lay there, I wondered whether Hendrix was in the same rain that caught me here. He certainly wouldn't be on the coast by now.

Taking the long way around like that, Hendrix would be bucking ter-rible brush along the Copper River for at least two more days, and maybe three. Then he'd come out onto the Copper River Delta mud flats and have to work to bypass Cordova. So he was at least three, perhaps four, days behind me.

This would give me time to do the snooping I needed to do in this vast beautiful land of fiords and glaciers and mystery. With luck, I'd have found what I needed before Hendrix came through this way and. . . .

I sat straight up in bed.

Retrieving the letter I had written to my unseen host, I rewrote the last page and signed it with Danny Manning's name and my Anchorage phone number on it. If I had found this cabin, Hendrix could certainly stop here, too. It wouldn't do to tip him off that Jeep George hadn't limped back to the Richardson Highway and out of his life.

There was another thing, too. If for some reason I wasn't able to repay my host, Betsy and Danny would see to it.

With the new signature on the letter, I stretched out and let some quiet rain music come back into my head. I was close now. I was getting close now.

Sometime in the night my eyes closed and I slept.

CHAPTER 25

The rain quit about midway through breakfast. As I cleaned up and hauled more wood into the cabin for my host, the world dripped quietly and the trees slipped in and out of fogs and ground clouds. A mysterious country, all in all.

I closed up well, took up my pack with the borrowed booty, and started walking the coastal bear trails again.

For miles and miles, the rugged coastline makes life difficult for a man on foot. I kept looking around each bend, checking the head of each little fiord. Around noon, a fishing boat sailed past with her outriggers set, and I stepped back into the trees until she had gone. Until I either proved or disproved my theory about Hendrix, I didn't want to have to answer questions about who I was and what I was doing out here alone.

The rain held off overnight, but I stuck a lean-to together anyway, far up the hill from the bear trail. Late the second day I found another cabin to bunk in. This one hadn't hosted anything but porcupines and bears for years, and it took me the best part of an hour to swamp it out and make it livable. There was a nest of red voles under the sink, and I dispossessed them and moved my things into the cabin.

It began raining in the morning, and I hiked through a drizzle into deep coves, around the end of fiords, and out around the points of land that stick out into the sound. Each time a new headland would go behind me, I'd get confident and hopeful, much as a man with a trapline will, but I found nothing.

Until late that afternoon.

The waters of Simpson Bay were roiling from a storm coming in off the Pacific, but I looked across the fiord and noticed a hidden headland sticking out. It would have been unrecognizable but for the waters at its entrance, which were calm as glass while the rest of the bay seethed with trouble. I marked where it was, and continued walking around the head of the fiord until I thought I must be fairly close to the calm waters I'd seen.

It was completely dark by this time, so I climbed well up the mountain away from the trail. I built a tiny fire, covered myself with the blankets, and slept.

I was up before the sun, with light filtering through the foggy forest making dull the mountains rising above, and the soft smell of the ocean to my left. I chewed a piece of salmon as I walked through the silent forest, and then there was the whuff, whuff, whuff of wings and the raven flew across my path.

"Good morning, Chulyen," I said. "May your children all be fat, and may you show me what I need this day."

The raven turned and came back across my path, probably out of curiosity, before heading down through some trees toward tidewater. I followed him.

I heard the waterfall before I saw it, coming down a steep rock cliff to the right. I stepped through the mossy rocks around it, and remembered Mrs. Hansen's description of her husband's *Crab Cove*, with the waterfall. But I'd already passed a dozen such falls, or what could have passed for waterfalls, since reaching the coast. Why would this one have to be the one?

Well, there were the two passes of the raven. There was the quiet water I had spotted from across the fiord, indicating some kind of cove or hideaway over here. Then there was just this feeling I had, a feeling that things were coming together, a culmination of trails, if you will.

This almost had to be the place Lee Hendrix was heading for, because he was that kind of man, and sometimes when the feelings are so strong, you don't argue with them, but accept them and save the analysis for winter nights in front of the fireplace.

I heard the soft lapping of water in some tall brush to my left, and headed that way. My foot slipped on a smooth rock and I grabbed a branch to steady myself and nearly fell headlong. The branch had come loose in my hand. So did the next one.

Very slowly, I stepped into this pseudo-thicket of rootless brush, walking out into deeper and deeper water as I did so. Just before the seawater crested over my hip boots, I pulled one more branch aside and there it was.

I didn't have to go to the bow or the stern to read the words "*Crab Cove*" on it, but I did, anyway. It was a white boat, with neat red trim . . . the boat of someone who loved boats. The name was in red, too. Hendrix hadn't painted that out yet. I scrambled aboard and looked at the stack of crab pots piled in the stern, then pulled some more camouflaging brush to one side and entered the wheelhouse.

There was nothing there, nor down in the hold, that could shed any obvious light on the fates of Captain Pete Hansen or his deckhand Chip.

The galley was well stocked with food, the diesel tanks nearly full. There were oilskins and clothes for the fishermen still in the lockers. There were no keys in the ignition, but I knew where those keys had to be, and where they had undoubtedly been for more than half a year. Built into the cabinetry was the boat's radio, but the large dent in the front, along with the smashed glass, spoke of why Hendrix wanted to buy a new one. But nothing there explained how it had happened, or why. Springlines held the *Crab Cove* firmly to trees ashore, and the camouflaging with brush was so thorough it would be little short of miraculous if someone sailing by found this boat.

No wonder Pete Hansen had liked this little cove. From the boat's wheelhouse roof, I could see that it had everything a man could want for a retirement home—the waterfall just feet away, huge timber cloaking the shore like mossy blankets. A cove enclosed by wooded spits jutting out into the fiord, snugging this little piece of calm water within its arms. Ahead of the boat about a hundred yards was a flat where the ground leveled off away from the ocean and extended back, cloaked in bright green grasses until it was swallowed up by the blackness of the forest. That would be the place where Pete Hansen would have built his retirement cabin, of course.

The boat was tied to timber on a shore that rose in a series of terraces up the mountainside to the right. This was primeval rainforest. You could go twenty feet into this and completely vanish.

I checked the boat's engine, which seemed to be in good working order, then quickly borrowed a couple of parts that would keep this boat right where it was until they were put back.

I took some food out of the galley, along with extra matches and both sets of oilskins and hats from the lockers. I also found several hundred feet of line and took that with me. I left the boat, stashed the goods well back in the woods, and then came back.

Where were Pete Hansen and Chip—what was his last name? Browning? That was it. Chip Browning. Well, Pete Hansen and Chip Browning, you're dead of course, but what kind of death did you have? Despite a thorough search, I found no blood on the boat. Out on the deck, I looked through the stack of crab pots, and there was the answer. There was the answer that stopped me cold in my tracks and made me shiver under those warm sweaters.

A crab pot is a round basket of sorts that sits on the bottom of the ocean. It is baited with a dead fish in it. A crab walks in to eat the dead fish, but he can't walk out again. The pot is attached to a long line which is attached to a float with identification and a number.

Six pots were stowed on the deck. They were all numbered. Numbers 2 and 5 were missing. I wondered if Hansen had Number 2 or Number 5 for his final resting place beneath Prince William Sound.

I never knew Pete Hansen, but I knew his kind. Alaska's fishing industry exists only because there are men like Pete Hansen who go out on the rough seas and risk their lives, and fight a frustrating battle against foreign interests, low prices at the canneries and high costs for fuel and ice.

Commercial fishermen in Alaska have to be impassioned about the way of life even to consider it. Someday, I always told myself, someday I was going to find someone like Pete Hansen who would let me go along and help for a trip, just so I can see what is so alluring about Alaska's waters that men will face seas as high as hills to earn their living.

There were some dirty dishes in the galley, and I went back in and checked them carefully this time. The two coffee cups had a gritty residue in them that shouldn't have been there from just a cup of coffee. I took them carefully out, holding them by a twig through the handles so I didn't touch them, and hid them up in the brush, then replaced them with two other cups. The boys at the state crime lab might like to take a close look at that residue one day soon. It might clear up another mystery.

I thought I knew, though. When Hansen and Browning were deep in the grip of whatever kind of dope that had been, Hendrix had taken the *Crab Cove* to sea, probably at night. For a big man like Hendrix, it wouldn't have been much trouble at all to put the unconscious men in the crab pots and toss them over the side. He'd have cut the buoy ropes; there'd be no trace left on the surface.

Before the icy waters took them, did they awaken just for that second or two? Did they have any idea what was happening to them as they went to the bottom to feed crabs?

I was really happy at that moment that I wasn't the police officer who would have to tell Mrs. Hansen how her Pete and that nice young man Chip had died. Nobody could pay me enough money to take a job like that. I wondered if police officers knew a way of sugarcoating such news, or if they just called a friend to come over, or a minister as they did with Karen, and tell her that her husband's body was forever attracting crabs at the bottom of the sound.

With the buoy missing, no one would ever be able to locate and recover those two grisly pots. When the crabs had finished their business, they wouldn't be able to leave. They would starve and die, attracting more crabs. It would go on like that, I knew, until time and sea water were able to break down chicken wire and rebar and stop the years of killing.

This was enough for me. At least for now. I gathered my gear and went ashore with it, then carefully replaced the brush Hendrix had used to hide the boat. I just wanted to get away from this death boat and sit on a rock and think.

By walking on rocks and tree roots, I was able to climb up to the first terrace, some thirty or so vertical feet above the boat, without leaving any tracks. When I reached the second tier of terraces, I walked away from the boat more than a quarter of a mile and set up a dry camp there for the rest of the day.

How much time did I have to decide what to do? One day? Two? How fast could Hendrix walk down the Copper River? Did the town of Cordova slow him down more than he planned? He would still be moving at night for the most part, but if he stayed back in the trees, away from the shore, he could march along with a red suit and a brass band. You could hide whole towns in this rainforest.

How many weeks had it been? I'd long ago lost track of what day it was. This trail seemed awfully long, but it had ended at last. All that was left now was to let the police know where this boat is and let them handle it.

There was just one little problem with that. If I walked back to Cordova to tell the police, I'd meet Hendrix on the trail.

There was always the chance I could flag down a passing fishing boat and call police that way, I supposed. But was this the end of it for me? Did I want to let it end there? He was coming, and there was a little time. Without those two engine parts he wasn't going anywhere except on foot, and he couldn't replace them anywhere short of Cordova, unless he should happen on another fishing boat tied up, waiting out a storm. I shuddered to think of what would happen then to whoever was on board.

No. Somehow, I had to find a way to hold him for the police.

I ate some canned chili, cold, that long afternoon and evening, enjoying the luxury of it. It began raining just before dark, and I sat there in oil-skins with my head on my knees and just let it rain. There was the comfort of the boat's cabin, of course, but to be caught there would be instant death. Also, I doubted I'd get much rest in it.

So I sat, shivering occasionally, and dozed while I waited out the night. It wasn't the first time, and I was getting used to it. After this hunt, going after bear from a tent camp would seem like calling room service from a suite in the Captain Cook.

Hendrix had to have some vulnerable spot. He had to have that Achilles heel that could be worked against him. But every time I considered differ-ent possibilities, I kept coming back to the undeniable: this was a dangerous, crazy man with a rifle, and I was just a hunting guide who hadn't come out too well the last time we met.

A guide's job is to lead the way to the quarry, of course. I'd done that. But somehow I couldn't simply wash my hands of this sordid mess.

Not now. I'd have to think of some way of keeping him here until the police could get here, or he'd be gone, at the first sign of trouble, into that dark timber, and we'd be right back where we'd started.

If I could turn the tables on Hendrix some way, if I could get him in a position where I could give him a smack on the head with a good club and truss him up as he had done to me, he'd be a much more manageable package for the Alaska State Troopers.

This would take some thought, but it was a long, wet night and I didn't have a whole lot else to do. I even allowed my thoughts to return to Betsy and that last evening together. That seemed so long ago, but it had been just a few weeks.

She would be worried, now, but I guessed she was worried when I left, so it probably didn't make a lot of difference for her. But our last night in town had made a big difference to me. I had no idea if anything would come of it, but the memory and the hint of promise was enough for now.

I didn't have to wonder what Betsy would suggest doing. She'd have had flares going off to attract police the second she discovered the *Crab Cove*.

I was going to do things differently. If what I had in mind was to work, Hendrix would have to hold off another day before arriving at the boat. I needed that day.

By morning the wind had shifted around and was blowing from the boat toward the point where my overnight camp was. Right there I had a good supply of the dry lowest branches of spruce, and in spite of the saturating wetness everywhere, I built a hat-size fire and watched carefully as the tendrils of smoke dissipated into the trees and were carried away from the direction of the boat.

I heated up some coffee in one can, and in the other, I put some scrapings I'd taken of the top of a nearby fly amanita, which is the prettiest and one of the nastiest of all Alaska's fungi. It always seems such a shame to me that the amanita has this beautiful red top with white speckles, an oasis of color in what can be sometimes drab forest, but that this banner of beauty can be so dangerous to careless mushroom gatherers.

When the scrapings were dry, I crumbled them into powder, finished my morning coffee, and started back for the boat. The camouflaging brush was exactly the way I'd left it, so I moved it and went on board again, wondering as I did so how far away Hendrix was. If I were caught aboard . . .

Into the half-can of coffee I found in the galley, I put the merest pinch of the amanita scraping, hoping it wouldn't kill him. I stirred it in well, and then turned my attention elsewhere.

It had occurred to me the night before, as I was holding up that spruce tree with my wet back, that crab-pot floats cost money. No matter how good a case could be built for declaring Hendrix loony, there was no evidence he was stupid. I started looking.

It took me about an hour, and I was just about to give up, but I finally found them under the bunks up in the forward part of the boat: Number 2 and Number 5, their lines neatly cut.

In another minute, I had them right where I wanted them. Then, as closely as I could recall, I laid silverware out on the table in the rough shape of the design Hendrix liked to use to ward off evil. The two coffee mugs that I'd left in the sink I brought out and placed in the middle of the design.

There were a couple of empty sea bags in the clothes locker, and I took them with me. I checked as carefully as I could, but I couldn't think of anything else, and I had no idea whether this would work. All I knew was that I had to try something.

I put the brush back carefully around the boat, putting one branch in particular in a way so I would know if it had been disturbed. Then I backed away on rocks and roots and turned and scrambled up to that first shelf about thirty vertical feet above the boat and set about rigging a surprise for Lee Hendrix. This was not my field of expertise, so it took me longer than I had expected.

Something within me was rebelling at everything I did then. There was a chance things could go wrong. In fact, there was a better than even chance things wouldn't go my way. After all, he was the one with the rifle. I had to try to think like Lee Hendrix. As with hunting moose, I had to put myself in his place and ask myself what I'd do if confronted with a certain set of circumstances.

But this was serious business. He had that rifle, and I wanted that rifle. I wanted him trussed like a turkey and ready for the troopers. I wanted to be done with this trail. I wanted to catch a flight back home. I wanted to go to the South Seas roadhouse and have an orange soda pop and listen to the wild yarns spun by those grand old sagamores of the mountains. I wanted a steak at a nice restaurant in Anchorage. I wanted to soak in a bathtub and not have to worry about who might be coming along on the trail or waiting up ahead of me. I wanted to go see Betsy and maybe buy the girl a cup of coffee or even a steak. I wanted to talk to her about this until it was gone.

But first I had to get out of this situation, and I had to do it with a lot of luck and every bit of skill I had.

When all was ready, I stayed away from the boat. I went back to where I'd sat the previous night out, well away from anywhere Hendrix would be likely to go. From now on, it would be too dangerous to have a fire, even this far away from him.

Before dark, I had fashioned a fair cudgel out of peeled green spruce, three feet long and almost as well balanced as a baseball bat.

The only question I still had was if I was ready for this. Part of me said I was a fool and not a small bit suicidal to boot. The other part of me argued that I was the right man at the right time to get this job done. From the first day Chada took me out to look at ptarmigan tracks, I'd been working up to this. If I had Hendrix figured out at all, it would be due in part to my Gramps Jepsen, too. He had spent the last years of his life watching the world go by and commenting on it. When I spent time with him, I tried to guess what people were like by watching them, as he did.

I wondered what he'd make of Lee Hendrix. He'd probably tell me to get out of here.

But the die had been cast now.

After dark, taking my bat with me, I washed carefully down at the creek. Then I went back to where I'd had my fire and blackened my face and neck and hands with soot.

It took me about an hour to walk back to a point on the second terrace where I could watch the *Crab Cove*. During the last hundred yards, I took off my boots and walked in both my pairs of borrowed heavy wool socks.

Hendrix might accidentally come around the bay and end up on the first terrace above the boat, but I knew he wouldn't get up this high.

I thought of staying awake all night, for safety's sake, but I was pretty confident he wouldn't be there, so I dozed and rested, then returned to my backpack and camp with first light.

The clouds that had been staying away nicely for a day or two were back, turning the coast into a murky house of horrors, speaking silently of little deaths and crimes that had gone unnoticed since the Great One put the rocks here. The coastline is at once one of my favorite places and a spooky spot. A man with a little imagination on a foggy day can scare himself half to death without even trying hard.

You think there should be more . . . something. More sound? More light? More activity? You keep trying to think of what it is, but you never quite get it. You look around, and you know it's beautiful and haunting, and you learn to live with the other part.

I finished a cold lunch and stretched out—but then I knew: Hendrix was coming.

CHAPTER 26

I couldn't see him or hear him. There were no outward signs that anything was different in the forest, but I knew.

As Chada once told me, "No dog has ever seen a flea, but he knows where they are."

An hour later I was in position on the second terrace above the *Crab Cove*. I could see the brush pulled away from the boat, pulled clear back away from the boat, uncovering the pretty little vessel completely. No wonder he liked it.

Hendrix was in plain view. He had the engine cover off and was swearing and throwing tools. How much did he know about engines? He wouldn't have to know much to decide someone had sabotaged him. But who had done it? There was the message of the twin coffee mugs and the silverware on the table in the galley. Would that mean anything to Hendrix? I was betting heavily that it would. I didn't want him leaving this boat so a stranger could have it. Whatever he was going to do should be done right here. I had high ground and surprise, but that was all I had. No one ever intended a homemade bat to equal the smashing power of a bullet from a .375 Holland & Holland Magnum.

The rain began then. It was a soaker. It fell in sheets and buckets and must have been washing the soot from my face. I pulled the borrowed black rain hat down a little tighter and was thankful I'd had the foresight to bring the oilskins.

With the rain came the mud, thick mud that oozed around my stockinged feet, making those thick socks unbearably squishy and uncomfortable.

Soon it was two inches deep and getting deeper. This was a hard rain, the kind that makes these coastal forests so drab during the storms, and so green and pretty when the sun comes out.

Maybe this would be my last rainy vigil, I thought, so I stayed up there on that second terrace and waited for things to happen.

The rain had driven Hendrix inside, and when he moved, the boat would rock a little, sending waves out into the machinegun spats of the rain on the quiet cove. In about an hour, I smelled coffee and wondered how Hendrix was going to enjoy the extra touch I'd given it. I flexed my arm muscles over and over, then stood and walked a few paces back and forth as the total blackness of a rainy night set in. I had to stay loose.

Hendrix screamed about eleven o'clock. He kept screaming and I watched through the darkness as he opened the hatch and threw both those floats out into Prince William Sound. It could be a bit unnerving, I'm sure, to pull back the covers on the master's bunk and find those two crab-pot floats waiting.

I could hear him yelling and screaming, but I couldn't hear what he was saying. The rain was still too heavy. It was the perfect time to work my way closer. In half an hour of tiny silent steps, I was on the first terrace, only thirty feet above the boat and about forty yards away.

The lights were still on in the cabin. It didn't surprise me that he wasn't getting a lot of sleep. Things hadn't gone his way today. First, the boat he'd been waiting for, had walked so far for, had killed for, wouldn't run. Then there were those floats in the bed, and the coffee mugs on the table, and the pattern made by the silverware. Those men were dead, and those things shouldn't have been there.

There was something else, too, because he was seeing and hearing some strange things now and he couldn't understand it. I'd bet he hadn't even noticed that the coffee tasted odd.

The familiar smell, heavy and fresh, came to me through the foggy night. Perhaps to calm himself down, to think, he had made some more coffee.

From here on the near ledge, I got a much better view of the boat. When Hendrix was quiet, the boat looked comfortable and friendly, a place that was warm and dry out of the rain. But that boat was nothing but horror inside now. I wondered how it was that someone could sit in something a man he had killed had treasured for years, and there weren't any lightning bolts, there wasn't some instant judge to tell the killer to get out. There was just a friendly looking little fishing boat that from the outside seemed no different than it was when Captain Pete and Chip had their last cup of coffee together in it.

The rig I'd fixed was tethered to a certain spruce tree, and I eased up and sat in front of it. I touched that razor-sharp Marble's knife I'd borrowed from the cabin down the coast, just to be sure I knew where it was.

Sitting in front of a tree is even better camouflage than sitting behind one, as a person behind a tree can't move much. If you're in front, you can move your arms without being seen easily.

So far Hendrix didn't seem to know I was around, but that was about to change. Figuring he must have enough of that special coffee in him by now, I quietly slipped out of the oilskin and laid it out of the way. They are a marvelous invention, but they're noisy. Then I chucked a rock onto the top of the boat's cabin and hooted like an owl.

He boiled out of that cabin, flame stabbed through the rain, and bark and branches blew off a tree somewhere farther up the hill.

He kept screaming, then. No words. Just a scream that held all the ghosts and terrors of the world in it and he turned more to the left and fired again.

Then the rain stopped, and the clouds broke enough to let the light of a full moon down. It was at once the most beautiful of sights and the most terrifying. Here was a fiord with a waterfall and glaciers gleaming in the moonlight like dreams, with a madman in the middle.

I chucked another rock, this time along the shelf I was on. Hendrix fired in that general direction, flame stabbing six feet out from the muzzle of that cannon. He took two more shells from his pocket and reloaded, all the time sobbing quietly to himself.

"Pete!" he finally yelled. "Is that you, Pete?"

And just then a real owl answered from farther along this same shelf. Hendrix fired twice, crying and whimpering, and came climbing up the shelf in the moonlight. He reached the terrace about forty feet from me and was looking the other way. I tightened my grip on my club, but didn't move.

I was trying my best to will myself invisible.

He looked even larger in the moonlight than he had on the hillside above Tazlina Lake, a lifetime and a mountain range ago.

"Pete?" he said, in a whisper. "I didn't mean it, Pete. You know that."

He kept the rifle pointed away from me toward where he'd heard the real owl. There was a light rustling down that way, and he fired and backed up a few steps closer to me.

"I didn't mean it," he whimpered, his breath making small whining sounds. "I didn't mean it."

I slipped the sheath knife out, reached over and cut through a cord right next to my hip. There was a swishing sound and a clunk as the good-sized rock I had used for ballast hit the ground. And a strange thing was happening: About fifty feet to my right, and rising straight out of the ground in front of Hendrix, was the dummy I'd rigged out of Pete Hansen's old oilskins and a sea bag full of moss. The stone's falling pulled it gently into his view and he backed up three steps and fired. The bullet slipped through the dummy and whined on into the darkness of the night. The dummy shivered and came back toward him. He took two more steps backward, screaming wordlessly into the moonlight, and fired again. This left him almost on top of me. Before he had time to throw the bolt on that last cartridge, I rose up and swung that club with all my strength right at his head.

Baseball has never been my thing.

CHAPTER 27

He had the rifle to his shoulder as he reached for the bolt to chamber that round. When my club hit, it caught his shoulder and the buttstock of that rifle with great force, but only glanced off his head. He screamed and flew down—face down—into the mud.

He turned his face toward me and I knew I couldn't get to him for another swing before he brought that rifle into action. He was screaming again, with wild eyes, as he threw the shell into the chamber and swung it toward me. I saw one last time the look in those eyes that no one would ever really understand, and I could feel his finger tightening on the trigger and knew my life would now end.

I winced at the flame and explosion before me. I kept hearing his screams, but I couldn't see his right eye any longer. That part of his face was gone.

He stumbled backward and fell from the terrace, and then everything was quiet again.

Even in the moonlight I could see what was left of his rifle. The most powerful charge of powder in the world can't push a bullet past a barrel plugged with mud. The rifle had been a strong one but it was now a mass of splinters, with several long pieces of the barrel and action missing. I could guess where at least one of them had gone.

Such was the fear Hendrix instilled in me that I took my time in walking to the edge and peering over. I shouldn't have bothered. When a neck is bent like that, it can mean only one thing, and his horrible face lay right in the path of light coming from the door of the boat. His headfirst plunge backwards off the terrace had ended when his head struck the gunwale of the boat.

I sat in the rain, never taking my eyes from him, for an hour. No movement. I crept down silently, more out of habit and instinct than anything else. Finding a branch, I reached out with it and touched the open left eyeball of the man who had destroyed so many lives. It didn't blink. With any animal, if there is any life left, the eye will blink.

Lee Hendrix was dead.

At last the rough world of Alaska could start to smooth the violent ripples he'd made and return to normal. Karen and the kids could put some of the nightmares away. Finally Jeep George could try to find his own life again. It wouldn't be easy for any of us.

I left that terrible scene in the moonlight and slogged in muddy socks back to my backpack and salmon. I suppose I could have moved into the cabin of the *Crab Cove* that night, but nothing would have induced me to do so.

When full daylight came, I returned to the boat and found Hendrix was still dead, which somehow surprised me. I spent an hour replacing a few things, like the oilskins and lines and sea bags. Engine parts found their way back into the engine. An open can of coffee in the boat accidentally got spilled over the side.

I felt no elation at the outcome. Just relief. When Jim Strickland and the others arrived, they'd find just what they wanted to find . . . that Alaska had taken care of another one of its miscreants. In this case, a breech blown into the face and a fall.

No trial. No sanity hearings.

But I'd wanted a trial. I'd wanted sanity hearings. I had wanted Lee Hendrix to know why he was in the courtroom and had to face society.

But I was just a hunting guide, and Jim Strickland had been right about one thing: Alaska does have a way of taking care of things.

So I walked down the shore for about a mile until a long beach spread before me, and I readied three evenly spaced signal fires there, to be lighted when I saw the first fishing boat go by.

My face was already blackened from last night's duel, so I wondered if there would be enough time before the plane came to sing the old songs for my friend Bill Turner.

There was.

Slim Randles considers himself an outdoorsman first and a writer second. His career spans more than three decades as a journalist, but is heavily dosed with life in the outdoors.

He began his career as a cowboy and mule packer in the California High Sierra, then spent a decade in Alaska as a "resident adventurer" for The Anchorage Daily News. While writing columns for the paper, he built a cabin twelve miles from the nearest road and lived in it eight years, drove a team in the first (1973) Iditarod sled dog race, and spent eight seasons as an assistant hunting guide in the Alaska Range and the Talkeetna Mountains, working primarily for the late Clark Engle and several other fair chase guides.

Randles has also been associate editor of Petersen's Hunting Magazine, author of hundreds of outdoor magazine articles, adjunct professor of journalism at the University of New Mexico, and is currently a columnist for the Albuquerque Journal. He is also a registered guide and outfitter in New Mexico. Like Jeep George, he enjoys taking a handful of picked gun, bow or camera hunters for elk, bear and cougar each fall and winter.

Slim, his wife, Jeannie, and daughter Bridget, live in the tiny village of San Ysidro in northern New Mexico with too many bluetick coonhounds.

Raven's Prey

Book and cover designed and composed by Paula Elmes,
ImageCraft Publications & Design, Fairbanks, Alaska

Typeset in Goudy Old Style, Giotto and Futura
using Adobe PageMaker on a Macintosh

Cover and artwork created in Macromedia FreeHand on a Macintosh

Printing and binding provided by BookCrafters, Chelsea, Michigan